Searching for Right

Searching for Right

Brittney Holmes

www.urbanchristianonline.com

Urban Books, LLC
97 N18th Street
Wyandanch, NY 11798

ISBN 13: 978-1-60162-829-9
ISBN 10: 1-60162-829-3

First Printing September 2013
Printed in the United States of America

10 9 8 7 6 5 4 3 2 1

This is a work of fiction. Any references or similarities to actual events, real people, living or dead, or to real locales are intended to give the novel a sense of reality. Any similarity in other names, characters, places, and incidents is entirely coincidental.

Distributed by Kensington Corp.
Submit Wholesale Orders to:
Kensington Publishing Corp.
C/O Penguin Group (USA) Inc.
Attention: Order Processing
405 Murray Hill Parkway
East Rutherford, NJ 07073-2316
Phone: 1-800-526-0275
Fax: 1-800-227-9604

Searching for Right

by

Brittney Holmes

For all of my sister-friends who've seen me at my best and my worst, those who've allowed me into their lives to share unforgettable moments, those who've taught me things I never knew I'd learn, shown me things I never thought I'd see, and those who've loved me unconditionally.

Acknowledgments

As always, I'd like to give honor and praise to God—my Savior and keeper—for all He has done for me. Lord, I can't thank you enough for all you have done for me and all you've given to me. Thank you for the blessings and life-long lessons that you've instilled in me. I pray that the words in this book connect to the souls of your young people and will guide them from wherever they are, to you. Thank you for this gift; I give it back to you.

To my parents, Jonathan Bellamy and Kendra Norman-Bellamy, thank you for being the great parents that you are. It's because of you guys that I have grown into the young woman I am today. Both of you inspire me to live out my dreams and to touch the lives of everyone I come in contact with. I love you both.

To Jimmy Lee Holmes: Daddy, the legacy you left behind showed me what it means to be a genuine person and to give to others as much, if not more, than I receive. Thank you for living a life that would never let your memory die.

Crystal, my li'l sis, it still amazes me that you're a young adult, experiencing college life, away from home. Believe it or not, I learn a lot from you. Despite our many tit for tats, we have many great experiences and stories to share with our kids later in life. Thank you for being a great sister.

To my grandparents, Bishop and Mrs. H.H. Norman, Mr. Jesse and Mrs. Dorothy Holmes, and the late Elder Clinton and Mrs. Willie Mae Bellamy, and the rest of my extended family (uncles, aunts, and cousins): I can always feel your prayers no matter where I go in life. Thank you for being the loving and supportive family that you are. I love each and every one of you.

To one of my bestest (yes, bestest) cousins ever, Terrence Wooten! You, along with mom, do a lot in order to make sure that my career stays intact. Thanks for always being there whenever, wherever, no matter what J.

To all of my friends at the University of Georgia—you know I wish I could name you all—you have made my college experience one to remember. Even though I'm graduating (yay!!!), the memories I have with my Bull-dog family will never fade away. To my family within the Black Affairs Council, the National Association of Black Journalists, *The Red & Black,* Rocksprings Com-munity Center (I love my kids!), and *InfUSion* maga-zine—thank you for cultivating me into the leader I am today.

To my sisters and sorors of Delta Sigma Theta So-rority, Incorporated (specifically the Zeta Psi Chapter at the University of Georgia, and even more specifi-cally D.O.F.–Spring 2011), I absolutely love you ladies. We know what it means to be the scholar, the student leader, the socialite . . . always on the go and still keep it all together as if we have nothing going on. I've been through so much with you, D.O.F., that there's nothing that could happen to break the bond that we share with one another. We may be sisters by choice, but what's most important is that we are sisters for life. OO-OOP!

To all of my true friends, thank you for the listening ear, the laughter, the nights downtown, the all-nighters the evening before the test, the pep talks, etc. etc. You have been there for me for so many things and I pray that you'll continue to remain the roots in growing tree of life. May God bless you all in your future endeavors . . . because I know we'll all be successful!

To the Great Redan High School—faculty, staff, and students—I miss RHS so much! I appreciate the love and support I continue to receive from you.

To my Teach For America family: Thank you for making my transition to Jacksonville more welcoming than I could've ever imagined. To my new church family, Household of Faith Church and spiritual father Bishop Lewis Williams: it's been a short time, but I already feel at home with my spiritual family. I look forward to growing in Christ under your care.

To those inspiration authors who've paved the way for me—thank you for being great role models in work and in life that I can look up to as I mature. Your literary works have inspired me beyond comprehension and I pray that my work is continuously blessed through you words.

To my publishers, Urban Books (Urban Christian), you have opened doors for me that I never would have imagined walking through. Thank you for aiding in the fruition of my dreams. Special appreciation goes out to my editor, Ms. Joylynn Jossel. Thank you for your openness, your keen eye and constructive criticism. Because of you, I have grown to understand my writing style and technique. Thank you for cultivating my creativity.

And finally, to my readers, this book will touch on everything from divorce to the taboo subject of student-teacher relationships, but I hope that in the midst of it all, you will understand that without God, peace, love, forgiveness nor hope is possible. It is my hope that as you turn the last page of this book you will know what it means to have God on your side as you search for right.

Chapter 1

Lauren

Lauren Hopewell walked down the senior hallway with her friends, Jayda, Danielle, and Brenda. They attracted deep, longing stares of approval from every guy in the hall and they loved the attention. The harmonious sway of their hips mesmerized the male eye and caused the green-eyed monster to come out in many females. The four girls reached their destination and entered the combinations to open their lockers.

Lauren was the leader of the pack and was considerably the most attractive. Her five foot seven shapely frame, brown eyes, and silky reddish brown hair, trimmed in an asymmetrical style, awarded her the admirable eye of several guys. But all those who tried gaining the title as Lauren's boyfriend hardly ever succeeded.

Jayda Henderson was equally as tall, but much slimmer than her best friend. Her smooth, dark brown skin was her best physical feature and her dark brown eyes were labeled as mysterious. She had the potential to be the most outspoken of the group, but was known to usually keep her strong opinions to herself, unless she felt the need to speak out.

Danielle Brookes was slightly shorter than Lauren and Jayda, but more curvaceous than the two put together. Her inherited form received daily praises, but she never let the compliments get to her head.

Brenda Killian was the most flirtatious one out of the group. Her long blond hair stopped midway down her back, and her baby blue eyes were strikingly beautiful. Though her appearance caused many of her peers to stereotypically label her as the "dumb blonde," Brenda constantly proved them wrong by attaining a 4.0 grade point average. She was smart, but she also loved the attention she received from the guys.

Growing up in a black neighborhood and attending predominately black schools throughout her life, Brenda found herself strongly attracted to African American males and found the males of her own race utterly "average looking." She never felt out of place when hanging out with her black girlfriends, and when dating black males, the stares and comments she received from those she referred to as "haters" never fazed her.

The girls used the mirrors in their lockers to make sure their hair was intact and their faces were continuously flawless. They grabbed books for their first class and simultaneously closed their locker doors. As they began down the hall once more, Jarred—an average-height, considerably good-looking senior who had been after Lauren for some time but had yet to be given the time of day—blocked their path. His perseverance was slightly admired by Lauren, but his continuous attempts to pursue her were nothing less than annoying.

"Hey, Lauren." Jarred greeted the leader of the group with a one-sided grin.

Lauren tried hard to suppress the loud sigh that had the potential to silence the entire hallway. "Hey, Jarred," she greeted him evenly. She heard Jayda laughing softly behind her and could tell that they were thinking the same thing: *this guy never gives up*.

"I was wondering . . ." Jarred began before pausing dramatically, as was usual for his character. "I'm falling slightly behind in calculus. Can you give a brotha some of your precious time and tutor me?" His brown eyes playfully pleaded puppy-dog style.

Lauren laughed. "You've got the wrong one," she told him and pointed toward Brenda. "Bre here is the math wiz, not me."

Brenda gave Lauren a cold stare, signaling that if Jarred even approached her to ask her any type of question, math related or not, Lauren would owe her big time.

Jarred shook his head, to Brenda's joy. "No, see, I would prefer if *you'd* tutor me."

Lauren decided to play along and allow Jarred to think that he was actually getting somewhere with her this time. "Okay, Jarred, I'll tutor you." He began to smile, but she spoke again before the ends of his mouth could reach his eyes. "Here's your first lesson: what is me *plus* you *divided by* my fist *multiplied by* your eye several times?" she asked with a scowl across her face.

Jarred's expression revealed his confusion. "What? I don't get it."

"It's a severely blackened eye, Jarred. Now I suggest you step out of my face before this problem is solved."

Lauren could see the mounting anger in Jarred's eyes as he walked away dejectedly for the millionth time in the last couple of months, but she felt no remorse for him. She knew she was much too good for him and felt that he should be aware of that. Having to humiliate him every time he approached her wasn't a satisfaction for her, but if it was the only way he would learn to back off, then she had to do what she had to do.

"Lauren, that was cold, girl." Danielle laughed as they began walking again.

Lauren shrugged and continued down the hall. Once the girls reached the commons area, they separated.

Lauren and Jayda headed toward their history class, which was their favorite class because their teacher was a young, laid-back male who taught not through boring lectures, but through films and hands-on activities.

"Good morning, Mr. Sterling," Lauren and Jayda sang as they sashayed into the empty classroom.

Sterling Daniels looked up from his work and smiled toward the two girls entering his room. "Good morning, ladies," he greeted them smoothly. "The first as always, I see."

The girls took their front-row seats and watched students fill the room, some entering the room just before the late bell rang.

"Morning, Mr. Sterling," most of them greeted him. Sterling allowed his students to refer to him by his first name because he said being called Mr. Daniels made him feel as old as his father, who wasn't even fifty yet.

From her seat, Lauren gazed at Sterling and almost laughed aloud as he tried to focus on his work and ignore her enticing stares, but she knew that her smile alone had a huge effect on his work ethic. Lauren was seventeen years old and Sterling was twenty-three, but that didn't stop her from making several attempts to get him to notice her, and after a short time he had, but he hadn't made any advances toward her. She knew why, of course, but she didn't care that he was her teacher or that his job would be at stake if they were to get involved. All Lauren cared about was that in a few weeks she would be eighteen, making her legally available to do whatever she pleased.

Sterling looked up into Lauren's brown eyes and held her stare for a fleeting moment before clearing his throat and standing from his seat. "How's everyone doing this morning?"

The class gave various responses, but one sultry voice stood out among the rest, and Lauren watched as Sterling tried not to look in her direction. Jayda glanced at Lauren and both girls smiled knowingly.

Jayda leaned into Lauren and said, "Girl, you better leave that man alone before you run him out of this school."

"He's not going anywhere." Lauren laughed. "He's not even scared, just a little nervous, and that's a good sign." She returned her attention to Sterling, who had for only a moment been able to teach without distraction, but as soon as Lauren looked at him and crossed her smooth, shapely legs at the knee, he was once again fumbling over words.

By the end of the class, Sterling had been able to teach without becoming sidetracked by Lauren's alluring gaze because the students had been into the lesson, asking several questions, and offering various opinions on the topic. When the bell rang, Lauren and Jayda waited for all the students to leave, as they did every day, and then walked up to Sterling's desk.

"Mr. Sterling."

Sterling watched the movements of her full lips as she spoke his name. "Yes, Lauren?" he asked, his voice cautious as if he were afraid of what she might say.

Lauren licked her lips slowly and asked, "I was wondering if you could help me out with chapter twenty-one's work. I didn't really understand what was going on."

"Well, I do have an afterschool tutorial every Tuesday and Thursday. The class is usually full of students who basically want to me teach the entire lesson over again, just for enjoyment."

Lauren shook her head. "I can't stay after school." She looked over at Jayda, who smiled. "We have cheerleading practice every afternoon. I was thinking that you could make a house call for this one?"

Sterling stood and his six foot five frame seemed more massive up close. Lauren gazed at the bulging muscles in his arms and almost whimpered out loud. He was a shade darker than Jayda, but his skin was just as smooth. His eyes were slightly lighter than the average brown, and their contrast to his skin tone only complemented his appearance.

Sterling looked toward Jayda. "Ms. Henderson, could you give us a minute?" His request caused Lauren to practically jump out of her skin.

Jayda only hesitated slightly before she walked out of the classroom and waited for Lauren outside of the door.

Sterling looked down at Lauren and said, "Lauren, I don't think that's a good idea." He moved toward the dry erase board and began cleaning it. "You know just as well as I that there is enough tension between you and me while in this classroom full of students. I don't think I'd want to experience what it would be like with just the two of us."

Lauren pretended to be clueless and shrugged her shoulders innocently. "I don't know what you're talking about, Mr. Sterling. I don't feel any tension at all."

Sterling laughed and looked toward Lauren. "Lauren, I'm not gonna lie." He spoke softly as he grabbed her left hand, giving Lauren the opportunity to step closer to him. He smiled and lowered his voice to nearly a whisper. "I am attracted to you. You're a beautiful, young woman and very mature for your age. You make me feel different from any woman I've ever been with and we're not even together."

His smile coupled with the endearing words caused Lauren's heart to flutter. She'd never had a guy compliment her in such a way before; but this just wasn't a guy, this was a *man,* and that made Lauren feel even better.

"But, Lauren, I'm your teacher," he said as he released her hand. "And you're my student. There's too much on the line, namely my job and freedom." He paused. "So our relationship must remain strictly professional."

Lauren nodded as if she understood. "For now." She smiled as she turned and walked out of the classroom, bypassing Sterling's second-period students who were entering the class. Lauren barely noticed Jarred standing in the doorway as she joined Jayda and they walked to their next class.

Chapter 2

Brenda

Brenda turned around slightly to pass the stack of papers on to the person behind her, and smiled at him as he slowly took them out of her hands. He grinned and winked at her before passing the stack on.

"So what are we doing tonight?" he asked once he'd turned back toward the front.

Brenda laughed playfully. "Whatever."

His eyebrows rose at her response as she turned back around and focused her attention on the lesson.

Brenda inwardly complimented her ability to keep her composure while speaking to her big-time crush, Zane Timbers. His smile caused her stomach to jumble into knots, while his caramel skin forced her to try her hardest to keep from running the palm of her hand down the side of his smooth face. His sometimes-hazel, sometimes-light brown eyes always smiled at her and made her feel warm inside. He had finally asked her out—well, he'd implied that a date was optional and that was good enough for Brenda. But she wondered if Zane finally taking notice of her was a good thing.

As she focused on her teacher's lecture, Brenda tried hard to keep her mind on the work, but the mental image of Zane's smiling face continued to distract her. That fleeting thought reminded her exactly why she never got seriously involved with any guy. Brenda was a scholar and she planned on staying that way. She hated letting anything come before her schoolwork, especially guys. Brenda was very career-oriented and that was the reason she worked hard to keep her grades up. The only way she was going to become the successful businesswoman she wanted to be was by focusing on her studies and keeping guys at a reasonable distance.

Zane was getting closer and closer, though. They hadn't even had their first date and he was already having an effect on Brenda's ability to focus. He was a really nice guy and made her feel good, but Brenda had always been and would forever be considered a flirt; her past had shown that she was not girlfriend material.

Her last boyfriend had ended their relationship because of Brenda's flirtatious tendencies. Flirting came so natural to her that she didn't seem to find anything wrong when her boyfriend had found her flirting with one of his friends. Obviously, to her and everyone else around her, she was meant to remain single, but that didn't mean she couldn't have a little fun.

The bell that signaled the end of second-period sounded and Brenda gathered her things and headed toward the door.

"Hey, Bre," she heard Zane call after her.

Brenda turned on her heels, causing her shimmering blond hair to swing around and land gracefully against her back and shoulders. The movement captivated Zane and several other admirers as they passed. "Yes?" She smiled.

Zane grinned and said, "Do you practice that hair thing in the mirror?" Brenda laughed. "But for real though, I was serious about us hookin' up tonight . . . or sometime soon," he stated as he pulled at the waistband of his pants.

Brenda watched as his eyes searched hers and felt herself falling for whatever spell his gaze was casting, but she promised to catch herself before she got too caught up in the feeling. "I don't know, Zane. I'm not really good at the whole dating thing."

Zane laughed softly and moved in closer. "Bre, I don't want anything from you. I just wanna chill wit' you 'cause you real cool. I know you're a flirt and that's why I just wanna be friends . . . that chill."

Brenda's lips curved upward at the way Zane said the word "chill," as if he meant it as something other than just hanging out. She was close to laughing out loud at the serious look on his face, but managed to keep her cool. "Zane, I'm not like those cheap females you talk to, okay? I'm a flirt, but that doesn't mean I'm the promiscuous type of girl who opens her legs for anyone."

"So . . . are you saying you're a virgin?"

There was a twinkle in her eyes when she said, "That is strictly classified information."

"There's that teasing thing you do." Zane shoved his hands in his pockets. "I like it."

"Zane, I'll think about hanging with you, and if I do, there will most definitely be rules and boundaries," Brenda said as Zane teasingly rolled his eyes.

"That's cool, Ms. Killian. I will *definitely* be talking to you soon."

The late bell sounded, signaling that both Brenda and Zane would be marked as tardy once they entered their classrooms.

"See what you're doing?" Zane spoke as he backed away. "You got me so caught up that I'm gonna be late to class."

Brenda laughed and shook her head as he took one final gaze at her and walked down the opposite hallway.

By the time Brenda reached her next class, the teacher had already begun calling the roll. The woman said

Brenda's name just as she walked through the door with an apologetic grin on her face.

"You should've seen the crowd in the girls' room," Brenda offered as an untruthful excuse.

Her teacher offered a "don't let it happen again" look and continued checking class attendance, as Brenda took her third-row seat next to Ken Sato, another guy she periodically flirted with. He was a biracial senior with African American and Japanese heritage running through his blood. With slightly slanted, dark eyes, full lips, and smooth, wavy hair that he kept in a low cut, shaped to perfection, he'd inherited a variety of physical traits from his ancestors. The absence of facial hair made him look younger than his seventeen years, but his personality was much more mature than his age accounted for.

He smiled at Brenda as she pulled her hair over her right shoulder. "Hey, Brenda. How are you?"

Brenda flashed him two rows of perfectly even teeth, the kind that had clearly been corrected by years of wearing braces. She replied, "Well, today seemed like an ordinary day, but all of a sudden I feel wonderful." She watched as his smile widened, deepening his already-deep dimples.

"I wouldn't have something to do with that, would I?" Ken asked.

"I would say you do," she responded before winking at him.

As she focused her attention on the teacher, Brenda thought about how much she flirted with so many guys, causing many of them to think she was easily accessible, though they soon found out she wasn't. Brenda loved being a flirt or, better yet, a tease. There was something about the game that she loved too much to let go. The thrill of the chase excited her to no end.

In this game of cat and mouse, she always played the mouse with intentions of never being caught. Sometimes having two cats on her tail made the challenge more enjoyable.

She wondered though, would she ever be able to settle down with just one guy? She, along with her friends, was scheduled to graduate in three months and would be off to their respective colleges. Brenda just knew she would continue to be the same coy tease she was today. There was nothing that could change that.

She would occasionally date, but if things progressed too far, she would end things, or purposely have the relationship ended, before she could get hurt. Deep down, she knew that she had intentionally fooled around on her last boyfriend just because she felt they were becoming too serious, something she was fearful off. *Guys are the key to heartbreak,* Brenda often thought. She knew that before Zane or Ken could get comfortable with her, she'd begin running, in an attempt to escape their harmful paws.

As Brenda listened and took notes during the math lesson, her phone began to vibrate. She discreetly reached down and retrieved her phone from her back pocket and looked at the screen. She had a text message and decided to read it.

Wud u like 2 go out wit me Sat nite? The message was from Ken. Brenda looked to her right and smiled at him; he smiled back and his eyes questioned her.

Brenda couldn't pass this up. She momentarily forgot about Zane's pending question as she readily agreed to go to the movies with Ken on Saturday evening. Zane would soon have his turn, though. Nothing was ever wrong with casual dating. As long as Brenda made sure things remained in her control, she could handle it.

Chapter 3

Danielle

Jayda pulled her black Ford Focus into the parking lot of Freedman Elementary School. Danielle released her seat belt and jumped out of the car along with Jayda, while Brenda and Lauren decided to wait in the vehicle. The girls walked into the building and were greeted by the secretary in the front office.

"Hi, Danielle. Hey, Jayda," the woman greeted them.

Danielle waved to the middle-aged woman with slightly graying hair. "Hi, Mrs. Leola. How are you to-day?"

"I'm blessed as always. Are you girls excited to be almost out of high school?" Mrs. Leola asked both girls.

Both girls nodded so hard that they looked like life-sized bobble-head dolls.

"I'll take that as you're itching to graduate." The woman laughed. "Well, I know you're here for pickup, so you can go on back." She motioned for the girls to head toward the afterschool program facility.

Danielle walked ahead of Jayda and turned down a decorative hall with walls covered in finger paintings and drawings. She entered one of the kindergarten classrooms where the elementary school housed its aftercare program. The program had been set up for children whose parents or caretakers were unable to pick them up once regular school hours were over.

When Danielle entered the room, a small girl in braids ran toward her with a wide smile.

"Mommy!" the girl squealed with delight.

Danielle opened her arms and received her daughter. "Hey, sweetie. How was preschool today?"

"Fun," the girl answered, and looked toward Jayda. "Hi, Jayda."

"Hey, Kennedi." Jayda smiled down at the four-year-old.

The last four years had been slightly harder on Danielle than they had been on the rest of her friends. At the age of thirteen, she learned she was pregnant, and had decided to keep the child despite the fact that her boyfriend persistently denied parental responsibility. Her mother refused to allow her to drop out of school, but she also refused to allow Danielle to become a charity case, so she was forced to get a weekend job that paid well enough for her to take care of her child. On weekends that Danielle worked, her mother was compassionate enough to keep Kennedi. Danielle had her hard times, especially when Kennedi was younger and would get sick or would misbehave, causing Danielle to miss work or school, but as the years passed things became routine.

Kennedi was a very active four-year-old. She loved to run around with her friends and have fun, just like most four-year-olds. She loved to shop, which was something Danielle was trying to break her out of. Though she loved to shop herself, most times when Kennedi wanted to spend a day at the mall, Danielle's funds wouldn't permit it. Kennedi also loved getting her way, which sometimes caused friction between Danielle's tendency to allow her daughter to have what she wanted and her motherly instinct that told her if she allowed the child to control her now, she would still be in control later.

"Come on, we're going to the store before we go home," Danielle told Kennedi.

The young girl's eyes opened wide and she jumped up and down. "Let's go, Mommy." She grabbed Danielle's hand and pulled her toward the exit. "Bye, everybody." She waved to her friends as she practically dragged Danielle out of the door.

After Danielle situated Kennedi in the car, between herself and Brenda, Jayda headed toward the mall. Lauren and Brenda quickly got out of the car and headed toward the entrance, while Jayda waited for Danielle to help Kennedi out of the car. As soon as Kennedi placed her feet on the ground, she ran toward the mall eagerly.

"Kennedi!" Danielle's heart nearly stopped when she saw a car slam on its brakes as her daughter carelessly continued running until she reached Lauren and Brenda, who were waiting for them. "Kennedi Camille Brookes! I'm 'bout to beat your behind," she threatened as she and Jayda crossed the street after the car had passed.

Danielle grabbed Kennedi by the arm and smacked her behind one good time, causing tears to flood the girl's eyes.

"Dang, Danni." Brenda scowled. "You ain't have to hit her like that."

"Bre, please don't tell me how to raise my daughter. How's she gonna learn if I don't teach her?" Danielle rolled her eyes. "Now, Kennedi, I've told you about running off like that. You almost got hit by that car back there. The stores ain't going nowhere. You stay with me. Now, give me your hand," she commanded.

Lauren shook her head at how strict Danielle was being, but Danielle simply ignored the gesture. Her friends just didn't understand.

Lauren opened the mall's door. "Come on y'all. I wanna get to 5-7-9. They got this sale that I don't wanna miss."

They walked into the mall full of young shoppers; many of them had come straight from school. During this time of the year, everyone was stocking up on clothes for the spring for less than half the usual price.

"Mommy, I wanna go over there," Kennedi said, pointing toward a store full of kids' clothing. Danielle knew Kennedi recognized the store as one they sometimes visited when they came to the mall.

"No, Kennedi," Danielle said, pulling her along. "We're going to a different store."

Kennedi snatched her hand away from Danielle. "Nooo, I wanna go over there," she whined.

Danielle looked down at Kennedi, raising her hand as if threatening to physically reprimand her. Immediately, Kennedi grabbed her mother's hand and continued walking with the girls.

They entered 5-7-9 and Jayda, Lauren, and Brenda began looking through clothes while Danielle perused the jewelry, purses, and other accessories.

"Whew, I'm glad coach cancelled practice today. I didn't feel like going anyway." Lauren sighed as she admired a long-sleeved, yellow V-neck top.

"I know, but we do have a game tomorrow, so you know she's gonna work us overtime in practice before we go out on the court." Jayda grimaced as she sorted through the rack of jeans. "So I would've rather had practice today and been able to relax a little before the game tomorrow."

Brenda shrugged her shoulders. "Regardless of all that, you guys always put on a great show, so it seems like it would be worth the overtime to me." It almost seemed as if she wouldn't have even been listening to the conversation with the way she was studying her reflection in a mirror that hung over the jewelry stand.

"Yeah, I guess." Jayda breathed heavily.

"You know, y'all make me sick when y'all bring me to this skinny-mini store, knowing I can't wear a doggone thing in here," Danielle complained, interrupting their conversation. "All I ever get are some earrings or something that will turn colors after a few weeks."

Lauren laughed. "Well, you should've taken your daughter to get some new spring outfits instead of coming over here with us."

Danielle sighed. "Kennedi, come on," she called to her daughter, who was playing with necklaces. "I'm only getting two outfits because Grandma just bought you some clothes last month."

"Yay!" Kennedi grabbed her mother's hand and they walked out of the store.

Sometimes Danielle felt ostracized by her friends just because she was a teen mother. She knew they loved her and she felt the same way about them, but it seemed as if they treated her differently because she had more responsibilities than they did. They, hopefully unintentionally, threw in her face the fact that she had to watch and care for Kennedi, and sometimes told her what she should and shouldn't do because of the effect it would have on her daughter. Danielle was well aware of the fact that she had to look after Kennedi, which would sometimes call for her to forgo some social activities, but the realization of it all seemed worse when her best friends reprimanded her.

When they walked into the children's store, a male worker with a bright smile greeted them. Danielle had never seen him before and figured he must be a new employee. However, he bore a strong resemblance to the older woman who, Danielle knew, was the owner of the store. She immediately found herself attracted to the worker's hazelnut complexion and luscious full lips. His brown eyes seemed to hold delight and pleasure that were unknown to Danielle, and she instantly wanted to get to know him in order to find out why he seemed so elated.

"Hi, my name is A.J. Can I help you find anything?" he asked Danielle.

Kennedi jumped up and down. "Yes! I want a pink dress."

A.J. smiled down at her. "What's your name?"

"Kennedi Brookes and this is my mommy, Danielle."

A.J. smiled at Danielle before returning his attention to Kennedi. "So you like pink, huh? Well, I'll go get my sister and she'll help you and your mother find something you'll really like." He looked up at Danielle. "I'll be right back."

"Thank you," Danielle responded as she watched him walk toward the back of the store. "Kennedi, why are you so hyper today? What did you have for lunch?"

"A sandwich, chips, and milk," Kennedi answered. "Oh, and Jalen had candy for snack." She smiled as she spoke of one of her school friends.

Danielle shook her head. Kennedi hardly ever ate candy, but when she did it caused her to become hyper and had lasting effects on Danielle. She tried to keep her daughter still as A.J. walked from the back with an attractive young woman following him.

"Hi, I'm Déjà and my brother tells me that you want a pink dress." The woman addressed Danielle.

Danielle pointed toward Kennedi. "Not me, my daughter."

Déjà looked down at Kennedi and smiled. "Well, let's go find a pretty one that you'll like." She extended her hand and Kennedi took it.

"Mommy, stay here," Kennedi said. "The dress is a surprise."

Danielle laughed. "Okay, Ms. Kennedi. Please pick something affordable."

"I can tell she's a handful," A.J. commented after his sister walked off with the toddler. "But she's a cute little girl. She looks like you."

Danielle blushed. "I'll take that as a compliment."

"You should," he told her. For a moment, he gazed at her as if he was analyzing her physical appearance. "How old are you?"

Danielle averted her gaze. "Seventeen."

"And Kennedi?"

She hesitated and looked back up into his eyes. She wanted to ask him why he was being so forward with his questioning when she didn't even know him. She'd been asked the question before by those who were just trying to be nosy and figure out Danielle's age when she'd given birth. But A.J. didn't sound as if he was trying to be judgmental, so she answered timidly, "She's four, almost five."

He continued gazing at her and Danielle was becoming afraid that maybe he was going to judge her. But as he continued to watch her, a smile spread across his face.

"You don't have any more, do you?" he asked teasingly.

Danielle laughed out loud. "If I did, I would seriously be in a straight jacket. One is enough . . . for now."

"So you plan on having more?" he asked.

She gave him her "why do you care" look. "Maybe, but if I do, I will definitely be married."

"That's good," A.J. responded as he continued to stare at Danielle. "You are very attractive," he told her shamelessly.

"Thank you," Danielle answered softly.

He continued gazing at her. "It's something about your eyes. You seem familiar to me."

Danielle wanted to laugh away the nervousness she felt, but all she could do was return his intense gaze. They seemed to be speaking to each other not with their minds, but deep down in their souls. The connection Danielle felt with this unfamiliar gentleman was strong and she couldn't break it.

"Hey, Danni," she heard Lauren's voice call.

Danielle blinked and held her head down in embarrassment. When she turned toward her friends, they were all standing behind her with wide smiles, their gazes shifting between her and a complete stranger.

"You guys done already?" Danielle asked tightly.

Brenda smiled sweetly. "Yes, but we see you're just getting started."

A.J. laughed as he introduced himself. "I'm A.J."

"Hi," the girls sang.

"A.J., this is Brenda, Jayda, and Lauren," Danielle said, pointing at each of the girls. "My friends, unfortunately."

She turned her attention back to A.J., but his gaze was steadfast as he continued to openly stare at her, despite her friends' presence. She knew she had to avoid eye contact or she wouldn't hear the end of it from the girls. She was glad when Kennedi came running toward the front with two summer dresses in her hand.

"Surprise! Mommy, look. I got two of 'em like you said. One pink, one yellow."

"Both under fifteen dollars," Déjà added as she noticed the three girls at the counter. "Oh, we have more customers."

The girls laughed.

"No, we're with her," Jayda informed her, pointing at Danielle. "I don't think we would be able to fit into anything in this store." They laughed again.

"Mommy, are you gonna buy these?" Kennedi asked, holding the dresses in the air.

Danielle took them and looked at A.J. "I'd like to purchase these, please."

A.J. unhurriedly took the dresses from Danielle with a small smile on his face and walked behind the counter. He rang up the items and bagged them, barely taking his eyes off of Danielle in the process. Danielle could hardly control her eyes either. It was hard trying to discreetly watch him when her eyes seemed to have a mind of their own.

As if in the distance, Danielle could hear her friends' snickers as she stood before the counter, smiling at A.J. as if he were the only man on earth. And Danielle was positive that A.J.'s sister was surprised at the way she had come in and taken his professionalism from a ten to barely a one.

Other customers walked through the door and broke the silence in the room with their own conversation. Déjà greeted them and urged A.J. to hurry with Danielle's purchase. After paying, Danielle grabbed her bag and Kennedi's hand as she prepared to leave.

"Wait," Brenda said. "After all that grinning you just did, you're not even gonna get her number?" she asked A.J.

"Bre," Danielle scolded, trying to hide her embarrassment. "I'm sorry," she told A.J.

"No, I would like your number, if that's okay with you." A.J. smiled as he pulled a BlackBerry from his pocket and handed it to her.

Danielle smiled brightly as she took it and programmed her name and number into the system.

"Oh, Mommy, let me see." Kennedi eagerly grabbed at her mother's arm.

Danielle quickly brushed Kennedi's hand away and gave A.J. his phone back with a smile. "I'll hear from you soon?"

"Most definitely," A.J. answered as he watched her and her friends leave the store.

Chapter 4

Jayda

After taking Danielle and Kennedi home, Jayda drove home and was glad when she pulled into the driveway of her family's townhouse. She was so tired that it felt like a chore to shut off the car's engine, climb out of the vehicle, and head toward the front door. As soon as she walked through the door, she heard her parents arguing in their bedroom.

"I'm sick of this, Preston!" she heard her mother yelling. "You're always doing crap like this. Now, I want to know whose number this is."

Her father answered, "Heather, I don't know what you're talking about. I don't know how that got into my pocket. It's not mine."

Jayda shook her head and went upstairs to find her thirteen-year-old twin siblings in her room watching television.

"Hey, guys," Jayda greeted them.

"Hey," they somberly answered.

"How long have they been arguing?" Jayda asked as she placed her book bag on the floor next to her bed.

"About twenty minutes," her brother, Cameron, answered.

"Mom called some lady's number she found in Dad's stuff," her sister, Candice, added nonchalantly.

Jayda sighed and sat on her bed as her siblings continued watching television. They'd been enduring arguments like this for the last several months. Their dad's infidelity had caused strife between their parents and stress between themselves. Jayda was glad that in a few months she would be leaving for college, but she felt sorry for her brother and sister, who would have to continue living in this house for another four years.

She'd often prayed that her parents would put themselves out of their misery and just divorce, but she'd soon pray that they would just work everything out and stay together. She knew that none of them—she, her siblings, nor their parents—wanted to split up their family, but it seemed as if they had no other options.

"Hey, you guys," Jayda called for her siblings' attention. "Do you wanna go somewhere?"

"Please," Candice begged. "I need to get out of this house."

Jayda laughed and said, "Let's go."

"Where are we going?" Cameron asked.

Jayda shrugged. "Anywhere but here."

The kids were able to leave the house without their parents' knowledge because they were too busy screaming to hear the front door open and the car pulling out of the driveway. Jayda drove around aimlessly for about ten minutes and then realized that a baseball practice was in progress at her school tonight. Because the team wasn't the best in the county, their practices usually ran extremely late and were sometimes open for visitors to watch. She figured that watching the guys try to better their game before the start of the season in March was much better than staying at home and listening to her parents argue. So she made a sharp right turn and headed toward Freedman High School.

"Guys, please stay with me," Jayda instructed her siblings. "And, Candice, don't try to talk to these high school guys because they are way too old for your fast tail," Jayda told her sister, who had a habit of being flirtatious.

They got out of the car and headed toward the baseball field. Jayda looked around for Lauren, knowing her friend would be here because Sterling, who'd played baseball throughout high school and college, was the coach. She knew exactly where to find Lauren, so she walked directly toward the dugout.

"Hey. What are you doing here?" Lauren asked when she saw Jayda walk up with Cameron and Candice behind her.

"It was too much drama going on in my house for us, so I decided to come out here." She looked over and saw Sterling standing next to the dugout. "I knew I'd find you over here," Jayda said to Lauren before turning her attention to Sterling. "Hey, Mr. Sterling."

Sterling smiled toward Jayda. "Hi, Ms. Henderson. Are these your siblings?"

"Yep." Jayda proceeded to make introductions. "Cameron and Candice, this is my history teacher, Mr. Sterling."

Cameron barely waved, but Candice was showing every one of her teeth as she smiled wide and giggled. "Hi."

Jayda elbowed her sister and shook her head. "He's taken," she casually informed her as she looked at Lauren.

Lauren glanced at Sterling, who only shook his head with a faint smile tugging at his lips.

"Mr. Sterling, do you mind if we sit in on your practice?" Jayda asked her teacher, and when he shook his head, she told Lauren, "We're going to watch from the bleachers. You make sure you behave." Lauren laughed as Jayda and her siblings walked off.

They took their seats and watched as the guys practiced. They started off practicing their swings and throws, but after about a half hour, Sterling asked the guys to play a mock game. They divided the team in two and prepared to show their skills to the few visitors who'd decided to watch the practice.

The first two players up to bat struck out miserably; then Jayda noticed one of her good friends step up to the plate and prepare to bat. His name was Evan Patterson and he was one of the all-star players on the team and in the top 10 percent of the senior class. He was about five inches taller than Jayda and his brown skin was almost as dark as hers. His long hair was neatly twisted into dreadlocks and his mustache trimmed. Some called him a pretty boy, but Jayda thought he was just concerned about his appearance, unlike many of the other guys who attended their school. Jayda found Evan very attractive, but had never thought about approaching him romantically, especially since he seemed to only see them as just good friends.

The pitcher threw the ball toward him, and with one strong swing Evan sent the ball far into the outfield, giving him the chance to score the first homerun of the game. Though this was just a practice, Evan's homerun caused a cheer to erupt among the small audience. Jayda used to wonder why Evan didn't attend a school where the baseball team was actually receiving positive publicity. But she'd found out that though he was passionate about his favorite sport and wanted to make a career out of it, he not only needed but wanted something to fall back on.

"At Freedman," he'd told her, "I get an education I can't get anywhere else in the district. I need this place." Jayda was glad to see that his priorities were straight.

Throughout the game, Evan scored three runs and one more homerun that allowed three players, including himself, to score for his side of the team; and he also pitched a couple of times, striking out several of the opposing team's players. Unsurprisingly, Evan's team won the practice game.

"Man, this team is gonna have a crappy season," Cameron proclaimed as they descended the stands. "But homeboy Evan got some serious talent."

Jayda smiled. "Yeah, there's talk about him going pro."

"I wanna meet him." Candice was grinning from ear to ear. "He's cute."

"Well, I wanna meet him too," Cameron admitted, "but it ain't 'cause I think he's cute." He cut his eyes at his twin sister.

Jayda chuckled as she walked over to the dugout once more, to find the players who'd lost sulking. There was one guy who was throwing bats around in a hissy fit. Sterling was standing before them, trying to give an encouraging speech about teamwork and relentless practicing. Jayda stood next to Lauren, who was in awe just of Sterling's presence alone.

"Isn't he wonderful?" Lauren said, mostly to herself.

Jayda shook her head silently and wondered if Lauren was digging herself into a deep hole that she would never get out of if things progressed as they were. Jayda was happy that her friend had found someone she was actually interested in, since Lauren hardly ever paid attention to the guys who usually approached her. However, Jayda honestly believed that Lauren had found the wrong person . . . Her timing was off. Maybe if it were a year, or even three months, from now, Lauren wanting to be with Sterling and Sterling possibly wanting to be with Lauren would be okay.

Jayda had been listening to the radio a few nights ago and the DJ was answering e-mails sent in by her listeners. One letter had been submitted by a woman who said she was a twenty-something teacher who was attracted to her eighteen-year-old male student. She was wondering if a relationship between them would be okay, even if she waited for the student to graduate. Many people had called in and openly disapproved of the relationship, but one caller had said it would be okay as long as the teacher waited until the student graduated. Jayda couldn't say she disagreed with the latter, but she did agree that a relationship between her friend and teacher at this moment shouldn't be an option. Stating her opinion, though, wasn't necessary, because Lauren would only do what she pleased.

Once Sterling finished with his speech, the guys grabbed their bags of equipment and prepared to leave. Jayda walked up behind Evan and tapped him on the shoulder. The gentleman turned around and smiled at her.

"Hey, Jayda, I didn't even know you were here," Evan said. "You don't ever come to the open practices."

Jayda smiled. "I'm not a big fan of baseball, but I didn't have anything else to do tonight."

Evan's smile grew wider. "Well, I'm glad you came. I don't get to see you much outside of school."

Jayda raised her eyebrows. She saw an opportunity she couldn't pass up. "Well, that's because you never ask to see me outside of school."

"Looks like some changes are in order," Evan responded, much to her pleasure.

Jayda looked down at Candice, who was noisily clearing her throat for attention.

Evan looked at Candice and smiled. "Who's this pretty young lady?"

Candice giggled and blushed and Cameron rolled his eyes as Jayda replied, "This is my sister, Candice, and my brother, Cameron. They wanted to meet you."

Evan shook Candice's hand softly and gave Cameron a firmer shake. "Well, it's nice to meet you. Are you guys twins?"

"Yeah," Cameron answered. "Your game was on point, man. Too bad the rest of your team wasn't."

Evan chuckled softly, but didn't comment because a few of his teammates were still nearby. "Thanks," he said. "Well, I need a shower, so I'ma head home. I'll see you later, Jayda."

"Okay," Jayda said as she watched him pick up his bag and leave.

"Jayda, you are so sprung," Cameron told her matter-of-factly. "You better watch yourself. Don't end up with some jerk like Dad."

"Don't talk about Daddy like that," Candice said, hitting her brother's arm.

"Well, he is a jerk." Cameron shrugged. "Anyone who plays a good woman like Mama *is* a jerk."

Jayda wanted to agree, but decided against it. She didn't want to cause her siblings to believe anything negative about their father. If they wanted to think he was a bad guy that would be their own opinion.

"Come on, you guys, let's go home. I'm sure Mom and Dad have calmed down by now." Jayda placed an arm around both of her siblings and began walking to her car.

By the time Jayda pulled into her driveway, it was almost nine o'clock. Her brother and sister were nearly falling over in the car; the day had apparently worn them all out. Though she was ready to fall into the softness of her bed sheets, Jayda dreaded going back into the house. Being away from the turmoil in her home had been too precious to waste, so she savored every minute.

"Cam, Candi," she called to them. "We're home. Wake up! Dang, y'all act like we've been on the road for hours."

"Feels like it," Cameron said somberly as he yawned and stepped out of the car.

When they walked into the house, they found their father bringing several suitcases out of their parents' bedroom. Jayda watched in confusion, although she knew exactly what was going on.

"Daddy," Candice called cautiously as she walked toward Preston, "where are you going?"

Preston looked at his children, who stood waiting for an explanation. "Kids, sit down for a minute."

The twins obeyed, but Jayda continued standing. She stood with her arms folded and left foot tapping against the carpeted floor. She glared at her father and wished he would just leave because there was no excuse he could give them that would justify him turning his back on his family.

"Jayda, please don't do this," Preston begged as he looked at her pleadingly.

"Dad, please. *I'm* not doing anything," she spat. "*You're* the one walking out on us."

Preston shook his head vigorously. "I'm not walking out on you guys. Your mother and I just need a break from each other. It's not permanent; maybe a few weeks . . . or months."

Candice was crying, but Cameron had the same firm, uncaring look on his face that Jayda had. Preston pulled Candice in his arms and hugged her tight, allowing her tears to wet his shirt.

"Princess, everything's gonna be okay. I'm always going to be here for you. I promise."

Jayda had had enough; she didn't want to watch her father walk out of that door and possibly never come back. She ran up the stairs, but stopped midway when Preston called her name.

"Jay baby, I love you," he told her.

"Yeah, Dad, I know. You've shown us all just how much you really care," she replied sarcastically before resuming the walk to her room.

Jayda sat in her room, fighting oncoming tears. For the past several months, she'd asked for this war in her house to end, but now that it seemed like it was, she realized that this was not what she really wanted. She wanted her father here with his family. She'd always liked the fact that, unlike some of her friends, she still had both parents at home with her, to care for and love her. Now, as she heard the garage door raising and soon her father's car driving away from the house, Jayda wondered when, or even if, she'd have both parents at home again.

Chapter 5

Brenda

Friday morning, Brenda woke up with the sun shining through her sheer pink curtains. She turned toward the alarm clock that was blaring in her ear and slapped the "off" button. After stretching her body out like a limber cat, Brenda relaxed her muscles and sighed heavily. The week was finally coming to an end. Friday was the best day of the week, in her opinion, and she couldn't wait until the day was over so she could come home and unwind.

She climbed out of bed and walked over to her dresser. As she looked through her drawers for something to wear, Brenda noticed that she had a voice mail on her cell phone, which was sitting on top of her dresser. Whoever had called her last night must have called extremely late because she had stayed up until midnight, but had not heard her phone ringing. She picked up her phone and dialed her voice mail number to listen to the message.

"Hey, Bre, it's Ken. I'm sorry I'm calling so late, but I just wanted to make sure we were still on for tomorrow night. I hope so because I can't wait to show you how a queen should be treated. Well, I guess I need to get to bed. I'll see you at school. Bye."

Brenda smiled as she ended the call. She'd almost forgotten about their date. Homework had consumed her thoughts all last night; she didn't even get a chance to eat dinner, settling for a granola bar to partially satisfy her stomach's hunger.

Brenda wished that she didn't have to work so hard to keep her grades up. She remembered a time when learning came natural, but now her Advanced Placement and gifted courses had her staying up late in the evenings, sometimes until well after midnight, studying and doing homework. It paid off though; she was a straight A student and was in the running to become valedictorian for her senior class.

By seven-thirty, Jayda was outside waiting for Brenda to come out and get into the car. Brenda knew she was running behind, but there was no way she was going to leave the house without her eyeliner, mascara, and blush. When she finally emerged from the house, Jayda was blowing her horn like a madwoman. Lucky for Brenda, only one of her younger siblings was still at home waiting for her bus, so no one was around to nag her about the excessive noise.

"You know, you do this every day. I'ma stop waiting for your slow behind," Jayda fussed as Brenda stepped into the car. "You know I have to pick up Lauren and Danni, and Danni needs me to drop Kennedi off at school today."

Brenda rolled her eyes. "Why? Doesn't her mom take Kennedi to school before going to work in the mornings?"

"Well apparently Ms. Beverly had to go into work earlier than usual today and didn't want to have Kennedi standing outside of the school, waiting for the doors to open," Jayda answered snidely. "Besides, I have no problem helping Danni out because she's a good friend and she is always ready when I get to her house."

"Whatever." Brenda smacked her lips. "I can't wait 'til I get my own car."

"Me either," Jayda agreed as she pulled out of Brenda's driveway and drove toward Lauren's home.

After picking up Lauren, Danielle, and Kennedi, Jayda dropped Kennedi off at school, and was parking in the student parking lot one minute before first bell was to ring.

"Look," Jayda said as she turned off the car, "we cannot be just getting here when the bell rings, so I'ma need to pick y'all up earlier or something. That or you guys just need to be ready when I get your house."

Danielle's face tightened. "I'm sorry if I'm making you run late, Jayda, but I didn't know until last night my mom had to go to work early today. And if it's a hassle for you to take me to pick Kennedi up in the afternoons because of cheerleading, then I can just ride the city bus. I don't wanna be too much trouble."

Jayda shook her head. "*No,* Danielle, that's not what I'm saying. The only person who holds me up in the mornings is Bre. And in the afternoons . . . I mean it does take a minute for me to drive over to the elementary school and then take you and Kennedi home before practice starts, but I always make it, so it's no trouble."

Danielle opened her door. "Like I said, I don't want to be a hassle, so I'll just ride the bus. It's not a big deal." She got out of the car and began walking toward the school.

Brenda looked at Jayda and shook her head. "See, I don't even understand why you do what you do for her. She doesn't even appreciate it." Brenda got out of the car and sashayed toward the school building.

The girls barely had time to retrieve their books from their lockers before having to rush off to class before the late bell declared them tardy. Brenda walked into her first class two minutes late without an excused tardy pass.

"Excuse me, Ms. Killian, do you have a pass?" her teacher questioned as Brenda sat in her desk.

Brenda offered the older woman a smile. "No, ma'am, I just got here and they just told me to go ahead to class."

Her teacher nodded apprehensively. "Okay, well, please try to make it to school on time."

"Yes, ma'am," Brenda replied, though she knew she hardly had any control over what time she got to school when she was relying on someone else for transportation.

Brenda opened her calculus book and began studying the chapter that they'd been working in for the last couple of days. She couldn't stay focused, though; her mind wandered to her date with Ken tonight, and she was excited and afraid at the same time. She wanted to go out with him, no doubt, but she was afraid of getting caught up and losing sight of the goals she'd set for herself. Brenda was extremely frightened of becoming a lovesick puppy, and the thought of her grades falling scared her even more. She couldn't let that happen; she had to stay focused.

Suddenly, a thought popped into her head. If Brenda could entertain both Ken and Zane at the same time without making any commitments, she could prevent herself from falling for either one of them. She smiled inwardly; that was her plan and she would stick to it no matter how much Zane smiled his gorgeous smile or Ken batted his long eyelashes. Brenda was only committed to focusing on her schoolwork and academic achievements, and she was not going to let any guy come between her and her run for number one in her class.

Danielle

Danielle tried to concentrate on what her drama teacher was telling the class about placing themselves in the character's shoes, but her mind was elsewhere. She had known that it was just a matter of time before her friends got tired of caring for her and her daughter. Not wanting to be the charity case her mother despised, Danielle acknowledged the fact that maybe she was placing too much responsibility on Jayda by asking her to transport her daughter from school every day.

Now that Danielle thought about it, the only payment that she had offered Jayda for her kindness was a "Thanks, Jay. You're the best." She hadn't offered to pay Jayda or to give her gas money to refill her tank each week. She figured the reason Jayda never asked her for money or why she, herself, never felt bad about not offering Jayda a few dollars was because Jayda drove around to each of her friends' house to pick them up for school and work. None of them had offered her a tribute of appreciation and they had gotten used to the arrangement.

Now that Danielle didn't have a free ride, she would be paying money every day to take public transportation from school to the elementary school in the afternoons to pick Kennedi up, and finally back home. Not to mention, it would be her transportation to work on the weekends as well. Suddenly, Danielle regretted her emotional decision to abandon her free ride, but she was much too proud to change her mind and ask Jayda to dismiss her decision.

Even though her day had started off slightly bad, Danielle wasn't feeling terribly low because she had heard from A.J. last night. She had been surprised that he'd called so soon. Kennedi had answered her cell phone because Danielle had been in the bathroom, and she had been so embarrassed when she heard Kennedi say, "My mommy's sitting on the toilet," that she almost didn't call A.J. back like he'd asked.

When she did, though, A.J. answered the phone laughing, only causing Danielle's embarrassment to escalate. Once his laughter subsided, their conversation flowed smoothly. She had been surprised to hear that A.J. was actually a sophomore at Morehouse College. He didn't look to be nineteen, but after talking to him for a while, Danielle could tell that he was much more mature than his age. He had just started working at the children's clothing store that his mother owned so that he could save up the extra money for his first apartment.

After talking about himself for a few minutes, A.J. coerced Danielle into telling him about her life. She knew it would only be a matter of time before the conversation switched from school to Kennedi, but she hadn't been prepared to tell A.J. about her daughter's absentee father.

"His name was Keenan Hobson," Danielle told him.

"His name *was* Keenan?" A.J. questioned. "Is he dead or something?"

"Sometimes I wish," she answered honestly. "But, to me, he is nonexistent. He's not around for Kennedi. He actually moved away when he found out I was pregnant."

"His parents actually picked up and moved because he didn't want to take care of his daughter?" he asked disbelievingly.

Danielle laughed dryly. "Unbelievable, right? But his mother still lives somewhere around here. He went to North Carolina and moved in with his father, who, before then, hadn't seen Keenan in about two years."

A.J. breathed deeply into the phone. "Wow, and yet, you've raised a beautiful little girl all by yourself. I commend you."

"Thank you, but if it weren't for my mother's negativity I wouldn't have the motivation to continue doing this."

When A.J. had questioned her statement, Danielle went on to tell him about how she and her mother had been really close before Kennedi came into the picture. Not only that, but Danielle had been closer to God as well. She and her mother would go to church every Sunday and Danielle would even spend quiet time alone reading the Bible. Now, not only had she strayed away from her Heavenly Father, but she'd also shied away from spending time with her mother, Beverly, who criticized her constantly about the way Danielle disciplined, raised, and treated Kennedi. Either Danielle was whipping Kennedi for something too minor or she wasn't disciplining her enough or she was too strict for one thing and a week later she was too lenient concerning the same situation. It was as if Beverly was punishing Danielle for just being the mother she thought she was supposed to be.

Danielle honestly felt that her mother was the reason she was no longer as close to God as she once was. Church had been their mother-daughter time, but Danielle had stopped going, even picking up a Sunday morning shift at work, to spend less time around her cynical mother. Although Beverly, along with Kennedi, continued to occasionally attend Sunday morning worship, Danielle refused to go. Because of that she no longer felt that strong connection she once had with Christ. Not that her mother should have been a hindrance, but Danielle was sure Beverly was part of the reason why she struggled with finding her way back to her faith. She'd been through so much and received so little support that she felt that both Beverly and God had left her alone to endure the trials that came along with motherhood. The only time Danielle felt as if she was doing a good job with Kennedi was when her daughter would tell her how much she loved her. Hearing Kennedi tell her that she was loved made all of the trouble and stress worthwhile.

"Well, I've only known you for a day and I can tell that you're a good mother," A.J. told her. "And God hasn't left you, Danielle. He's the only reason you're continuing to press on in spite of the difficulties."

Talking to A.J. made Danielle feel more comforted than she'd felt in a long time. Though she surrounded herself with a group of girls who were constantly admired by their peers, Danielle felt the least confident in the group. She exhibited pride and poise when walking through her school's hallways and she pretended to be into the attention she received from guys, but honestly, their compliments and come-on lines meant zero to her and they did even less for her self-confidence. However, when she talked to A.J., she felt special and her confidence level rocketed.

Danielle wasn't necessarily looking for a boyfriend and she definitely didn't need one, but she knew it would be nice to have someone to call her knight in shining armor. She was a sap for romance, and indulging herself in romantic novels and movies made Danielle long for that one guy who would come and sweep her off of her feet. She was no fool, though. After her relationship with Keenan, Danielle had learned that not just any guy could come up to her with sweet, endearing words and get her to fall for him instantly. Forcefully being taught to rely on herself, Danielle was strong in her belief that she didn't need a male companion in order to survive. It seemed that, aside from Jayda, she was the only one of her friends who believed there was more to a guy than just his physical appearance. As a result, she was known for being the picky one among her friends when it came to who she would date.

A.J. had already told Danielle that he wasn't looking for a girlfriend, and she respected that, but she could tell that resisting the urge to fall for this intelligent and endearing guy was going to be one of the hardest tasks she'd ever had to undertake.

Chapter 6

Lauren

Friday evening, Jayda, Lauren, and the rest of the cheerleaders changed out of their uniforms and into their dance attire for the halftime show during the basketball game. While they undressed, Lauren listened as Jayda talked about Danielle's decision to stop allowing her to pick Kennedi up from school.

"I just don't get what the attitude was about." Jayda wiggled out of her cheerleading skirt and pulled on her dance tights. "I was just saying that I needed to pick you guys up earlier or y'all needed to be ready on time. And I was really referring to Bre when I was saying that. I don't see how I offended her or what the big deal was. I like picking Kennedi up from the center. It gives me a chance to help Danni out, especially since I know she has a hard enough time concerning other things."

Lauren sat on the bench in the girls' locker room and placed her dancing shoes on her feet. "Maybe Danielle's having her own issues. If you haven't noticed, none of us are as close to her as we used to be back in middle school. Kennedi's changed some things, mainly our relationship with Danni." She stood up and shrugged her shoulders while Jayda finished dressing. "Maybe she thinks she's being a burden and feels like you think the same thing. I don't know what the problem is, but you don't need to worry about it, because you know Danni's gonna make a way for herself regardless if she has your help or anyone else's."

Jayda sighed heavily and folded her arms across her chest. "I guess you're right. Danielle's as stubborn as she wants to be. Even if she has no other way to get Kennedi to school, she still wouldn't come and ask me for a ride."

"She's just like that," Lauren said, "but I love it because that's what makes her strongest out of all of us."

"And her being strong keeps me lifted," Jayda added with a smile. "It makes me feel like I can get through anything."

Lauren smiled also. "Now, let's take that lifted spirit out on the court. We go out in two minutes."

Jayda rubbed her hands together anxiously. "I don't know why I always get so nervous before dancing at halftime," she said, "but I do. I don't even have anyone to dance for, unlike you."

Lauren looked at Jayda in confusion. "What are you talking about?" She paused and then placed her left hand on her hip. "I know you're not talking about Jarred . . . that stalker. I do not dance for him."

"No, I'm not talking about Jarred," Jayda's stated casually, and Lauren felt completely clueless.

"Then *who* are you talking about?" Lauren asked.

Jayda shook her head. "No one. C'mon, the game's at halftime."

The cheer coach walked into the locker room and clapped her hands noisily. "Hey, let's line it up, girls!"

As captain, Lauren took the head of the line as the rest of the girls assembled behind her. They strutted out onto the court as their schoolmates cheered for them. As they stood in formation, the music began to play and the girls began to dance uniformly. As she danced, Lauren kept her required smile in place. She loved dancing, as well as cheering. She danced with the drill team for the football season and cheered during the basketball months. Not only did the sports keep her fit, but they also gave her a chance to do something other than academic-related activities at school.

Her mind wondered back to Jayda's comment about her having someone to dance for, and as she continued moving to the music's beats, Lauren tried to look around to see who might be here for her to entertain. She was moving so fast, though, that she had no time to look at any particular person. She mentally counted the last sixteen counts of the routine and was finally able to stop dancing. As she stood in a squatted position with her left leg stretched out beside her and both her arms extended high in the air, her plastered smile widened at the sight of Sterling standing near the entrance of the gym.

Oh my God. What is he doing here? Lauren's heart raced. Was he here to see her or the game? The basketball season had started back in November and if Sterling was just coming to see how well the team played, he could've done so months ago. Lauren's heart told her that he was here to see her in action. As his eyes locked with hers, she knew she was right.

The second track began playing and Lauren was determined to dance with more passion and vigor than she had in her entire lifetime. By the time the team finished this routine, the entire crowd was on their feet cheering them on. The girls strutted off of the court and to the stands, taking a seat on the bottom two rows of bleachers on the home side.

As the step team took the court, Lauren elbowed Jayda and whispered, "Why didn't you tell me he was here?"

Jayda gave a slight smile and they looked at Sterling. He nodded in their direction and they waved in return. Lauren could barely contain her glee and knew that Jayda was trying hard not to laugh out loud at her. Lauren knew she was acting as if she were having her first elementary school crush, but that's how she felt.

"I didn't know he was coming, but I saw him earlier when I came out to watch a minute of the game while we were waiting for halftime. He had to come here for you because the basketball team has been playing for months now, but we just told him yesterday that we were cheerleaders," Jayda reminded her friend.

"Well, he's had to have known that we were cheerleaders," Lauren countered, though her heart was still fluttering. "I mean, we wear our uniforms every week and I know he's been noticed that."

"I guess he finally wanted to see his eye candy in action."

Lauren shoved Jayda playfully.

By the time the second half of the game started, the girls had changed back into their cheerleading uniforms and Sterling had left the gymnasium, much to Lauren's disappointment; but she was happy to know that he had come just to see her moves. Maybe she would ask him how much he enjoyed the show on Monday.

"Oh my goodness!" Jayda exclaimed, laughing. "Lauren, look who they're putting in the game."

Lauren was forced to take her mind off of Sterling and focus her attention on the court. Jarred, who hardly ever received any playing time, was running out onto the court. He looked to where the girls stood on the sidelines and pointed toward Lauren as he nodded his head.

Lauren shuddered. "Eww, why is he looking at me?"

Jayda turned slightly toward her friend with a question in her eyes. "Why are you so mean to that boy? He's nice, he's cute, and he's practically in love with you."

"Jayda, you know me. I don't like begging guys. I like a hard catch . . . like Mr. Sterling."

"Yeah, he's nearly unconquerable." Jayda cringed.

Lauren could read the expression on Jayda's face and knew that her friend wished she hadn't just said that out loud. "And what is that supposed to mean?" she questioned, with a fierce glare.

Jayda shook her head and shrugged. "I just think that you should turn your efforts toward someone more your speed. Someone who won't get fired from his job or go to jail for being with you."

Lauren stared at Jayda as her attitude began to flare. "Jayda, since when are you against me and Mr. Sterling? You were all smiles about it just a few minutes ago."

Jayda refused to look at Lauren as she concentrated on the game. "I just think you should stop while you're ahead."

"Girl, you just gave me motivation to work harder to try to get what I want," Lauren said tightly. "And you know I always get what I want. Why do you think my parents are spending out money they don't hardly have for my birthday party?" She laughed before shouting out a cheer to the girls.

Jayda

As Jayda drove home that evening, she pondered over her conversation with Lauren. *I should've just kept my mouth closed,* she inwardly scolded herself for sharing her true feelings toward Lauren and Sterling's relationship with her friend. But for some reason, the issue wouldn't stop taunting her mind. She laughed and encouraged Lauren's infatuation in order to avoid conflict. Lauren wasn't one who liked to be called out about anything she was doing, whether it was positive or negative, so Jayda just kept her opinion to herself and allowed her friend to believe she supported her. But the last thing she wanted was for Sterling to get fired for fooling around with Lauren. Though the age of consent was sixteen, Jayda was glad Lauren seemed to have sense enough to wait until she turned eighteen before really getting involved with Sterling. But even if they waited, his job would still be on the line. Jayda was extremely afraid of what would happen once Lauren's birthday arrived; her becoming legal would probably give her the gas she needed to put her move on Sterling in complete motion.

Sterling was first on Lauren's birthday party guest list and Lauren had already stated that no one, not even her three closest friends, would receive their party invitations until Sterling got his next Monday. Lauren's party was supposed to be the bash of the year and only those with invites were welcome. She was planning on having so many attendees that she had her parents hire security to monitor every corner of the ballroom they had rented. Lauren was hoping for a car to commemorate her eighteenth birthday, but Jayda knew that if Lauren were given Sterling on a silver platter, she would be happy.

Lauren's adamant declaration about getting what she wanted caused Jayda to cringe in disgust. She loved Lauren to death, but she was much too cocky. She needed to be put in her place and Jayda knew that someone would soon do it. It would take Lauren messing with the wrong person and them being upset enough to set her straight.

By the time Jayda reached her house, she was worn out. She planned on heading straight upstairs for a shower before going right to bed. When she entered the house, she saw her mother sitting on the sofa in the family room, reading a novel. Jayda quietly greeted her mother, hoping Heather wouldn't stop her for a long conversation.

"So, how was the game?" Heather asked as she placed the book face down on her lap.

"We won," Jayda responded unemotionally.

Heather smiled. "Congrats. I'm sorry I couldn't come, but I wasn't feeling up to it."

Jayda shrugged. "I understand." She honestly couldn't care less if her mother came just to watch her cheer during the game and dance at halftime. Jayda wanted to spend as little time with her family as she could right now. Her mother was so depressed, and being around her made Jayda feel the same emotion. Jayda liked being happy and being around her family didn't afford her that luxury, so she was glad that her mother had decided to stay home and mope instead of bringing her disheartened attitude to the basketball game.

"Jay, I don't know how this is affecting you, but I want you to know that your father and I did what we thought was best for all of us."

Jayda rolled her eyes heavenward as she wondered how many parents used that same excuse when they separated. "Mom, I'm fine. I'm glad Dad left."

"You are?" Heather seemed surprised.

"I mean, I'm not happy about the circumstance, but all of the arguing was working my nerves. It was either one of you guys leave, or I would've been living out on the streets." Jayda looked into her mother's eyes. "I just hope that this is not permanent."

Heather didn't respond to her daughter's comment; instead, she changed the subject. "Are you hungry? I can warm up some dinner for you."

Jayda shook her head. "I'm just gonna shower and then turn in for tonight. Good night." She went upstairs to her room, only to find Candice on her computer.

"Candi, what are you doing?" Jayda asked in frustration. She was already tired and her siblings, namely Candice, always bothering her things agitated her to no end. She was the only one of her siblings who had her own laptop; everyone else in the house used the office desktop. But whenever one of the twins lost their computer privileges for whatever reason, they tended to sneak in and use her personal computer. Not only was her sister on the computer, but she was using the webcam to converse with someone over Skype.

Candice told her friend to hold on before muting the microphone. "I'm on Skype, obviously." She rolled her eyes and resumed talking.

Jayda hastily walked over to the computer and discontinued the video call. "Candice, I'm telling you for the last time to stay off of my computer. Now, get out of my room!"

Candice stomped off and Jayda slammed the door behind her. She was so tired of her entire family that she wished she could just move out on her own. She couldn't wait until the time came for her to move into her college dormitory. She'd finally be away from the people who annoyed her most.

Her cell phone rang and an unfamiliar number appeared on her caller ID. She hesitantly answered, "Hello?" Her voice was laced with aggravation.

"Hello, may I speak to Jayda?" a male voice asked apprehensively.

Jayda scrunched her face at the voice; it seemed vaguely familiar. "This is Jayda. Who is this?"

The male laughed. "Jayda, after four years, you don't know my voice?" he asked. "It's Evan."

Jayda's mood lightened and her spirits lifted. "Evan?" She wondered why he was calling her. "How'd you get my number?"

"Umm . . . I've had your number for a couple years now. Why *don't* you have mine?" he asked, sounding almost offended.

Jayda remembered exchanging numbers with him awhile ago, but she'd gone through two cell phones since then, and because she and Evan rarely talked outside of school, she never thought to get his number again. "Uh . . . I guess I never asked you for it again after I got my new phone a few months back." She chucked softly. "But I'll be sure to save it now. Anyway, what's up?"

"I was just calling to see if you were doing anything tomorrow night. And if you aren't, would you like to go to the movies with me?"

Jayda knew to play it cool, though she wanted so badly to scream yes. "Well, I'm not sure. It is kinda short notice and I don't usually accept invitations for a date unless they're at least three days in advance."

Evan's laugh was mellow and deep. "Well, do you think you could make an exception for a friend?"

Jayda smiled as she thought about his proposal. "I guess. What do you have in mind to see?"

"Whatever you want is fine with me," he said, causing Jayda's dark cheeks to flush.

"Well, anything funny or scary will do," she told him.

"Okay, we'll see what's playing tomorrow around . . . seven?" he suggested.

"Sure. Can't wait. Bye." She hung up the phone.

She was so excited that she could hardly contain the shout of joy that wanted to erupt from the pit of her stomach. Her computer began to make a noise and she noticed the Skype tune warning of an incoming call. She figured that it was the same guy she had hung up on earlier.

"Candice!" Jayda yelled to her sister. "Come here please." She didn't want to yell for her sister to answer the call and cause her to get into trouble; she hoped Candice would just come and see what she wanted.

When her sister entered her room, Jayda pointed toward the computer, signaling that it was for her. She was too happy to deny the young teens a chance to speak to one another. Everyone deserved their chance at love, and tomorrow, Jayda would get hers.

Chapter 7

Brenda

Brenda smiled as Ken handed her the movie ticket he'd just purchased. He'd chosen to take her to a scary movie, definitely a plus as far as Brenda was concerned. As they headed toward the food counter to purchase a few snacks, she noticed Jayda and Evan exiting the line.

"Hey, Jayda," Brenda called out, surprised to see her friend out on a date.

Jayda turned to face the voice and smiled at the sight of Brenda. "Hey, Bre. I didn't know you had a date tonight." She gazed up at Ken and gave him a smile.

Brenda laughed. "Well, I didn't even know that you came out of your house on a Saturday night."

Evan looked down at Jayda, who almost seemed embarrassed. "Oh, I'll definitely have to change that." He took her hand. "Well, we have to get in our seats before the movie starts."

Brenda watched as they walked in the opposite direction of where she and her date would be going. Ken ordered a huge tub of popcorn to share and two sodas. They headed toward their theatre and took their seats.

As the previews played, Brenda hoped that this date would go well. She prayed that Ken would raise the bar between him and Zane and make Brenda increase her standards for them both. If all things went well, this little competition between the two guys would be very entertaining. She gazed at Ken and smiled when he looked back at her.

"You all right?" he asked her.

Brenda nodded as she settled into her seat. "I'm great."

When the movie began, Ken placed his arm around Brenda's shoulder and she moved in closer and settled into the embrace. *This feels kinda nice,* Brenda thought, but she reminded herself that she was not to fall for this guy, because if she did she would end up just like her mother.

Brenda's mother, Eileen, had given her heart to man after man only to have it repeatedly broken. After her third divorce, Eileen vowed to her children never to put herself in the same situation again, but, as Brenda suspected, Eileen couldn't keep her promise. At the age of forty-five, she was once again going through a bitter divorce after only a year of marriage.

Brenda and her four brothers and sisters were tired of getting attached to the men in their mother's life only to have them leave and never come back. Brenda was the second oldest child. Her older brother, Chase, who, along with Brenda, was the product of Eileen's first marriage, was off serving in the Navy. Brenda rarely ever got to see him because he was stationed in Corpus Christi, Texas, but when she did, she clung to him as if her life depended on it. He was the only man in her life who actually did all he possibly could for her and the rest of his family. He had promised Brenda that he would always be there for her and Brenda held that promise in her heart because, at this point in her life, it was the only thing she had to depend on.

Under Brenda were Taylor, who was thirteen; Maya, who was nine; and David, who was seven. Maya and

David were biracial and were the only two who cared to see their father, who was black. Taylor was at the rebel age and only did what she felt like doing. She was the one who caused the most trouble in the house, claiming that no one cared for her and that Eileen only gave birth to her because she felt she had to. Brenda had occasionally heard her younger sister say that if she committed suicide no one would care, but when she had taken the information to Eileen, her mother brushed it off as if it were not a big deal.

"She's just acting out," her mother would say, and Brenda hoped that she was right.

Brenda's life was always full of stress and she dealt with it by carelessly flirting with guys who would openly flirt in return. She felt that as long as she never became attached to any of them, like her mother tended to do, she'd be okay and her heart would stay in one piece. She hoped she was right.

Suddenly, a frightening scene in the movie brought Brenda's attention back to the present.

"Oh my God!" The horrific image caused her to nearly jump out of her seat.

Ken laughed as Brenda buried her face against his chest to block her vision of the bloody figure carrying a sharp machete in his hand.

Jayda

The theatre was full of laughter, and Jayda was cackling so hard that she was almost choking on her nachos. She picked up her soda to wash down the food as the laughter died down.

Evan had done an excellent job in choosing a funny movie because Jayda had been in need of a good laugh. It had taken her mind off of all the troubles at home, and had relieved some of the burdens concerning

Lauren from her back. She could hardly allow the first laugh to die down before another scene in the movie caused another round of laughter to erupt. Jayda had never seen such hilarity in one film before; this was too much, but she was enjoying every minute of it. She looked over at Evan, who was practically falling out of his seat. His mouth was wide open and his laughter came from deep within his belly. She was glad that they were both having a good time.

Jayda hadn't thought about having a boyfriend and the thought was still near the back of her mind, but she wouldn't mind taking it into consideration if things continued to progress with Evan. He was a really nice guy, and Jayda was glad that they had been friends for so long because she didn't have to worry about getting to know him. She'd known him for four years and Evan was consistent in character. He was sweet, honest, goal oriented, and respectable. He'd had only one girlfriend during the time Jayda had known him, and their relationship ended because the girl had been too clingy and always wanted to know what Evan was doing when she wasn't around him. Evan was a good friend, but Jayda wondered how good of a boyfriend he could be. She would love to find out.

She watched his movements and noticed how distinct his jaw line was and how sensual his lips looked. His mustache was neatly trimmed and only enhanced the appearance of his full lips. Jayda practically melted in her seat as she watched him laugh. She hadn't noticed that she'd been staring at him until he began staring back. It seemed as if time had stopped as he slowly leaned in and kissed her lips tenderly. Suddenly, he pulled back. The kiss was brief, but left a lingering feeling on her lips, that pladed Jayda in state of shock.

"I'm sorry," Evan said softly. "I've always wanted to do that and I couldn't help myself."

Jayda was momentarily speechless as she shook her head. "Oh . . . no. Umm, it's cool."

Evan smiled slightly at the shocked look on her face. "Are you sure? You seem a little caught off-guard."

She chuckled nervously. "I was, but it was okay, really."

He looked a little anxious. "So . . . you wouldn't mind if I did it again?"

Jayda had never considered herself to be the type of girl to kiss on the first date, let along in a dark movie theatre, but the brief peck Evan had just given her seemed right. She settled his anxiety with a small smile and shook her head. "No, I wouldn't mind."

Evan placed his arm around her shoulders and leaned in once more for a firmer, more sensual kiss. The laughter in the background went unheard as Jayda allowed herself fall deeper and deeper, hoping that Evan wouldn't let her land flat on her face.

Chapter 8

Lauren

Lauren walked to her locker on Monday morning, along with her friends, and wasn't shocked to see several students standing around the area anxiously awaiting the distribution of her party invitations. She turned toward Jayda with a smile as she opened her oversized purse and pulled out the silver envelopes labeled with each person's name. The first one was labeled MR. STERLING, and no one else was getting theirs until he received his.

She laughed aloud as the students followed her like newborn ducklings following their mother. Jayda, Brenda, and Danielle were supposed to help with keeping order as she gave out the invites, but they were too busy laughing at the individuals acting as if they had never been invited to a party before. The crowd came to a halt right outside of Sterling's classroom.

He was sitting at his desk, waiting for the first bell to ring, and looked surprised to see several students standing outside of his door as Lauren walked in. She smiled at him as she stopped right in front of his desk.

"Good morning, Mr. Sterling," Lauren greeted him cheerfully.

Sterling gazed at her with caution. "Hello, Ms. Hopewell." He glanced in confusion at the students standing in his doorway.

She smiled slyly. "I saw you at the game on Friday. Did you enjoy it?"

"If you're referring to the halftime show . . . yes, I did. You ladies were great," he said, to her pleasure.

"Did you enjoy any one dancer more than another?" she asked in a lowered voice.

Sterling laughed as he shifted several papers on his desk. "You are a very talented dancer and cheerleader, Lauren."

Lauren was content with his answer, imagining there was a deeper meaning, so she changed the subject. "You're not busy on March tenth, are you?"

"Not that I know of. Why?"

She handed him the invitation with a smile. "Well, I'm having a birthday party that night at eight o'clock," she told him. "I'm turning *eighteen,*" she emphasized. She noticed how Sterling's eyebrows rose with interest, but he caught himself before he let his guard completely down.

"And I'm invited?" he questioned. She nodded. "Are there any other teachers who are going to be there?"

Lauren scrunched her eyebrows together as if she was deep in thought. "No, not unless someone else invited them." She paused. "But if you would feel more comfortable around other adults, there's gonna be a few adult chaperons."

He smiled. "I guess I can squeeze you in," he said, to her excitement.

"Great, I'll save you a dance," she stated as she sauntered out of the classroom.

Lauren began passing out invitations and the students grabbed them as if they were one-hundred-dollar bills. She hoped Sterling would show up at the party, and, even more, she hoped he'd make the night an especially memorable one for her.

Danielle

Danielle laughed with Jayda as they waited for the bell to signal that their third-period class was to begin.

"Girl, this party is gonna be crazy," Jayda said as they continued laughing. "Did you see those people this morning?"

"Ooh, me, me! I want one!" Danielle imitated her peers. "They sounded like Kennedi."

"Oh, and did you see Jarred?" Jayda asked as she shook her head. "He looked so upset when Lauren didn't give him an invitation. I kinda felt sorry for him."

"Yeah, you know if Lauren wouldn't get upset about it, he would probably be my guest to the party."

"Why him?" Jayda asked.

"Well, she did say that if there was someone we wanted to come with us who wasn't on her list, we could bring that person, and Jarred looked so pitiful that I would take him just out of sympathy."

Jayda shook her head. "I think that's worse than not inviting him at all, but I thought you would invite that cutie from the mall to the party."

Danielle shrugged. "I thought about it, but I've talked to A.J. almost every day since we've met and the more I learn about him . . . Well, I'll just say that this party doesn't seem like his scene. He's really conservative."

"I think that's good for you, though," Jayda stated. "You know, he could be someone who could keep you focused on what's important."

"Like Kennedi?" Danielle asked; her smile had suddenly vanished.

Jayda shook her head. "No, not just Kennedi, but with school and work and anything else that's really important to you."

Danielle's face softened. "I'm sorry, it just seems like you guys sometimes put me on blast when it comes to Kennedi and how I raise or take care of her."

"Danni, I'm sorry if we've ever made you think that we feel like we're better than you, or we don't like spending a lot of time around you just because you have Kennedi, because we don't feel that way at all. As a matter of fact, I really admire you for being a single mother and still in school, even though it's not the best position to be in. Plus you're an honor roll student. You're doing better than all of us . . . well, except for Brainiac Brenda."

"Thanks." Danielle smiled. "I also wanted to thank you again for picking me up this morning and agreeing to pick Kennedi up from school again. Girl, I didn't know who that was blowing outside my house this morning. I almost ignored it until I looked out the window and saw you outside yelling for me to come on before I got left." She laughed.

Jayda chuckled. "You know I wasn't even listening to you on Friday with that mess. I gave you one afternoon to see how it was riding the bus and after that I knew you wouldn't like it."

"Yeah, I don't have the money to ride the bus." Danielle shook her head. "But because I've never told you this, I'ma say it now. I really, really appreciate you taking the time out to pick Kennedi and me up. I know it takes up a few gallons of gas and—"

Jayda stopped her before she could complete her sentence. "Don't even say that you're gonna start paying me for gas. I'm good and I don't have a problem taking my friend wherever she needs to go . . . for free."

"But gas is ridiculous and I don't feel comfortable using up yours without reimbursing you." Danielle spoke as the bell rang, signaling the start of the period.

"Seriously, Danni. My parents take care of that so I'm cool," Jayda insisted.

Danielle sighed and relented. "Okay, but if you ever need help, let me know and I got you."

"Mr. Patterson, you're late," they heard their teacher tell Evan as he walked through the classroom door seconds after the bell had rung. "Sign the tardy log."

Evan did as he was told and smiled as he sat in the desk positioned on the other side of Danielle.

Danielle watched as Jayda's face brightened at the sight of their mutual friend. She looked over at Evan and noticed that he was gazing at Jayda intently. She realized that the look in his eyes was different than it had been in the past and she wondered what was going on between the two.

"Hey, Evan." Danielle chuckled.

Evan barely took his eyes off of Jayda as he quickly nodded in Danielle's direction and replied, "Wassup, Danni." He took in Jayda's appearance and he smiled in approval. "Hey, you," he greeted Jayda.

Jayda was smiling as if she'd just been presented with a Publisher's Clearing House Sweepstakes million-dollar check. "Hey."

Danielle was dying to get the details surrounding this new relationship, but their teacher was beginning the lesson and there was no way she would be able to concentrate with these two lovebirds staring at each other.

"Hey, guys, I'm gonna need for you two to break this up until after class," she whispered to them, but it was as if she were like an invisible spirit that couldn't be heard within a dream with the way they were ignoring her.

Danielle looked at Jayda as if her friend were a stranger to her. She had never seen Jayda act like this before, but it was nice to know she had found someone who made her happy. "Okay, how about this," she tried

again. "Jayda, would you like to switch seats with me?"
She tried not to draw the teacher's attention by laughing aloud when Jayda jumped up, gathered her things,
and moved to Danielle's desk.

Danielle sat down in Jayda's seat just as the teacher
turned around to see what the commotion in the back
of the classroom was all about.

"Evan, Jayda, Danielle, is there a problem?" she
asked them.

Danielle looked at Evan and Jayda, who seemed
to be too wrapped up in each other to notice that the
teacher had addressed them. Danielle turned toward
the teacher and shook her head. "No, there's no problem," she answered.

The teacher turned back toward the board and
Danielle glanced at her friends once again and shook
her head. The two were practically in love and anyone
watching them could tell.

Brenda

Brenda took a seat at her usual lunch table next to
a few of her friends in her Advanced Placement psychology class. She wished that her usual friends were
bold enough to take the college accredited class, but
they all protested when she suggested that they sign up
for it, saying that it took up too much time and none
of them needed the class for their college majors. So
Brenda had been forced to make a few new friends this
semester, which was slightly harder for her than usual
because many females saw her as a potential threat,
especially if they had boyfriends with wandering eyes.
Almost anyone who knew Brenda knew that she flirted
with any guy, whether he was spoken for or not. But,
despite her reputation, she had successfully made
friends with a few people in her class.

"Hey, Bre," Daphne greeted her as she sat down at the table. "What's goin' on, girl?"

Brenda smiled at the dark-haired, hazel-eyed girl. "Everything. Tryin'a balance school along with helping Lauren put the finishing touches on her party plans. Are y'all going?"

Daphne nodded enthusiastically. "Yep, got my invite this morning." She held up the silver envelope.

"Me too," another girl, Traci, replied as she pulled at her shoulder-length dark brown hair, which had recently been streaked with red highlights. "I'm going shopping for my dress this weekend."

Brenda noticed that the other two girls at the table remained quiet. "What about you guys, Kara, Erin?"

Kara rolled her eyes. "We didn't get invites."

Brenda knew that the two girls hadn't received invitations and she was glad that they hadn't. Kara and Erin were known for starting drama, mainly among girls. It was as if drama followed them wherever they went and Lauren had stated that she wanted her party to be fun and drama-free. So, Brenda couldn't feel sorry for the girls.

"Well, it don't even matter," Erin said with a smack in her tone. "My brother's half sister's boyfriend is having a party that night and we're going. It's gonna be off the chain, probably better than Lauren's *bourgeois soiree*," she commented exaggeratedly.

Brenda laughed; she could tell that Erin was really upset about not being invited and she tried to hide it by acting as if she didn't care, but Brenda knew the truth. "I doubt that," she retorted evenly. "Lauren's parents are going all out for this one. It's not every day a girl turns eighteen." She turned her attention back to Traci and Daphne. "So, are you guys bringing dates? You know whoever you go with has to be someone who's been invited."

Traci nodded. "I have a few prospects in mind. What about you, Daphne?"

Daphne shrugged. "I'm sure I'll find someone to hang with." She looked at Brenda. "While you're asking, Bre, do you have a date for the party?"

Before Brenda could answer, Zane smoothly slid into a seat next to her and said, "Of course she does. She's going with me." He looked at her and placed his arm around her shoulders. "Right, Bre?"

Brenda smiled at her friends. She raised her eyebrows and laughed. "I guess so."

"Hi. How are you?" Zane asked as he licked his lips and stared at her intently.

Brenda smiled. *He could certainly give LL Cool J some competition.* "I'm good."

"Just good, huh? Well, how about I make you feel great?" he suggested.

Brenda glanced at Daphne and Traci; the girls' eyes were wide open, as if they'd taken Zane's comment to mean something other than what it really meant.

"Okay," Brenda responded. "How do you plan to do that?"

"By taking you out Friday night."

Brenda heard the two girls giggle as if they both found the real meaning behind Zane's initial statement funny. "Well, I'm sure I'm free. What do you have in mind?"

He shrugged. "Maybe dinner or a movie; maybe both."

Brenda remembered the movie she'd just seen with Ken on Saturday and a sudden surge of deceit ran through her heart. She didn't understand why she was feeling guilty about accepting a date with Zane; she and Ken weren't exclusively dating. Though she'd had a blast with him on Saturday, she reminded herself that she wasn't looking for a boyfriend, just someone to hang out with, and that's exactly what Zane wanted. *Friends who chill,* she remembered. Zane understood where she was coming from, but would Ken? He seemed like the type who wanted a commitment, but because he had yet to say that, Brenda still felt comfortable just hanging out with him. She just hoped that the game would continue without anyone getting hurt.

She shook all guilt from her conscience and smiled at Zane once again. "Dinner would be nice," she answered.

He smiled. "Great. I'll call you by Wednesday with details." He stood to leave, but before departing, he turned toward her and asked, "How are you feeling now?"

Brenda laughed along with her friends. "Wonderful," she answered, to his delight.

He tilted his head with a smile. "Even better than great. My job here is done." He turned and walked off.

"Girl, he is so crazy," Traci said.

Brenda shook her head. "I know, but I like it."

Daphne chuckled. "I'm sure you do."

Brenda turned and saw Zane sitting at a table with a group of boys, but he was looking in her direction. She smiled as he winked at her. This game was definitely getting interesting.

Chapter 9

Danielle

Jayda pulled into the driveway of Danielle's home and Danielle and Kennedi got out of the car.

"Thank you, Jay," Danielle said. "I'll see you tomorrow. Kennedi, tell Jayda bye."

"Bye, Jayda." Kennedi waved as Danielle took her hand and led her toward the house.

Jayda waved good-bye before backing out of the driveway. Danielle unlocked the door to the house and walked inside. She looked around and saw several suitcases next to the sofa. Her mother hadn't told her that she was planning to travel so she wondered what was going on.

"Hello? Ma, are you home?" Danielle yelled out.

"Grandma? Grandma?" Kennedi screamed at the top of her lungs.

"Grandma's not here," a male voice yelled just as loud as the girls had.

Danielle spun around so fast that she almost lost her balance. Her frightened expression vanished as a wide smile spread across her face. "Jackson!"

"Hey, little sis," Jackson said, bending down to hug Danielle. "How are you?"

"I'm good." Danielle laughed.

"Mommy, who's that?" Kennedi asked as she drew closer to her mother as if she was afraid.

Jackson looked down at Kennedi as if he had no idea who she was. "I know this is not baby Kennedi?" Danielle nodded. "The last time I saw her she could barely talk."

Danielle smiled. "Well, she does a lot of it now and it drives me crazy. Kennedi, this is my brother, Jackson; you call him Uncle Jack."

"Hi, Uncle Jack." Kennedi waved cautiously.

"Kennedi!" Jackson scooped her up into his arms and swung her around. "Girl, you've gotten so big."

"Jackie, what are you doing here?" Danielle asked. "I know school isn't out in New York. Does Daddy know you're here?"

Jackson looked around nervously and Danielle knew something was up. "Umm, yeah, he knows I'm here."

Danielle could sense that her brother was hiding something, and she was going to sit him down and find out what was going on. "Kennedi, go upstairs and play in your room."

"Oh, Mommy," Kennedi whined.

Danielle placed her hands firmly on her hips and gave her daughter an unyielding look. Without words, Kennedi left the room and went upstairs to her bedroom.

Jackson laughed as he sat on the sofa. "Girl, you are just like Mama. That look you just gave Kennedi had 'Beverly Lowe' written all over it."

Danielle hadn't seen her brother in almost two years. After their parents divorced five years ago, they decided that it would be best for Beverly to keep Danielle and for their father, Neil, to keep Jackson. Danielle had been okay with the arrangement until about two years ago, when Neil was offered a job in New York and relocated, causing Danielle to resort to long-distance phone calls in order to be able to communicate with her father and brother. Seeing Jackson now was a re-warding surprise, but by the several suitcases in the living room and his demeanor, Danielle knew this was not just a regular visit.

"Jackson, what's going on?" she asked him after sev-eral minutes of silence. "Why are you here?" She sat next to him on the sofa.

Jackson smiled and shook his head. "Danni, can't I come visit? I haven't seen you or Mom in almost two years . . . That's about twenty-four months. I miss you guys." He placed his arm around her shoulder.

"Yeah, I miss you too, but it's the middle of the school year and I know that you wouldn't just drop everything and come down here for a visit. Something's up." She gazed at him. "Did Dad kick you out or something?"

"Please, like that man would kick me out."

Danielle noticed the animosity in his tone. "O-kay. I'm lost."

"I left. I can't stay there no more." Jackson's face was now full of anger. His left leg was shaking and both his hands were balled into tight fists as if he was ready to hit someone.

"Jackson, what is going on?" Danielle commanded.

Jackson blew out a stream of air to calm his nerves before replying. "Do you remember when Mom and Dad divorced, and they wouldn't tell us what was going on?"

"Yeah." Danielle nodded. "They just said things weren't working out."

"That wasn't the entire truth, and had I not been so nosy, I would've never found out." Jackson became si-lent and Danielle's impatience was rising.

"Jackson, you're scaring me. Please tell me whatever it is that brought you way down here."

"Dad has a son . . . He's younger than you, but not young enough for him to have been conceived *after* the divorce," he explained.

Her face was blank and she was literally speechless.

Jackson continued, "His name is Neil Jr., but Dad said his name was just Junior, so it wouldn't provoke suspicions. When I found out, I went ballistic. I actually hauled off and hit Dad in the jaw."

Danielle still couldn't even express how upset she was upon hearing this news.

"I had befriended this boy and everything. I didn't even know who he was; he doesn't look exactly like dad, though he has some of his features." He sighed heavily.

"How did you find this out?" she finally asked.

He shook his head. "Like I said, I was really being nosy. But I think I should start from the beginning. Neil . . . Junior is like this bad kid turned good. He was a part of the mentoring program that Dad works for on the weekends and Dad became his mentor. The thing is that Dad tried to make it seem like he and the boy had just met, but they obviously knew each other when he first joined the program, or else he wouldn't have been the reason Dad and Mom divorced. When I met him, he was really cool. He was like a little brother to me.

"A few months ago, Junior's mom died in a car accident. We all attended the funeral, which was something I didn't find unusual because we'd grown so close. But things started moving so fast. Dad moved Junior into our house. I really didn't have a problem with that because I was living on campus, but when I asked Dad why Junior couldn't move in with his own father or another family member, he looked me dead in my eyes and told me a bald-faced lie. He said that Junior's father was dead and there was no one else who could take care of him." Jackson looked at Danielle, and she was still staring blankly at the floor.

"Jackson, all of this is useless information to me," she said quietly. "None of this is proving to me how Junior is Daddy's son."

He got up and stood, facing her. He began speaking faster. "Last week, I came home, but Junior and Dad weren't there when I got there. I had been upstairs doing some research for about thirty minutes when they came home from wherever they had been. I heard Junior in the living room crying, and then I heard him say, 'I miss my mama, *Daddy*.'" He paused, looking for a reaction from his sister.

"So, you heard that come out of his mouth?" she asked.

"Yes."

"Well, how do you know that he and Daddy didn't just get so close that he felt comfortable calling Daddy his father?"

"Danni, don't be so naïve," Jackson told her. "As soon as I heard the word 'daddy' come out of Junior's mouth, I ran downstairs so fast. I started asking questions and making assumptions. Because Junior was so upset, Dad said he'd talk to me about it later. So I stormed out the house. When I came back later that evening, Dad sat me down and told me everything. We ended up arguing and I hit him. We both were in shock. I couldn't even apologize and I didn't want to, so I stormed out again and I haven't been back since."

"I can't believe this." Danielle lifted her head. Jackson could see tears in her eyes, but she refused to let them fall. "So why did you come here? Why didn't you just stay on campus?"

Jackson shrugged. "I really don't know. I kinda did everything in haste. I haven't withdrawn from school yet, but because I enrolled in the summer quarter, I have enough credits to pass my freshman year. So as soon as I hear back from Clark Atlanta, UGA, Georgia State, or anywhere except NYU, I'm moving on." He sat back on the sofa.

Danielle shook her head. "I can't believe this," she repeated. "Daddy has a son by another woman, who is apparently part of the reason Mama divorced him. Was this woman living with Daddy when you first moved in with him?"

"No, because she lives in New York. Daddy apparently had been sending child support to her even before he and Mama divorced."

"Wait," Danielle said, confused. "So how in the world did Daddy cheat on Mama with this woman if she was all the way in New York?"

Jackson sighed. "Dad went on lots of business trips," he reminded her. "He had a few to New York and I guess he would visit this woman while he was up there. Those trips are also how he got the job up there." He shook his head. "Daddy told me that the woman had been tryin'a reach him on his cell phone one day, but he had left the phone at the house, 'cause Mama answered the call. That's how she found out about Junior and that was the end of their marriage."

Danielle began rubbing her temples. "How old is Junior?"

"He's ten," he answered. "He's young, but old enough to know how to keep a secret when his *daddy* tells him to."

She began shaking her head vigorously. "Ten! I can't believe Mama never told me. They've been divorced for five years. They were only married for twelve," she fussed as she tried to calculate the time in her head. "This is just too much. I need to get out of this house before Mama comes home."

"Why?" Jackson asked. "She knows I'm here. She picked me up from the airport and rented a car for me and everything."

"But I'm afraid that if I see her I may do to her what you did to Daddy. I can't take that chance right now." Danielle grabbed her purse. "Kennedi! Kennedi, come down here. We're going to the store."

Kennedi could be heard yelling joyfully as she came down the stairs.

"Are you coming, Jackson? If not, I can certainly find a ride."

Jackson pulled the keys to his rental car out of his pants pocket. "Let's go."

As they headed down to the garage, millions of thoughts ran through Danielle's head. The main thing she was focused on was what she was going to say to her father the next time she spoke to him.

Chapter 10

Brenda

"Brenda! Brenda, come watch this chicken for me. I need to run to the grocery store real quick for something," Eileen yelled to her daughter.

Upstairs, Brenda rolled her eyes and spoke into the receiver of her cell phone. "Zane, I have to go. I gotta finish cooking dinner and if I try to multitask by talking to you at the same time, I'm liable to burn the house down."

Zane laughed. "All right. I'll talk to you later."

Brenda hung up the phone and dragged her feet down the stairs to do as she'd been told.

"I need for you to turn these once they finish frying on this side. It may take awhile because these are the breast pieces. I also need for you to watch this corn-on-the-cob. When this timer goes off, they're done," Eileen instructed.

"Mother, I know how to cook. I got this," Brenda said sarcastically.

Eileen glared at her daughter. "Brenda, do not start talking on the phone or get so distracted to where you let this food burn."

"Mom, I got it," Brenda stressed agitatedly.

"You better watch your tone, girl," Eileen warned as Brenda rolled her eyes. "Now, Maya and David should be home from soccer practice in about an hour. If I'm not home by then, make sure you thank Ms. Jean for dropping them off."

Brenda gave her mother a suspicious glance. "Why wouldn't you be back from the store in an hour? It's like five minutes away."

Eileen glared at her again. "You need to mind your business and don't worry about mine. Now do as I said and I'll be back *whenever* I get back." She walked out of the kitchen and left the house.

Brenda shook her head and muttered under her breath. She knew her mother wasn't just going to the grocery store. It was just a cover story so she wouldn't have to tell her children that she was going to her husband's house for an evening rendezvous. Even though they were going through a divorce, Eileen couldn't seem to break herself from the man she claimed loved her as much as she loved him. Brenda hated seeing her mother run after that man like a dog. It saddened her to know that Eileen was so dependant upon companionship that she would lie to her children concerning her whereabouts.

Brenda thought about how her father had treated Eileen. He wasn't abusive, but extremely negligent. He could hardly ever be found at home. He never gave information on where he would be and never felt as if he owed anyone an explanation for his actions. He did as he pleased and no one, not even Brenda, his little princess, could stop him.

Taylor's father *was* abusive, though. Not physically, but verbally. He called Eileen, Brenda, and Taylor all kinds of names. He put Eileen down and crushed every last one of her fairytale dreams. No one could question his authority. Whatever he said was law. After a while, Chase got sick of his verbal lashing and decided to physically solve the problem. Chase nearly killed

Taylor's father by giving him a brutal beat down, but before he could finish the job, Taylor's father put them all out of their misery and left. Not too long after, he was imprisoned for picking up streetwalkers.

David and Maya's father was a pretty decent man, in Brenda's opinion. Even Chase thought he was okay. None of them seemed to have a problem with the fact that he was black, though it was a slight change of pace for the household. The reason for the end to that relationship was because of his and Eileen's difference of opinions in various areas. He believed in strict discipline, though he only practiced it on his own children. Eileen saw his discipline as abuse. He believed that Eileen should work to help bring in a household income. Eileen loved being a housewife. Their opinions and beliefs were so contrasted that Brenda didn't understand how they lasted nearly five years.

Then there was Steve, the man Eileen was now divorcing. Brenda called him a bum because she honestly believed that Eileen had been so desperate for a husband that she'd gone out and found some strange man off the streets and fell in love with him. He didn't do anything except sit around the house, watch television, and eat. He completely ignored all of the kids unless it was to tell them to keep quiet while the game was on. His laziness had forced Eileen to go out and get a job, something she refused to do with her last husband. But with no experience or accreditation, she found a job that barely paid minimum wage. Steve and Eileen's marriage had been a living nightmare for the children and they were all glad that it was over.

Now if she would just leave him alone, Brenda thought as she turned the frying chicken. Eileen didn't know when to let go and she was determined to hold on to Steve, despite the fact that he'd found another family to feed off of. Brenda prayed that her mother would come to her senses and realize that she was strong enough to survive on her own.

By the time the chicken finished frying, Maya and David had come home and had started on their homework. Taylor had been blasting rock music for the past hour and it was starting to work on Brenda's nerves. She walked upstairs just as she heard her cell phone blaring its ringtone. She bypassed Taylor's room and made a mad dash across her bed in order to retrieve her phone from her bookshelf.

"Hello," she answered hastily.

"Hello, may I please speak to Brenda?" the caller asked.

"This is Brenda."

"Hey, Bre, this is Ken," the caller said. "Did I catch you at a bad time?"

Brenda's tone softened as she smiled. "Oh, no, you didn't. Could you hold on for one second?"

"Yeah."

Brenda walked back to her sister's room and began banging on the door covered in Do Not Enter and No Trespassing signs. It took Taylor much too long to answer her door, but when she did, Brenda noticed that she looked completely out of her senses.

"What do you want?" Taylor demanded.

Brenda scrunched up her nose at the stench coming from inside of the room. "Could you turn down the music, please? I'm on the phone."

"Okay. Anything else?"

Brenda reached up and held her nose. "Yes. Lay off the perfume."

"Bye," Taylor growled before closing the door.

Brenda waited to hear the volume of the music lower before going to her room and resuming her phone conversation.

"I'm sorry, Ken. My mom left me at home to baby-sit," Brenda explained as she sat on her bed. "So what's up?"

"This is probably a stupid question, but are you going to Lauren's party?" Ken asked.

Brenda laughed. "I would have to agree with you, Ken. That is a stupid question," she said as he laughed. "Of course I'm going to the party. Did you get your invite? I personally made sure Lauren didn't leave you off of the list."

"I appreciate that and I did get my invitation. I was calling to see if you wanted to go to the party with me?"

"Did you even have to ask?" Brenda said without thinking. "Of course I'll go with you."

"Great," he responded excitedly. "I also wanted to see if you'd like to go out this weekend. Maybe Friday or Saturday?"

The mention of a Friday night date made Brenda think of Zane and she realized what she'd just done. How was she going to go to the party with Ken and Zane? What had she gotten herself into? She couldn't suddenly change her mind and tell him that she already had a date for the party. She could tell by the way Ken had asked the question that he'd been anticipating her approval. She didn't want to hurt his feelings, so she'd just have to think of a way to hang out with both boys at the same time. But for now she would have to make sure she never made the same mistake again.

"Saturday is good," she said softly.

Ken must've noted her sudden change of tone. "Brenda, if you don't want to go out with me, you don't have to. I'm not forcing you to do anything you don't wanna do."

Brenda felt bad because she could tell that Ken really liked her. He was much different from Zane, who didn't want a commitment. She could tell that Ken was into exclusive relationships, but because she liked him so much, she couldn't force herself to place space between them like she usually did when she realized that she was getting too close to a guy. Brenda didn't want to get hurt, but she also didn't want to hurt Ken. *This is why I don't get into relationships,* she thought.

Brenda sighed. "Ken, I want to go out with you. It's just that I feel like we're moving slightly faster than I expected. I want to be honest with you." She paused for a long moment. She couldn't tell him that she was dating him and someone else at the same time, but she could make him understand why she was so apprehensive. "I'm afraid of relationships. I'm afraid of being hurt. You see me flirting a lot, but the last time I had a steady boyfriend was during my sophomore year and I purposely fooled around so he would end the relationship. I felt we were getting too close and I wanted to end things before I ended up with a broken heart."

"Brenda, I understand where you're coming from and I promise I'll take things slow with you, but I'm not gonna play games with you because I really do like you. I hope that you won't play games with me, either. I don't have a problem with casual dating, but hopefully our casual dates could lead to something more . . . when you're ready."

Brenda could feel herself falling for Ken. He was a really genuine and sweet guy. He was one of the few guys at her school who didn't try to put up a front for everyone in order to be perceived as cool. He was confident in himself and what he wanted to do with his life after high school. He was pretty much everything a girl would want in a guy, but she was going to keep her heart protected no matter what. "Thanks, Ken. You're really sweet."

"So, are we on for Saturday night?" Ken asked.

"Yes, we are."

"Great. I have to go, but I'll call you later."

"Okay. Bye," she said as she hung up the phone.

Brenda lay back on her pillow and released a heavy sigh. Ken was a really nice guy, but she didn't know if she could trust him with her heart. He'd said all the right things and made her feel special, but could she trust him not to hurt her in the end?

All Zane wanted to do was hang out and have fun. Brenda knew she couldn't get hurt doing that. There was no commitment, no promises, therefore no heartbreak. Deep down, though, Brenda knew she wanted to be with Ken, but she refused to allow him access to her most sensitive possession—her heart.

Chapter 11

Danielle

Jackson carried Kennedi on his shoulders as he and Danielle walked through the mall. They had been wandering aimlessly for nearly fifteen minutes and Danielle knew that Jackson was ready to go back home. She was too heated to face their mother, though, so, at her demand, they continued to walk from store to store with no intention of purchasing anything.

"Mommy, let's go see A.J.," Kennedi requested.

Danielle smiled at the mention of A.J.'s name. She was surprised that Kennedi hadn't said something sooner, considering the fact that she'd been running her mouth since they got to the mall. Jackson now knew the name of every one of Kennedi's preschool friends and all of their business. Kennedi's motor mouth was soon to run out of gas and she would tire out and want to go to sleep; Danielle was sure of it, especially since Kennedi's teacher had informed Danielle that she couldn't get Kennedi to sleep during naptime today.

"Who's A.J.?" Jackson wondered aloud.

Danielle looked up at him and noticed his eyebrow was raised in curiosity. He was waiting for an answer and Danielle had no problem giving him one. "Just this guy I met last week. He works in this children's clothing store here at the mall."

"Is he your boyfriend?" Jackson inquired, his tone showing his rising displeasure.

She laughed at the look of disdain on his face. "No, Jackie, he's not. He's just a friend."

"Well, I still want to meet him," he declared. "Where's the store?"

"It's on the lower level," she informed him. "But I don't even know if he is working today. He does go to school."

"Well, most of the high schools over here let out about three hours ago," Jackson said matter-of-factly.

Danielle shook her head. "But he's not in high school. He's a sophomore in college."

Her brother's eyes opened wide. "Oh, he's *older* than me and talking to *you*. I definitely want to meet him now, and if he ain't here today I'm coming back every day until I see him." He began walking toward the descending escalator. "C'mon and show me where this store is, girl."

Danielle sighed as she followed him. Once they reached the lower level, she led him toward the store where A.J. worked and prayed that he wasn't in today. She knew Jackson had no problems telling anyone how he felt about them, whether good or bad. He also had no problems confronting any guy who was seeing his sister to make sure he was coming correct, and the fact that he'd been away for so long would definitely have an effect on how he approached A.J. The last time Jackson had grilled one of his sister's male friends was the first time he met Keenan, and Jackson had scared him half to death.

Danielle took a deep breath as they entered the children's store and smiled when she saw Déjà at the counter reading a magazine. She looked up when the bell signaled that customers had entered the store.

"Hi, Danielle," Déjà greeted her with a smile. "Hey, Kennedi."

"Hi," Danielle greeted her as Kennedi waved. She looked back at her brother, who seemed to be captured by Déjà's beauty. "Déjà, this is my brother, Jackson. Jackson, this is Déjà."

Déjà extended her hand and greeted Jackson, "Hi. It's nice to meet you."

Jackson's face held a wide grin as he took her hand and shook it gently. "The pleasure is *all* mine."

Danielle laughed when her brother seemed to forget why they had come to the store while he gazed at Déjà openly, much like A.J. had done with Danielle the first day they'd met. Only A.J.'s gaze had been more confident, while Jackson was staring at Déjà as if he'd never seen a woman in his life.

Déjà was very pretty, Danielle thought. Her skin was pecan brown and her eyes were slightly slanted and light brown in color. She had high, exotic cheekbones and full lips that revealed a tiny gap between her two front teeth when she smiled. She was slightly heavyset, but her weight settled in all the right places. Danielle could see why her brother was instantly attracted to her, but Jackson was way out of his league because A.J. had informed Danielle that his sister was twenty-two. In her opinion, Déjà was much too mature and focused to get involved with her eighteen-year-old brother who could sometimes be childish and easily distracted from his goals.

Déjà smiled as Jackson stared at her as if he were in a daze. "Are you here to purchase sweet little Kennedi another dress?" she asked as she turned away from Jackson and looked at Danielle.

"Yes!" Kennedi sang from her uncle's shoulders.

"Umm, not unless Uncle Jack has some money." Danielle laughed.

Jackson seemed to come out of his daze at the mention of his name. "What's that?" he asked.

Kennedi pulled on his neck. "Mama said you can buy me a dress."

"Oh really?" Jackson laughed as he looked at his sister. "Well, that depends on one thing."

Danielle looked confused. "What's that?"

He turned and looked at Déjà. "Is there an A.J. here?"

Déjà smiled at Danielle, who was discreetly telling her to say no by slightly shaking her head and bulging out her eyes. Déjà laughed when she realized why the siblings had come to the store. "Well, I can't tell a lie," she started, to Danielle's disappointment. "He's in the back. Would you like me to go get him?"

Jackson nodded with a smile. "If it wouldn't be too much trouble."

She shook her head. "Not at all," she said as she walked from the counter toward the back.

Jackson watched Déjà walk away before he looked at his sister. "Danni, that girl is fine . . . and I mean fine . . . thick *and* fine," he digressed. "She look like that lady on the Food Network . . . Sunny Anderson."

Danielle's brows furrowed and she asked, "Since when do you like big girls? The last girl I saw you with was 'bout as big as Jayda. And if you don't remember, Jayda's 'bout as big as a branch on a tree."

"I'm eclectic when it comes to women, I like 'em all." He laughed as she rolled her eyes in disgust.

"Well, you might as well go somewhere with your tired game 'cause Déjà is too mature for it. She's twenty-two and has a lot going for herself," Danielle pointed out.

He shrugged indifferently. "And . . . ? I'm legal. Shoot, I'll be nineteen in a few months. And I have a lot going for myself too. Just wait 'til I get back in school."

Danielle laughed. "If you're not acting like Lauren, trying to get with someone too old for you."

"What are you talking about? Who's Lauren trying to get with?"

Before Danielle could respond, Déjà returned with a smiling A.J. right behind her.

"A.J.!" Kennedi yelled.

A.J. laughed. "Hey, Miss Kennedi. How are you?"

"Good," she sang.

"Hi, Danni," he greeted Danielle as he leaned against the counter.

"Hey, I didn't know if you were in today," Danielle said. "Well, actually I was kinda hoping that you weren't in today."

"Why?" A.J. questioned in confusion.

Danielle smiled tightly as she touched her brother's arm lightly. "A.J., this is Jackson, my brother. Jackson, *this* is A.J."

"Wassup?" Jackson forced his voice to deepen as if he was trying to intimidate A.J. "I hear that you and my sister are pretty good friends."

A.J. glanced at Danielle, who mouthed to him how sorry she was. He looked back at Jackson, who apparently was waiting for a response. "Uh, well, I just met her last week, but yeah, Danielle's pretty cool," he stated as if he didn't know what else to say.

"I also hear that you're a sophomore in college," Jackson added.

A.J. was trying hard not to laugh, but Jackson's forced attitude was amusing. "Yeah, I go to Morehouse."

"An all-male school?" Jackson questioned. "Umm."

"Jackson!" Danielle punched his arm, knowing exactly what he was thinking. "I didn't bring you here to judge him." She looked at A.J. "I apologize for his stupidity."

"It's cool," A.J. said. "I understand where he's coming from. I gotta keep tabs on this one all the time." He shoved his thumb in Déjà's direction.

Danielle laughed. "I'm sure you do." She glanced at Jackson, whose facial expression showed his surprise.

"Oh . . . that's your sister?" Jackson asked. A.J. nodded with a smile. Jackson glanced at Déjà before looking down at his sister and giving her a "you should have told me" look. He turned back toward A.J. and decided to soften his tone. "Man, I apologize. It's just hard tryin'a keep track of her when I'm almost eight hundred miles away. The last guy I got a chance to grill was Kennedi's jerk of a father."

"Jackson, don't say that out loud," Danielle admonished. She glanced up at her daughter, who was drearily listening to their conversation.

Kennedi had recently begun asking questions about Keenan's whereabouts and Danielle had answered Kennedi's questions as truthfully as she could. She had told Kennedi that her father lived too far away to come see her, and even though Kennedi would follow up with questions asking why, Danielle only gave the same response. She couldn't tell her daughter that her father didn't want her, but as Kennedi continued to get older, Danielle knew that she was going to have to reveal the truth.

"Where are you from?" Déjà asked Jackson, breaking the silence.

"I'm from here, but I've been living in New York for the past couple of years," Jackson informed her. "I attend . . . I mean, I *attended* New York University, but I'm moving back down here. I'm waiting to hear back from the University of Georgia, Clark Atlanta University, or Georgia State University."

"Oh, I'm a senior there." Déjà smiled. "At Clark Atlanta, that is." She watched as Jackson's smile grew wider. "Yeah, after I graduate, I plan on going for my PhD in psychology."

"Well, hopefully I'll hear back from them soon," he responded.

Danielle shook her head and grabbed his arm. "Well, we have to get going now. I'm hungry and Kennedi looks sleepy, so we need to get home."

Jackson pulled Kennedi off of his back and held her in his arms. "Well, if she's going to sleep, I don't think I can buy her an outfit. She'll be too tired to pick one out."

Kennedi raised her head. "I'm not sleepy," she said, though she was rubbing her eyes. "I want an outfit. Déjà can show you some."

Jackson looked at Déjà, who only smiled as she walked from behind the counter and led Jackson and Kennedi to the toddler clothing, leaving A.J. and Danielle alone at the counter.

"He's really protective of you," A.J. observed. "That's good."

"I haven't seen him in two years, so I guess he would be," Danielle said.

"Two years?" he questioned. "Why so long?"

"He moved to New York with my dad a few years after our parents' divorce. I had been hoping that once he started college, he'd come back down here, but I guess NYU caught his eye. The last time he saw me, Kennedi was barely two." Danielle sighed as she thought about what had brought Jackson back home. She decided to change the subject to something that didn't make her so angry. "A.J., do you go to parties?" she suddenly asked.

A.J. laughed subtly. "Well, I do, but I don't go to too many because of school and work. Why would you ask?"

Danielle shrugged. "My friend, Lauren—you met her last week—well, she's having this party on March tenth and I can invite one person who didn't receive a personal invitation. I was just wondering if you would like to go with me?"

"What type of party is it?"

"A birthday party. She's turning eighteen."

A.J. smiled mischievously. "I'm not too interested in going to a high school party—"

"Okay, well I'll just invite someone else." Danielle shrugged nonchalantly as a smile spread across her face.

"I was just playin'," he said. "I'd love go with you, but what are you gonna do with Kennedi?"

Danielle frowned. She hadn't thought about where Kennedi would go while she was at the party, but she had two weeks to find out. "I'm sure I can find someone to babysit for me."

Jackson and Déjà returned with Kennedi holding two outfits: one baby blue short set and a purple skirt set. Jackson held two shoeboxes in his hands. Danielle shook her head when she realized that Kennedi had hoodwinked her uncle into purchasing the items for her.

Jackson noticed the look on his sister's face. "*What?*" He smiled. "She can't even wear the last thing I bought her. I had to make up for lost time."

"Why are you trying to explain yourself?" Danielle asked. "It's your money."

She watched as A.J. scanned the items and totaled the costs. Once Jackson paid and received his receipt, he took the bags as Danielle took Kennedi's hand.

Before they left the store, Jackson looked at Déjà and asked, "Would you guys like to come to our house for dinner some time this week?"

"Are you offering to cook?" Danielle held a disbelieving gaze in her eyes.

"Can you cook?" Déjà asked playfully before Jackson could answer the first question.

"Not that I know of," Danielle answered with a small laugh.

Jackson tossed her an annoyed look before saying, "Actually, I do a little cooking. I can make some really good shrimp Alfredo and grilled chicken."

Danielle looked at her brother and figured that he really must be into Déjà for him to invite her and A.J. to dinner and to volunteer whatever culinary skills he had.

"Well, Saturday's good for me if it's good for A.J." Déjà looked at her brother.

A.J. gazed at Danielle and smiled. "I'd love to," he said, causing her to blush from his stare.

"Great, we'll see you on Saturday then." Jackson held the door open for Danielle and Kennedi as they left the store.

Danielle waited until they were a reasonable distance away before asking, "Why did you do that?"

"Do what?" Jackson pretended as if he had no idea what she was talking about.

"Jackie, I'm trying so hard not to fall for A.J., okay? The last thing I need is for him to be at our house."

"What? Are you afraid that you guys might . . . ?"

"No." Danielle gave Jackson a disgusted look. "I'm not easy like that and neither is he, but we've been talking for long hours for the past few days and I like him a lot already. I know the more time I spend with him the more my heart will draw closer to him. Plus, he's already told me that he wasn't looking for a girl and I definitely don't need a boyfriend, so the last thing that needs to happen is me giving my heart to him to just have it broken all over again."

Danielle's apprehension actually had very little to do with A.J.; her mind was wandering back four years and she was remembering how Keenan had left the state after finding out that she was pregnant. She had been so depressed after that incident that she wouldn't eat or sleep, which almost caused Kennedi to become malnourished, but for the sake of her unborn baby, Danielle began forcing herself to eat just enough to keep Kennedi healthy. Even after Kennedi was born, Danielle could hardly stand to look at her because she carried so many of Keenan's features. It wasn't that Danielle didn't want to spend time with A.J., but the possibility that she'd love only to lose once again was too much for her.

"Well, I don't understand how he can say he's not looking for a girlfriend with the way he was gawking at you in that store. If you ask me he's already fallen for you," Jackson stated.

Danielle shook her head. "Jackie, we've only known each other for a week."

"Whatever." Jackson opened the door that led to the mall's parking lot. "But as long as you don't put yourself in compromising positions with this dude, you shouldn't have to worry about having your heart broken."

Danielle could only try to take her brother's advice, but she could tell that it would be a hard task.

Chapter 12

Lauren

Lauren was sitting in her room, looking over her party plans. She was checking the guest list, making sure that everyone had gotten their invitations. There were several people who hadn't received one and many of them went to a different school. She still needed to get in contact with her party planner to make sure that everything that she was supposed to take care of was set, so Lauren picked up her cell phone and decided to do that now.

"This is Nira," the party planner answered after the second ring.

"Hi, Nira, this is Lauren."

"Hey, Lauren, I was just about to call you. How's everything?"

"Everything's good. I do have a few more invitations to send out and I wanted to make sure that all loose ends were tied on your end," Lauren informed her.

"Well, that's what I was going to call you about," Nira said. "I'm sorry to tell you that the DJ for your party has backed out. Apparently, someone else is having a party that night and offered him twice as much money as we offered."

Lauren sighed heavily. She couldn't believe this. Two weeks before her party and she didn't have a DJ. "Well, what am I supposed to do? How are we going to have a party without music?" she asked frantically.

"Lauren, calm down, honey," Nira told her. "I'm already in contact with someone else, but he might cost a few hundred more."

"I don't care, just please get him before next week," Lauren practically begged.

Nira laughed. "Don't you think you should consult your parents before giving the consent that they will spend more money on a DJ?"

Lauren knew she would have to ask her parents, but she needed to get this man before someone else did. She'd talk to her parents about it later. Besides, they gave her practically anything she wanted, so it shouldn't even be a problem. "I'll ask them, but could you please put an offer on the table and try to snatch him up before we lose him?"

"I'll do that, but I'm also going to call your parents to make sure they are well aware of their expenses."

"Okay." Lauren shrugged as if she really cared; she was having this party if she had to pay for it out of her own pocket. *Don't get carried away, Lauren,* she laughed to herself.

"I'll talk to you later," Nira said before hanging up.

Lauren tossed her phone onto her bed and exhaled. She was hoping that this party would be the party of the year. That's why she was trying to go all out regardless of the expenses. She wanted her peers to talk about this party at their twenty-year class reunion. She also was hoping that she could tell her children that her party was where she and their father first began dating.

Though she knew she was risking a lot, Lauren wanted to be with Sterling. She couldn't think of anything more that she wanted for her birthday than to just be his girl. She wanted him to hold her and protect her; she wanted to feel his warm, sensual lips against hers. She would love for Sterling to dance the night away with her and seal the magical evening with a good-night kiss; if she could get more out of the night and offer Sterling her virginity, Lauren's life would be complete.

She hated the fact that he was her teacher, but that didn't matter to her when it came to what she felt in her heart. Sterling was well aware of his position and the risks that dating her would have, but he had agreed to come to her party, not as a chaperone, but as a guest. He knew Lauren's intentions and he'd told her that they could have nothing more than a student-teacher relationship. Lauren felt as if he was sending mixed signals and to her that was a good thing because, though his actions showed that he was apprehensive toward her, they also revealed his interest in pursuing a relationship with her. Jayda had told Lauren that she was in way over her head and that only made Lauren's pursuit of Sterling intensify. She would get Sterling to fall for her if it was the last thing she did.

It wasn't that Lauren couldn't find a guy her own age; she was definitely capable of getting any guy's attention, but she liked a challenge. She was a lot like Brenda in that she enjoyed the thrill of the chase, except Lauren liked to play the cat and she loved a mouse that barely stayed within reach. Guys like Jarred were too accessible and much too clingy. Jarred would be perfect for Lauren if he would just back off and allow her to draw toward him. That's why she loved Sterling; he continuously pushed her away, knowing that she wasn't going to stop until she got what she wanted.

Lauren had been labeled as stuck-up and snotty by guys and girls, just because she knew what she wanted and set high standards for herself when it came to picking a mate or even a friend. She couldn't care less what people said about her though because she knew she was the best all around, and those who thought otherwise were considered jealous.

Lauren lay back on her bed and smiled; for someone who was envied and talked about by so many people, she was extremely popular. *How ironic,* she thought. She shrugged; as long as her popularity status didn't waver, she'd let what others said about her roll through one ear and right out of the other.

Jayda

"Mama, do you need any help?" Jayda asked as she stood in the entryway of the kitchen.

Heather looked up at her daughter and smiled. "Why don't you come cut these onions for the spaghetti sauce?"

Jayda moved toward the island that sat in the center of the kitchen and began cutting the onions that rested on the cutting board. The kitchen was silent, with the exceptions of the knife slicing through the onion and the sound of the running water that Heather was using to clean off the tomatoes. Jayda knew her mother was still upset about her separation; her parents had been together since their college years, and if she excluded the last few months, Jayda couldn't remember a time when her parents didn't publicly or privately exhibit their love for each other. Sure, they had their disagreements, but so did every other normal couple. Jayda just didn't know what had gone wrong. Why had her father started to be unfaithful? That was a question she didn't know the answer to, but she was determined to find out.

"Mama." Jayda's voice finally broke through the lingering silence.

Heather looked up. "Yes, baby?"

Jayda inhaled deeply before asking, "What happened to make Daddy do what he did to you?"

Heather turned away and resumed slicing the tomatoes. The silence that had blanketed the room before returned and Jayda sighed, figuring that her mother didn't want to discuss the issue. She went back to chopping the onions and decided not to ask any more questions, but silently hoped that her mother would reveal what had disrupted their stable home.

"Your father doesn't know what he wants," Heather suddenly said.

Jayda turned and gazed at her mother in confusion. She knew there was more to the statement, but Heather didn't say anything else. Knowing her mother, Jayda decided not to pry, but knew she would find out the complete truth soon enough.

By the time dinner was ready, the twins had come home from their afterschool activities. Cameron was on the basketball team and Candice was a cheerleader. Their practices usually ran through the afternoon and to the early evening, but they always made it home for dinner. Jayda walked to the front door and waved to the woman who'd just dropped her siblings off before closing the door and locking it.

"Hey, guys," Jayda greeted them.

"Hey, Jay," they returned the greeting solemnly.

Their sister looked at them sorrowfully. "You can eat as soon as you guys take your showers."

She watched as they sulked up the stairs. Jayda knew they missed their father; so did she. Even though their home hadn't been its happiest in the last few months, they all knew that their family wasn't the same without Preston around.

While the twins showered, Jayda decided to call Evan. She needed someone to talk to and knew that he would provide a listening ear.

"Hey, babe. Wassup?" Evan answered on the first ring.

Jayda smiled as her face warmed to his voice. "Hey, Ev. Can I talk to you about something?"

"Sure," he replied. "I'm listening."

Jayda began telling him about the situation at home and how her parents had temporarily separated. "Everybody's just moping around as if the world has ended," she informed him as tears began to roll down her cheeks. "And it feels like it has. My dad's only been gone for about a week, but it feels as if he's been gone for years and I miss him so much. And my mom . . . she won't tell me anything. When I asked her about it all she said was that my dad can't seem to make up his mind about what he wants. I'm trying to be strong for everybody, but I feel so weak myself. I don't know what to do."

Evan listened as Jayda cried for a moment before offering his advice. "Jayda, I've known you for some time, a long time, and you are a strong woman—that's who you are by nature. So trying to force yourself to be overly strong for your family right now isn't necessary because even if you don't try, that characteristic is going to come out in you always. You need to let your guard down and show your emotions. Just like you're talking to me right now and showing how you truly feel about the situation, you need to do that with your parents. Let them know that this is bothering you; tell them that you're hurting. As long as you walk around as if everything's okay, they're going to assume that you're all right and you're not affected by the problem at all."

"But, Evan, I just told you that I asked my mother about it and she barely gave me a response," Jayda cried.

"That's because you haven't shown any emotions concerning it. I don't mean go to her crying and falling out, but let her see your heart and tell her how you feel about being left in the dark." He paused before adding, "Now, there are some things that go on in a marriage that parents will keep from their kids because it would be too much for them to handle. So if your mom tells you that it's something you wouldn't understand, trust me when I say that she's probably right. And if that's the case, leave it alone until she, or even your dad, feels like they're comfortable telling you what's really going on."

Jayda still had tears coming out of her eyes, but she felt slightly better. "I hear you, Evan, and I don't know when I'll be able to do what you're asking, but I know I will do it. Thank you so much, for listening to me." She chuckled softly. "I can't believe I just cried in front of you."

Evan laughed. "I'm sure you were beautiful doing it."

Jayda couldn't help but smile at his words. She hadn't known that he was so sweet. Though they hadn't formally begun dating, Evan was already treating her like his number one lady. She couldn't wait until they made it official.

"Thank you again," she said right before hearing her mother call her down for dinner. The way Heather screamed her name, Jayda was sure that she'd been summoned more than once. "Evan, I have to go."

"All right, babe, I'll see you at school tomorrow," he said.

"Okay, bye." Jayda was hesitant to hang up the phone, but when her mother called her name again, she knew she had to.

She smiled as she quickly placed the phone on the hook and went into the bathroom to wash her hands before heading downstairs to the dinner table. Cameron and Candice were already sitting in their usual spots and they were all waiting for Jayda to do the same so they could bless their food. As Heather said grace, Jayda felt it weird to not hear Preston's deep baritone thanking God for allowing him to share another meal with his family and asking that their food be blessed and nourishing to their bodies. But Evan's advice stuck with her and caused her smile to remain throughout the prayer in spite of the situation.

As they began enjoying their meals, Jayda hadn't noticed that her smile was still in place until Cameron snidely pointed it out. She realized that everyone was looking at her, waiting for an explanation.

"What? I was just on the phone with a friend," she said, struggling to remove the wide grin from her face. She had to admit that it was a hard task seeing as how Evan had shown her how caring he was. That was something she hardly ever saw in the guys who approached her.

"She was probably talking to that cute baseball player from her school," Candice chimed in.

"Evan?" Cameron asked as he shook his head. "I should've known."

"Evan?" Heather questioned with a raised eyebrow. "The guy you went out with Saturday?" she asked with a slight smile.

"Yes, ma'am," Jayda said. "He's really nice, Mama, and I've known him for a long time."

Heather put her hand up to stop her daughter's rambling. "If he makes you happy, that's good. Just try not to get yourself hurt, baby."

"Yes, ma'am," Jayda responded softly.

As they continued to enjoy their dinner, they shared light conversation, trying hard not to focus on the fact that their father was not at the head of the table. *Don't worry Mama,* Jayda silently said. *Evan won't hurt me like Daddy hurt you.*

Chapter 13

Brenda

Brenda was actually having a nice time with Zane. He was so funny and had Brenda laughing all night. The only problem was that Ken kept sneaking in and out of Brenda's thoughts. She felt slightly guilty for being out with Zane after Ken had told her how he felt about her. She felt as if she was being unfaithful to him, but they weren't even in an exclusive relationship. Besides, Ken said that he understood her position concerning their relationship and he was up for casually dating, so she didn't understand why her conscience was attacking her for doing something that they'd both agreed was okay.

"I hope you enjoyed dinner," Zane stated as they exited the restaurant.

Brenda smiled. "Yes, not only was the food good, but so was the conversation. You are so funny. I couldn't stop laughing."

"Oh, that was intended. I had to keep you laughing so I could admire your beautiful smile."

Brenda blushed at his comment.

"So, where do you want to go now?" he asked as they left the building.

She wasn't ready to go home just yet, so she said, "Wherever."

Zane smiled as he helped her into his car. They drove around for about ten minutes before he pulled up to a park where several other cars were parked. By the scenery, Brenda could tell that this was the romantic spot for many couples to visit after dates. Some couples walked around aimlessly under the night sky, while others took the opportunity to spend the time alone in their vehicles.

Zane placed his arm around Brenda's shoulder as he lowered the volume to the jazz station that was playing on his radio. Brenda smiled as he looked directly into her blue eyes.

"Can I ask you a question?"

Brenda laughed. "Well, you just did, but if you have another question, sure you can ask me."

Zane smiled as he continued to gaze at her. "How come I never see you with a white guy?"

She laughed, louder this time. "What kind of question is that?"

"One that I would really like an answer to," he said. "We have . . . a few white guys at our school, who I'm sure would love to be in my position right now, but I always see you with a black guy or a guy with some color in him . . . never any guy of the *Caucasian persuasion*."

Brenda couldn't help but to laugh again as he continued to stare into her eyes. It wasn't just his question that amused her, but the fact that he was very serious in his asking made the inquiry more humorous. It wasn't the first time she'd been asked the question; her friends used to wonder why she seemed to always be attracted to males of color. But even with the question being familiar to her, Brenda took the time to think about her response before answering. "I don't know why I don't date white guys. I find plenty of them attractive, but I guess it's because I'm just more attracted to what I know."

Zane's confused expression amused her even more. "What exactly do you know, Ms. Brenda?"

"I grew up in a black neighborhood. I've attended predominantly black schools, which is why I kinda stick with them. As you can see, I hang with a group of black girls. I have a few white girlfriends, but I don't relate to them like I relate to Lauren and the crew. We all like the same music and the same activities. I know that a lot of people would call me a wannabe sista or whatever, but I'm just being who I am."

"Well, that's true because you certainly don't try to *act* black, though you do have a little attitude about yourself." Zane smiled. "I like that. I also like the fact that you're real and honest."

"Well, that's who I am," Brenda replied as a sinking feeling passed through her stomach, knowing she was not being completely honest with Zane.

She watched his eyes move from her eyes down to her red-painted lips and her heart fluttered as he moved in slowly to kiss her softly. Brenda felt warm all over as she placed the palms of her hands on his face. She hadn't been kissed in a long time and it surely felt good. She reminded herself not to go further than this kiss, although her body was telling her that it wanted to. She liked the way Zane lightly held her waist and the way his warm breath tickled her face as they kissed. She could get used to this for sure.

Brenda's mind became a whirlwind of thoughts as she continued to kiss Zane. Soon, her mind was on Ken and she was imagining that he was the one caressing her mouth with his. She lost herself for a moment and allowed herself to long for Ken's touch and she wondered what his kiss felt like. She had hoped to experience this with Ken on their first date, but when he had walked her to her door last Saturday, he simply kissed her cheek and left, promising to call.

Her stomach was churning and she felt as if she were about to spill her insides out in Zane's car. She pulled back and searched the face of the one she was kissing, but she felt as if she were looking into Ken's dark eyes instead of Zane's hazel ones. She completely moved away from him and wiped her mouth.

"What's wrong?" Zane questioned as he stared at her.

She had moved close to the door as if she was trying to get out of his reach. "Nothing. I just think we should stop, that's all."

He looked at her for a moment longer before agreeing. "Should I take you home?"

"No, I'm good. Could we walk around or something? It's hot in here."

Zane nodded and turned off the car. They exited the vehicle and began to leisurely walk around the park. The streetlights provided a nice romantic field throughout the area and the full moon enhanced the night. Zane lightly held Brenda's hand as they walked in silence. She felt so uncomfortable and she didn't know why. She had never felt this guilty about dating two guys at the same time. Maybe it was because one of the guys really liked her and wasn't just trying to pass the time away until he stopped feeling attracted to her. She knew that's what Zane was doing. He did it all the time and Brenda didn't have a problem with it. As long as she didn't give her heart to him, she knew she would be fine. But Ken had already given his heart to her and she had accepted it, not out of obligation, but because she knew that deep down she shared his feelings. The last thing on her mind was hurting Ken, but she didn't know how she was going to try to spare his heart and hers at the same time.

As if he could tell Brenda's head was elsewhere, Zane stopped walking to gain her attention. "I want to tell you something."

Brenda looked at him and nodded for him to continue.

"I really like you, Brenda. I know you're probably thinking that I'm just saying this and that I say the same thing to a lot of other girls, but I'm being so serious right now. I think about you a lot and that's not something that usually happens when I'm with a girl. I know I flirt a lot and so do you. I also know that I said that I'm not looking for a relationship, but I'm really feeling you, Bre. I wanna be with you." He paused. "So . . . what do you say?"

Brenda was speechless. She couldn't believe the mess she had gotten herself into. Zane had never been in a committed relationship before. Why did Brenda have to be the first girl he wanted to be serious with? Why did it seem like the guys she talked to wanted her even though they knew they couldn't have her? Zane knew she was a flirt; it was one of the things they had in common. Why this sudden change?

"Bre." Zane called her name to fully gain her attention.

Brenda stared at him and took a deep breath. "Zane, I really don't know what to say. I'm not good with relationships; I never have been. I'm not going to say I don't like you, because I do, but I'm really afraid of committing because I'm afraid of being hurt. I really don't want to take my chances with you because I know you are just like me when it comes to flirting. So for now, casual dating is all that I can offer you." She waited for his response.

"That's cool," he said, to her relief. "*But* I'm going to do everything I can to show you that if you would be mine I wouldn't break your heart. I really do care for you and I want you to know that."

All Brenda could do was nod as they resumed walking. Almost a half hour later, Zane was standing with Brenda on her porch.

"I'll call you," he said before kissing her lightly on the lips.

Brenda unlocked her door and stepped inside. She watched as he left the porch before closing the door and going upstairs to her room. She'd made it home with a few minutes to spare before her twelve o'clock curfew. She slipped out of her clothes and into her pajamas as she thought about both Ken's and Zane's proposed commitments. She didn't know what to do. She just hoped that she was not digging herself into a deep hole with no hopes of getting out.

Chapter 14

Danielle

Danielle had gone all week without confronting her mother concerning the issue with her dad. She was sure that Beverly knew she was aware of the reason Jackson was in town, but her mother had yet to approach Danielle about the situation. She knew she needed to talk to her mother before dinner tonight because the last thing she wanted was for Déjà and A.J. to enter a house full of tension.

Barnes & Noble was as busy as it usually was on a Saturday. Danielle's shift would be ending soon and she had yet to take a break. She couldn't complain though because her hard work had awarded her a recent pay raise, and that alone was helping to pay for whatever her daughter needed. She turned and looked at her coworker, Selena, who was adamant about working, even at seven months' pregnant.

Selena was only nineteen and she wasn't married. Her boyfriend was a high school dropout who refused to stay out of trouble. Selena said that he'd vowed to take care of her and the baby, but she didn't buy into his empty promises because of his sketchy ways. She had told Danielle that at first she was going to stay with him and pray that everything worked out, but a few weeks ago, Selena had caught her boyfriend with another girl and that quickly diminished that decision.

So now she was working forty hours a week and saving every penny, hoping that she and her baby would be able to at least get by.

Danielle had offered her expertise concerning being a teen mother and Selena had been grateful for every piece of information she received. Danielle was glad that she could help, but at the same time she felt sorry that Selena was about to go through the same thing that Danielle had been going through for almost five years . . . all alone.

Danielle gained Selena's attention. "Selena, you can go sit in the back or something. Me and Blaire can handle the counter," she spoke of their other coworker.

"Yeah, Mama Lena, why don't you go take your break," Blaire assured her. "We got the counter."

Selena smiled her appreciation, but declined. "I wanna take my break with Danni." Danielle gave her a confused look. "I really need to talk to you," Selena explained.

"Okay, I'm taking my break as soon as Ingrid comes back from hers. I was just going to go over to Starbucks." She pointed toward the other end of the bookstore where the coffee shop operated. "But if you want some privacy we can walk down to Subway and grab a sandwich instead."

Selena nodded. "Yeah, I'd appreciate that."

Blaire looked at the two as if she felt left out. "Great, just leave me with the nightmare manager from Elm Street."

The girls laughed as they continued to work. Ten minutes later, their manager, Ingrid, came back from her break and allowed Selena and Danielle to leave. The girls retrieved their coats and walked out of the store and into the cold air. Danielle pulled her coat close to her body and blew out a stream of air.

"I'm in the mood for a hot sub," Danielle said. "What about you?"

Selena solemnly nodded as they continued walking along the storefronts. Subway was only a few stores down, so Selena didn't have to be on her feet for too long. They walked into the sandwich shop and ordered one foot-long, toasted Subway club to share, and a couple of bottled waters. Then they took a seat away from the door, resting in silence for a few moments as they enjoyed their lunch. Danielle soon noticed that Selena's eyes were tearing up as she barely nibbled at her sandwich.

"Lena, what's wrong?" Danielle asked, touching Selena's arm lightly.

"Danni, I'm so, so scared. I know you've told me everything about being a single mother and I thought I was ready, but I . . . I just can't do this. I think I'm going to have partial-birth abortion."

Danielle's eyes opened wide in shock. "No," she nearly screamed. She tried to remind herself to remain calm before she sent her coworker into hysteria. "No, Lena, you *don't* want to do that," she said in a softer voice. "I know you're not even going to do that because after carrying this child for the last seven months, you have to have some emotional attachment to your son. You have to. There's no way you can't love that little boy already." She had tears in her eyes, but she was not going to leave this restaurant until she knew Selena was going to have her baby.

Selena nodded. "I do," she assured Danielle with tears in her own eyes. "I do love my son, but I already hate the life I'm going to provide for him. I can't give him the clothes and the food and the type of living he deserves. And I'm surely not going to allow José to come in with his marijuana money and provide for my son. I just don't know how I'm going to give him the things he needs to survive."

Danielle pulled her chair closer to her friend and placed her arm around her shoulders. "Lena, you have a lot to offer your son. You can give him the love and care that he needs and everything else will work itself out. My mom always used to tell me that God never puts more on us than we can bear. Now I'm not about to preach to you, because I'm hardly a saint, but I believe that you will be able to care for this baby, emotionally and financially. You just have to believe that you can do it and I'm sure God will help you along the way."

"How have you done it for so long?" Selena asked as she wiped her tears. "How have you taken care of your daughter, gone to school, and held down a job all at the same time? You don't even seem to have mental breakdowns like I do, and I haven't even had the baby yet. What's your secret?"

Danielle smiled as she thought about her answer. She looked Selena directly in her eyes and replied, "Her name is Kennedi Camille Brookes. She's four years old and the light of my life. She keeps me on my toes and because I love her so much I do whatever I have to do to keep her well taken care of. When she was younger, she would whine and cry and keep me up all night, but there was not one day that I regretted having her, because she is my heart and I wouldn't trade her for anything in this world."

Selena was crying again, but this time she had been touched emotionally. "That's so wonderful. I want to feel like that about my son."

"Well give yourself a chance and you will." Danielle rubbed her shoulder. "Don't give up so easily, because this is only the beginning; and though it seems like your life has ended, it only gets better with time."

She paused. "Plus, when you have your son, you'll be thankful for each day that goes by because he will be that much closer to getting out of the house and moving out on his own."

They laughed, wiped their tears away, and continued to enjoy the rest of their twenty-minute break. As they walked back to their job, Danielle noticed her brother's rental car in the parking lot near the bookstore. When they walked into the store, they found Blaire smiling so hard that it seemed as if her cheeks would ache from being stretched to capacity.

"Where is he?" Danielle asked knowingly.

"In the children's section with Kennedi," Blaire answered.

Hearing her mother's voice, Kennedi ran up to the front of the store, wearing a bright smile. "Hi, Mommy," she said as she jumped into Danielle's arms for a hug.

"Hey. What are you doing here?" Danielle asked as she looked up and saw Jackson walking up behind Kennedi.

"Well, I thought she could use a few learning materials," Jackson said as he held up several books and learning tools.

"Aren't you the big spender," Danielle teased. "All you've been doing all week is buying her stuff." She laughed and then remembered her coworkers. "Oh, you guys, I'm sorry. This is my brother, Jackson," she introduced him. "Jackson, this is Blaire and Selena."

"Hi, how are you ladies?" he asked them.

"I'm fine." Blaire eyed Jackson was the finest man she'd ever seen in her life.

"I'm good, also." Selena smiled as she and Danielle walked back behind the counter.

Jackson placed the books on the counter in front of Danielle's register. After she checked the items out, giving him the employee discounted charge that she was able to use, Danielle bagged the items and handed them to him.

"Mommy, when are you comin' home?" Kennedi asked.

"I'll be there in a few hours," Danielle answered with a smile.

"Dinner's at seven," Jackson said. "I need A.J.'s number so that I can call him and tell him what time to be there, too. Do you have his home number? Maybe Déjà will answer."

Danielle laughed. "No, I only have his cell because he lives in a dorm, and Déjà has her own place. So either you can ask A.J. for his sister's number or you'll just have to let him tell her what time dinner is himself." She pulled her cell phone out and gave her brother the number. "Just make sure that dinner is ready, and it better taste good."

Jackson waved off her comment. "We'll see you later. Kennedi, tell your mama bye."

"Bye, Mommy. I'll taste the food so it's good, okay?" Kennedi offered.

Danielle came around the counter and hugged her daughter. "Thank you, baby. I'll see you later. Mommy loves you."

"I love you too, Mommy." Kennedi kissed her mother on the cheek.

They left the store and Danielle resumed working. She looked at her coworkers with a smile.

"Your brother is *so* fine," Blaire stated.

Danielle rolled her eyes and laughed. That was nothing new to her. Plenty of girls found Jackson attractive and he was. He was tall and handsome with skin the color of coffee. With his strong facial features and deep, dark brown eyes, he looked just like their father. Before any negative thoughts about her father could enter Danielle's mind, Selena gained her attention.

"I want what you and Kennedi have," she said. "She's so sweet."

"You *will* have what Kennedi and I have, if you allow yourself to," Danielle stated. "You know I'm always here for you."

Selena had unshed tears in her eyes. "Thank you."

Danielle made a mental note to pray for Selena and her baby. With that thought on her heart, she felt the need to pray more often. She had gotten too far away from God in the last few years and she needed to find her way back to Him.

Chapter 15

Danielle

Danielle walked into the house with Jackson following her. They saw their mother sitting on the sofa and Danielle knew that Beverly was ready to talk. Jackson excused himself and went upstairs to check on Kennedi while Danielle opted for the armchair that was situated a short distance away from the sofa.

"I know you want to talk about your father," Beverly announced with her hands clasped together nervously.

"As long as this conversation can end before A.J. and Déjà get here, I'm willing to hear you out," Danielle said.

At this point, she had no tolerance for any excuse that her mother had to give as to why this secret had remained for so long. Danielle just wanted the truth and if her mother couldn't give it to her, she definitely had other means of obtaining it.

Beverly excused her daughter's tone and went ahead with her confession. "I did know about Neil Jr. He was the reason for the divorce. Had he not been in the picture, your father and I would most likely still be together."

Danielle didn't need the preliminaries. "Mama, I don't care about the divorce or even the affair. I just want to know why no one felt that Jackson and I had the right to know about Junior? He's our brother, for God's sake."

"Danielle, you had just gotten out of your depressed state when your father and I divorced. You could hardly look at your own daughter. That made me wonder how you would be able to handle the situation. Would you shut the whole family out? Would you just ostracize your father or even me? Would you return to being miserable and helpless? Those were all of the thoughts that went through my head when I found out about Junior. I wasn't even concerned about my feelings because I knew that as long as I had God, I would be okay. I was concerned about your feelings. I was looking out for you . . . and Jackson, because Lord knows that if he would have found out sooner than he did, his temper would have just gone over the top."

Danielle shook her head as she tried to make sense of all of this. "Mama, if all of this was going on, why did you let Jackie move in with Daddy in the first place? You had to know that he would've found out sooner or later, especially after they moved to New York."

Beverly shrugged. "I didn't have a choice. Jackson wanted to go with Neil and Neil was threatening to take me to court if at least one of you didn't get to move in with him. The last thing I wanted was for you and Kennedi to move in with your father, so I let him and Jackson have what they wanted. I promised your father that I wouldn't say anything about Junior."

Danielle still didn't understand. "Daddy wanted us to find out," she said as if she knew it to be true. "He had to. There's no way he would've accepted that job in New York if he knew that woman was up there with *his* son. And then for him to take Junior in . . . He wanted the truth to come to light; he just wanted to do it in a way that made him not have to be a man and fess up to his mistakes."

"Danni, baby, please don't be angry with your father. He was just trying to protect you and Jackson," Beverly defended.

Danielle stood and proceeded up the staircase. She stopped midway up the stairs and looked down at her mother, sitting on the sofa. "I'm going to wash up for dinner. A.J. and Déjà will be here soon."

Jackson was coming down the stairs at the same time Danielle was going up. He glanced at her before continuing toward the kitchen to finish preparing dinner. Danielle went into her daughter's room and found Kennedi pulling clothes out of her dresser drawer.

"Kennedi, what are you doing?" Danielle asked as she watched Kennedi pull out a dress and place it against her body as she looked into the mirror on the wall.

"I wanna be pretty for dinner," Kennedi answered as she turned around and smiled at her mother. "You like this?"

Danielle laughed as she sat on Kennedi's bed. "Yes, I do, but I'm sure whatever you wear, you're going to look lovely."

"Mommy, I gotta be *really* pretty. A.J. can be my daddy."

Danielle's head snapped toward her daughter so fast that her neck popped. Massaging the side of her neck, she tried to calm the nerves that had arisen inside of her body. She felt as if she were about to vomit as she looked at Kennedi's smiling face and noticed how much she looked like Keenan.

"Kennedi, come sit next to me," Danielle said as calmly as she could. She knew that her four-year-old wouldn't understand why her mother looked so upset, but Danielle had to try her best to explain it to her. "A.J. is not your daddy."

"He's not?" Kennedi's downcast eyes revealed her disappointment. "Who is?"

Danielle sighed.

"Why I don't see him?" she asked. "He don't like me?"

Danielle was trying hard to hold back her tears. She didn't know how a four-year-old could ask such questions. Most children who didn't have a father didn't begin questioning his whereabouts this early in life . . . at least not that she knew of.

"Baby, your daddy lives too far away to come and see you. And I'm sure if he got to know you, he would love you just like I do." Danielle wanted to say more, but she couldn't offer her daughter a reasonable explanation concerning Keenan's absence, so she just left the situation alone, though Kennedi had tears in her eyes. "Come and put on your clothes before A.J. and Déjà get here," Danielle said softy as she helped Kennedi change.

After getting Kennedi dressed, Danielle sent her to watch television in the den and told her to call her when their guests arrived. Danielle went into her own room and looked through her closet. She didn't have time to shower, but she wanted to at least look decent for dinner, and the worn khaki pants and Polo-style shirt she wore regularly to work wasn't cutting close to being presentable. She decided to wear a pair of fitted blue jeans and a champagne-colored sweater. She slipped her feet into a pair of slides to match her top and that were comfortable enough to enjoy company in. After pulling her kinky hair up into a high, puffy ponytail, Danielle had a few minutes to spare, so she went downstairs to make sure that Jackson was finishing up the dinner.

"Hey, need help?" she asked him once she reached the kitchen.

Jackson looked up at her and smiled as he placed the top over his pasta. "Well, I'm finished with the food, but you can help me set up the dining room table." He reached into the cabinets that held their mother's special china, which was only used during Thanksgiving, Christmas, and when they were hosting guests.

Danielle took the plates while Jackson followed close behind with the utensils and drinking cups. Danielle spotted Kennedi watching television quietly in the den as she walked into the dining room. She prayed that her daughter would get past the "I want to see my father" phase because that was the one thing Danielle knew she couldn't provide for her little angel.

"Danni, are you okay?" Jackson asked when he noticed that she held a strange expression on her face.

Danielle looked at him and smiled. "Yeah, I'm cool."

They finished setting the table in silence. Jackson went into the kitchen and placed his feast on serving platters. He brought them into the dining room and put them in the center of the table. Afterward, he asked Danielle to check on their mother to make sure that she would be joining them as planned. Hesitantly, she obliged, and Beverly assured Danielle that she would be out as soon as the guests arrived. Then, she joined her brother and daughter in the den and silently watched the cartoons that Kennedi had chosen to enjoy.

At seven o'clock on the dot, the doorbell rang. Danielle watched as Kennedi jumped from the couch and ran toward the front door. She asked who was there and Déjà answered that it was she and A.J., Kennedi yelled for Danielle to come open the door.

"Hi." Danielle smiled slightly as she opened the door for her guests and stepped aside to allow them in the house.

"Hi, Danni," Déjà said, hugging her and Kennedi.

"Hey, you." A.J. smiled as he walked into the house. He bent down and gave Danielle a gentle hug and unknowingly sent a surge of warmth throughout her body.

Déjà and A.J. greeted Jackson just as Beverly came out of her bedroom. Jackson took the liberty of making introductions before leading everyone to the dining room table.

A.J. volunteered to bless the food and Danielle noticed how powerful his prayer was. Maybe he would be the one to help her get back on track with God. Maybe that was why she'd become acquainted with him. She decided to continue to get to know him and hoped that the purpose for their relationship would be revealed soon.

"I have to admit, Jackson, I had my doubts," Danielle said, "but this is really good." She savored the shrimp and pasta.

Jackson smiled and looked at Déjà. "Do *you* like it?"

Déjà returned his smile and nodded. "It's delicious. The chicken is really tender," she said as she cut another piece and put it into her mouth.

Danielle noticed that Kennedi was nearly talking A.J.'s ear off and her stomach sank. She didn't want her daughter to get too attached to her new friend; there was no telling what would become of their relationship and she didn't want to get Kennedi's hopes up.

"Danni, wipe Kennedi's face," Beverly said when she noticed that Kennedi had Alfredo sauce around her mouth.

Danielle did as she was told, forcing herself to subdue the loud grunt that threatened her lips. Her eyes revealed her rising irritation and she tried not to allow anyone to see it. Her mother was always trying to tell her how to handle Kennedi and it irked her to no end.

"Danielle, help her with that chicken," Beverly told her daughter, not a full five minutes later.

Danielle rolled her eyes as she looked at Kennedi and saw that the piece of chicken she was trying to eat was too big for her to consume, so Danielle reached over and cut it into smaller pieces. When she looked up, A.J. caught her eye and silently asked her what was wrong. She merely shook her head and continued eating.

The conversation was flowing around the table very smoothly. Déjà was telling Jackson about campus life at Clark Atlanta and he was soaking up everything she was saying. Beverly had taken A.J.'s attention away from Kennedi and had begun to ask him questions about himself. Danielle knew that her mother was prying for information about her relationship with the young man, but there wasn't much to tell, so she was really wasting her breath.

"Get that knife out of her hand!" Beverly suddenly shrieked, gaining everyone's attention.

Danielle had already been in the process of instructing Kennedi to hand her the knife, but Beverly's over-dramatic order caused Danielle to irately snatch the butter knife out of her daughter's hand and slam it on the table. "Mom! Please, I've got this." She was tired of her mother making comments every time Kennedi did or said something. This had been going on for so long that Danielle usually just let it go into one ear and out of the other, but tonight Beverly had made her look like an inadequate mother in front of her friends and that was embarrassing.

Everyone looked surprised at Danielle's tone, especially A.J.

Beverly glared at her daughter. "Well, if you paid more attention to Kennedi, I wouldn't have to come behind you and make sure that you're doing things right."

Danielle placed her fork onto her plate and stated, "I don't need help with raising my child. You had your chance a long time ago with me, now I can take care of myself and *my* daughter."

Beverly was taken aback by her daughter's attitude, but she surely was not going to back down. "Excuse me! Danielle, I need to speak with you."

"Now's not the time, Mom. We have guests," Danielle stated adamantly.

Beverly stood. "I think now is the time. Danielle Renée Brookes, come with me right—"

Before Beverly could finish her command, Kennedi's small voice piped up and said, "A.J., can you be my daddy?"

Every head snapped in the little girl's direction. Danielle's face instantly turned red in horrified embarrassment. She gazed at A.J. with tears in her eyes before getting up from the table and running out of the house.

Just before she closed the front door, she heard Kennedi ask, "What's wrong with Mommy?"

Chapter 16

Brenda

Brenda had met up with her girlfriends at Eastpoint Mall so they could shop for their dresses for Lauren's party, which was only six days away. The Sunday afternoon mall crowd was massive, but Brenda knew Lauren couldn't care less. She would be getting her dress from *this* mall. Only 4 U was a boutique housed inside of the two-story mall that designed custom-made dresses for all occasions. Lauren had the design laid out on paper weeks ago and now she was coming in to try on the real thing.

Brenda, Danielle, and Jayda would be buying their dresses from the store's racks. They were custom designs by the owner of the store and though they weren't one of a kind, they were still very rare in quantity. As Lauren tried on her dress, the girls looked around the store for something they liked.

"So, Bre, how was your date with the African American/Japanese—"

"His name is Ken." Brenda laughed as she cut off Jayda's question. "And the date was fun. He's really sweet and romantic. He took me to Olive Garden and, though I've been there a thousand times, I really enjoyed myself."

Danielle smiled slightly. "You sound kinda sprung, Ms. Killian. Are you falling for this guy?"

"No," Brenda answered a little too quickly. "I'm not.
If I was do you think I would be going out with him *and*
Zane?" She was boasting, but she felt bad about dating both of them at the same time. Last night Ken had
treated her like a queen and here she was going behind
his back and seeing another guy.

"Now that's the Brenda I know." Jayda chuckled
while shaking her head.

"You're not committed to either of them are you?"
Danielle questioned as she looked at the dresses on the
plus-size rack.

Brenda shook her head. "No." She decided against
telling them that both of the guys were looking for a
commitment. Her friends would surely begin lecturing
her about playing the guys when they truly cared for
her.

"Okay, you guys. Come look at this," Lauren called to
them when she stepped out of the dressing room.

The saleswoman helped Lauren onto a raised platform that faced three mirrors to allow her to view all
sides of the dress at once. The pink silk halter dress
stopped right at her knees. The A-line skirt and plung-
ing neckline with beaded flowers added elegance to the
dress, making it perfect for her party.

"Lauren, you look beautiful," Danielle admired.

Jayda nodded in agreement. "That dress is gorgeous.
I love it."

Brenda laughed as she walked up to Lauren. "If this
doesn't pull Mr. Sterling in, I don't know what will."
Unlike the rest of her crew, Brenda supported Lauren
wholeheartedly when it came to the situation surrounding Sterling. She honestly believed that if he was
who Lauren wanted, Lauren should go after him. Other
than the fact that he was her teacher, Brenda didn't see
any obstacle in the couple's way.

Lauren smiled as she stepped off of the platform and headed toward the dressing room. "I'm going to take this off. You guys find something and let me see it on you."

The girls went back to the racks and looked through more dresses. Jayda found her perfect party dress first. It was a red satin dress with an A-line skirt and a neckline that was accented by rhinestone buckles. Danielle found a blue chiffon dress with heavenly watercolors and a softly draped neckline that she knew would accentuate her curves wonderfully. Brenda thought both of their dresses were beautiful, but she immediately fell in love with a midnight blue velvet dress with V-cut straps that tied around the neck along with three rhinestone straps across the back. When she tried on her dress, she knew she looked good. Having her friends reinforce her thoughts only boosted her confidence. After seeing Jayda and Danielle in their chosen attire, Brenda was certain that they would be the best dressed girls at the party. They had no choice; they were the birthday girl's best friends.

Lauren's dad had volunteered to pay for all of the dresses, regardless of the price, and Brenda wasn't the only one who didn't object. She knew none of them had $200 to spend on a dress that they would probably only wear for one night.

After making their purchase, they decided to go to another store to find shoes that would complement their dresses. Lauren found a pair of silver five-inch heel sandals with beaded accents. Danielle also found a pair of silver heeled sandals to accompany her dress, but made sure that she and Lauren had very different styles before they purchased them. Brenda picked out a pair of dark blue heels and Jayda decided on a pair of red spike-heel sandals. Lauren also used her father's Visa to buy the shoes.

Afterward, Brenda suggested that they pack their items into the trunk of Jayda's car before stopping by the food court for lunch.

"So, Danni, how did dinner go last night?" Lauren asked.

Danielle stared at each of her friends and transmitted her thoughts to them.

"That bad, huh?" Brenda laughed softly.

"What happened?" Jayda inquired.

Danielle told them about her dinner with A.J. and Déjà. "And then while my mother and I were arguing, Kennedi asked A.J. to be her father."

"What?" Jayda shouted as Brenda gasped.

Danielle nodded. "I was so embarrassed. Everyone was looking at Kennedi as if she were crazy. All I could do was bust out crying before running out of the house."

Brenda chuckled. "You ran out of the house?"

"Bre, that's not funny." Lauren cut her eyes at Brenda.

Brenda returned the gesture. "I'm sorry, but that only adds to the embarrassment. If you were going to run, you should've gone to your room or something. Not out of the house." She shook her head as she continued to enjoy her meal from McDonald's.

Because Danielle was usually the strongest of her friends, Brenda hated when she allowed her weaknesses to show. And any discussion surrounding Kennedi's father was her weakness. As far as Brenda was concerned, Danielle should stay away from any man until she could solve the problems concerning the one who'd impregnated her with the child she'd birthed almost five years ago.

"Well that was the only thing on my mind. Getting away from that house and my mother," Danielle responded despairingly. "I walked for about a block before I saw Jackson coming after me. It took awhile for him to convince me to come back home, but I did."

"Were A.J. and his sister still there?" Lauren asked.

Danielle nodded. "They were waiting for me to come back, but when I did, they got ready to leave. Before they left, A.J. took my hands and said that he would call me so we could talk. I couldn't even look at him or respond 'cause I knew I was close to crying again."

"Has he called you?" Brenda wanted to know.

"Yeah, about three times. Once late last night and twice today, but I haven't answered."

Jayda gazed at Danielle confusingly. "Why not?"

"'Cause I don't want him to think that I've been filling Kennedi's head with that garbage about him becoming her father. He'll probably think that's the only reason I'm talking to him. He'll think I'm looking for a man just to give my baby a father."

"Are you?" Brenda questioned.

Danielle glared at her as if she'd lost her mind. "No!"

"I'm sorry, Danni, but if I were him and your daughter asked me that question, I'd definitely think that was the case."

"Well, it's not," Danielle shot back.

"Then, you should at least talk to him and tell him that," Jayda cut in, nudging Brenda in her side.

Brenda took the hint and the weariness in Danielle's eyes forced her to keep her mouth closed.

"And you need to do it before my party on Saturday," Lauren said, pointing her plastic fork at Danielle. "I don't want you showing up by yourself."

"Unless . . . you wanna bring Jackson." Jayda smiled dreamily.

Danielle smirked. "If I did you ain't gonna talk to him. You have a man. Remember Evan?"

"Evan and I are just friends," Jayda said, but Brenda noticed the smile on her face was growing wider.

"Sure." Brenda laughed. "Either you're lying or you're practicing for an audition for a Colgate commercial."

The girls laughed.

"Well, I do like him . . . *a lot*," Jayda admitted. "But he hasn't asked me to be his girl yet. I'm not going to push him, either. Part of me actually likes the way things are now, but my heart is like a magnet that is only attracted to him."

Brenda noticed how bright Jayda's eyes were and she could tell her friend was truly happy. Her heart felt heavy because she wanted to experience that same feeling, but her past experiences wouldn't let her. She inwardly sighed; romance had no home in her life.

"Well, girls, let's get out of here," Lauren said. "I have a meeting with my party planner in an hour."

"And I need to get to work," Danielle added as she looked at her watch.

The girls gathered their trash and threw it away before exiting the mall.

Danielle

Danielle sighed heavily when she heard Blaire call her to the counter. She had several books that she needed to sort out and place on the shelves before her shift ended. She had nowhere to place the ten books she was carrying in her arms, so she just held them as she walked out of the storage room toward the front of the store. When she neared the checkout counter, she gasped and dropped the books in her hand. Blaire and A.J. rushed over to her and picked up the materials. Danielle was too embarrassed to even help them. When A.J. stood, he held the books in his hands and gazed into her eyes.

"We need to talk," he said and all Danielle could do was nod.

"Blaire, could you handle this for me and let Selena watch the counter?" Danielle asked, forcefully breaking away from A.J.'s intense gaze.

"Yeah . . . sure." Blaire took the books from A.J. and walked away before calling Selena from the break room.

Danielle led A.J. to the back of the store, where a small section of chairs and tables were set up for children who wished to look through picture books while their parent shopped around. A.J. waited for Danielle to sit in one of the small chairs before taking one himself. Danielle couldn't even look at A.J., though his stare was unyielding. Being in his presence right now was too much and she fought the tears that she knew were threatening her eyelids.

"Why haven't you returned my phone calls?" A.J. finally asked.

"I . . . I didn't tell Kennedi that you could be her father. I promise I didn't tell her that," she cried, allowing her tears to fall.

A.J. moved his chair closer to hers and placed his arm around her shoulder. "I know you didn't," he said softly. "I'm guessing that's why you didn't want to talk to me—because you thought I would think that you did tell her that I could be her father."

Danielle nodded. "I don't know what to do with her." She wiped the back of her hand over her eyes. "She's been asking about her daddy for so long and lately it's become an everyday thing. Yesterday, she was trying to be so pretty for dinner because she thought that if she was, you'd be her daddy. When I told her that you couldn't be her daddy, she asked me if her real daddy even liked her." Her shoulders became heavy as she sighed. "I didn't know what to tell her."

A.J. removed his arm from her shoulders and turned her face toward his, using his index finger. "You need to give her what she wants . . . what she needs."

She shook her head at his command. "No, I can't just try to hook up with some guy to give Kennedi a father."

"That's not what I said," he told her. "She wants *her* father. Not some strange dude you might meet in a child's clothing store." He gave her a small smile. "She needs *her* father. The man who helped you create her."

Danielle sighed. "Keenan," she stated knowingly.

"Yes," A.J. answered. "You need to get in contact with him and find out where he is, what he's up to, and figure out if he's had a change of heart concerning Kennedi. It's been five years, almost, so it's not mentally possible for him to be the same immature, irresponsible kid he was back then."

"I wouldn't be too sure about that," Danielle said dryly.

"Just give it a try. Give him a chance to prove you wrong."

Danielle shrugged. "I don't see why I shouldn't." She paused and thought for a moment. "Other than the fact that he could say no and crush Kennedi's dreams of ever meeting her father."

"Or he could agree," A.J. said before she could begin crying again. "And he could get to know Kennedi and develop a relationship with her."

"But he's all the way in North Carolina," she noted. "How am I supposed to get in contact with him?"

"His mother still lives here right?" he asked. "Look her up and get in contact with her. I'm sure she can help you."

Danielle didn't know about that. Keenan's mother had never been too fond of her and the feeling was very much mutual. The woman had been seriously upset with Danielle for getting pregnant and causing her son to move so far away from her. Keenan had been a mama's boy and letting her son go was the hardest thing that Olivia Benson had ever had to do.

"I'll try," Danielle answered, though she was sure that Olivia wouldn't be of much help.

"Good." A.J. stood to his feet and pulled Danielle up with him. He wrapped his arms around her, giving her body a light squeeze.

Danielle felt weak in her knees. *This really feels good,* she thought. She reminded herself not to get too caught up; A.J. was just a friend.

"How'd you know I worked here?" Danielle asked as they walked toward the front.

"I stopped by your house first and your brother told me you worked here," A.J. explained. "So am I still invited to the party on Saturday?"

Danielle gave him a sideways glance. "Of course you are. Jackson's already agreed to keep Kennedi." She walked behind the counter and stood next to Selena.

"So, what time do I pick you up?"

"Seven. Lauren wants all her girls there an hour early to make sure everything is perfect. If that's too early for you, I could ride with Jayda and just meet up with you later."

A.J. shook his head. "No, that's cool. Oh . . . do I need to wear anything fancy?"

"Just a nice button-down shirt with a pair of slacks. Something you're comfortable dancing in," she said.

"All right," he said. "I gotta get back to work, but I'll call you later."

"Okay," Danielle replied. She watched as he left the store.

"Who was that?" Selena questioned.

Danielle smiled as she watched A.J. get into his car and drive off. "A really good friend of mine," she answered.

Chapter 17

Lauren

The night had come. Today, Lauren Hopewell was legally an adult. She had been waiting to turn eighteen for eighteen years and her wait was finally over.

Lauren looked around the ballroom of the hotel where her party was being held and tearfully placed her hands against her chest in amazement. The room was beautiful. A black and gold balloon arch stood at the entryway and several more balloons, with the words HAPPY 18TH BIRTHDAY, LAUREN printed on them, were spaced around the entire ballroom. Streamers, all black and gold, matching the rest of the decorations, hung from the ceiling. A large banner was positioned at the front of the room that had the same words that were displayed on the balloons printed on it in fancy calligraphy. Colorful lights hung from the center of the ceiling, surrounding a grand disco ball. A long table covered with a variety of hors d'oeuvres was positioned on the right side of the room and next to it sat a dolphin ice sculpture, spouting out her mother's special home-made punch. Two slide projectors were positioned on either side of the stage and showed photos of Lauren from the time she was born up until now. There was also a life-sized portrait of her that she'd had made a couple of weeks ago, which would hide the birthday girl until it was time for her to enter the party.

"This is so perfect," Lauren said to her friends.

"It's beautiful, Lauren," Nira, her party planner, said. "And everything is set. The DJ is here. Security is posted. And several of your guests are already lined up outside."

Lauren smiled to her parents. "Thank you, Mama and Daddy." She hugged them both. "This is so wonderful."

Her father, Rueben, hugged her tight. "You deserve it, sweetheart."

"Tonight is your night," her mother, Cathy, added.

Lauren turned toward her girls with a huge smile. Their expressions mirrored hers and she could almost feel the excitement pouring from her body into theirs. She opened her arms for a group hug. They ran toward her like small children flocking toward an ice cream truck. They hugged and screamed because they all knew tonight was going to be a wonderful night.

Nira pushed Lauren out of the ballroom, so she wouldn't be the first person seen when guests began to arrive. Lauren begged for her friends to come with her so they could help calm her nerves. They all anxiously sat in the small room behind the stage.

"When can we come out of these coats?" Brenda asked as she unbuttoned her long overcoat that each girl wore to hide her dress. "It's hot."

"Bre, nobody told you to wear velvet." Jayda laughed.

"Oh, I'm so nervous. This ain't even my party," Danielle said.

Lauren smiled. "You're just nervous 'cause A.J. is looking good tonight and you're afraid that you're falling for him."

Danielle only smiled as she thought about A.J., who was standing outside with the other guests waiting for the doors to open. Lauren wasn't ashamed about calling Danielle out on her relationship with A.J. She felt it was about time Danielle open up her heart again and A.J. seemed like a great catch, and his attributes went far beyond his physical appearance. Even if they didn't start dating, Lauren believed he had just as much to offer Danielle as a friend.

"So, Bre, how are you going to balance Ken and Zane tonight? They're both here already," Danielle pointed out, and Lauren knew she wanted to take the attention away from herself.

Brenda sighed and shook her head. "I don't even know. I barely escaped having them pick me up this evening. They both called yesterday asking if they could drive me here, but I told them that I had to meet up with you guys early to make sure everything was straight."

"Well, just make sure that you keep them a distance apart 'cause I don't want no drama tonight," Lauren instructed seriously. The last thing she needed was an altercation of any kind disrupting her special evening.

The girls heard the music blasting and guests could be heard entering the ballroom. Lauren's nerves shot to an all-time high and she could hardly inhale for a calming breath.

"Girl, you need to calm down," Jayda said as she fixed the tiara on Lauren's head. "You look great. The place looks great. Everything is going to be great."

Lauren looked up with a worried expression on her face. "What if Sterling doesn't show up?" she questioned anxiously and her friends realized the true reason for her jitteriness. She'd mentioned the party a couple of times since giving Sterling his invitation and he continued to avoid giving Lauren a direct answer. She wanted so badly to see him walk through the ballroom doors and if he didn't, she'd be devastated.

"He'll be here. There's no way he would miss this," Brenda assured her with her arm around Lauren's shoulder.

"Come on, girls." Nira clapped her hands as she walked into the room. "Out of those coats."

The girls removed their coats like snakes shedding old skin. They knew they looked good and they planned on having fun tonight. Everyone except Lauren and Nira left the room. Lauren wrung her hands nervously and settled into her seat. She watched as Nira spoke into the headset that connected her to all of the people who were helping make tonight a big success.

"Yeah, make sure they're tight at the door," Nira commanded and Lauren knew she was speaking to security. She turned toward Lauren with a smile. "Everything's going according to plan."

"Great," Lauren mumbled nervously.

Nira glared at her and studied her appearance. "Lauren, is everything okay?"

Lauren fumbled with her necklace. There was no way she could discuss the basis of her anxiety with her thirty-year-old party planner. Though there was a positive in that she probably would never see Nira again after tonight, which meant she wouldn't have to deal with the fact that she'd told her party planner her business, Lauren decided against it.

"Yes, everything's great. I'm just a little anxious, but tonight is going to be perfect," she claimed, hoping Sterling would make that declaration true.

"It is . . . as soon as you make your grand entrance." Nira motioned for Lauren to follow her.

Lauren felt the bass of the music pumping throughout her body as she stood backstage. She held a mental picture of the ballroom and smiled at the thought of everyone dancing to the music and waiting for her to make her grand entrance. Suddenly, she heard the DJ speak.

"Is everybody havin' a good time?" The teens screamed in response and Lauren shook in excitement. "Well, it seems like everyone's here to party, so why don't we bring out the lady of the evening. I guarantee if we scream loud enough, we'll get her out here." The DJ began chanting, "Lauren, Lauren, Lauren," and the partiers joined in.

The curtains on the stage closed, and the giant picture of Lauren slowly disappeared from her guests' view. Nira rushed the stage workers to remove the picture and position Lauren in the spot where the picture once stood. Seconds later, the curtains reopened and when they saw Lauren standing in her picture's place, with her hands on her hips and a smile on her face, everyone screamed as if she were a famous Hollywood star.

The DJ handed her the microphone and she began to speak. "Wassup, everybody?" In response, everyone screamed again. Lauren laughed because she loved every bit of the attention. "Thank you guys so much for coming out and celebrating this day with me. I'm eighteen, y'all," she said and they screamed and clapped again. "I hope you guys have the time of your life. So enough talking, let's dance." She gave the microphone back to the DJ.

When she looked up, she saw several students walking through the door, showing their invitations to the security guards, who, in turn, checked for their names on the list. Sterling was standing at the door. He seemed to be having a problem getting in and it looked as if he was about to leave. Lauren rushed off the stage and ran, in her heels, toward the door. Getting through the crowd of dancing teens and well-wishers was a chore, but she finally made it to the front door. Sterling was walking off when she called his name, nearly out of breath.

Sterling turned around and smiled at Lauren. "Hey."

"Hi." Lauren smiled. "Is there a problem?" she asked the guards.

The larger of the two guards replied, "This gentleman is not on your list, but he has a personal invitation."

Lauren waved her hand to dismiss his concern. "He's a chaperone. All of the chaperons got invites, but their names are on another list that the head chaperon has." She looked at Sterling and winked.

"Oh, I'm sorry," the other guard said. "Come on in, sir."

"Thank you," Sterling said as he walked toward Lauren.

"I didn't think you were going to show," Lauren told him as they walked away from the guards.

"I almost didn't," he replied honestly. "But I knew you would be expecting me. I didn't want to let you down."

"I'm glad you didn't." She smoothly reached up and locked her arm with his. "Would you like to dance with me?"

Sterling glanced around and noticed the crowd of partying teens. "Umm, maybe later," he told her as he eased his arm out of her grasp. "I think I'll just hang with the other *chaperons* for a while."

Lauren's face clearly revealed her disappointment.

"Please don't frown. You look beautiful tonight. I promise I'll dance with you . . . just not now." He began walking away from her, but turned back and said, "Happy birthday, Ms. Hopewell."

Lauren turned and dejectedly joined the rest of her guests out on the dance floor. She silently hoped that Sterling would make this a happy birthday for her.

Chapter 18

Brenda

Brenda had been dancing with Ken for several songs and she knew that Zane was among the crowd, waiting for her to come back from the bathroom . . . well that's at least where she'd told him she was going. She had to get back to him before he thought she'd gone missing. She pulled away from Ken and told him that she had to run to the ladies' room. He nodded and his approval allowed for her to search the crowd for Zane. She was glad that the ballroom was so big and the crowd so dense because that slimmed the chances of the two gentlemen running into each other.

She found Zane hanging by the gift table with a few of his friends. When he spotted Brenda, he smiled and excused himself. Immediately, he took her hands and began dancing with her.

"I thought you'd gone MIA," he said as they moved to the upbeat tunes of the song.

Brenda decided against making up an excuse and just continued dancing. She knew she didn't have much time to be with him. The girls' restroom line could only be so long. For the moment, she enjoyed the feel of Zane's hands on her hips as she swayed to the music.

Suddenly, the DJ came over the speakers again. This time it was to call Brenda, Jayda, and Danielle to the front along with Lauren's parents.

"I'll be right back, this won't take long," Brenda spoke as she stepped out of Zane's embrace.

She walked up to the stage and stood next to Lauren's parents, along with her two friends. She spotted Lauren standing at the very front of the crowd with a wide smile on her face. The DJ handed Lauren's father the microphone.

"Sweetheart, your friends came to us a few weeks ago and asked if we would allow them to do something special for your birthday," Rueben said before handing his wife the microphone.

"But we told them that this would not be a substitute for a birthday gift," Cathy added, to everyone's amusement.

"Let 'em know, Mama," Lauren yelled as laughter filled the building. "Let . . . them . . . know." She snapped her fingers with each word.

Her mother continued, "They have put together a little show to express just how they feel about you."

Her parents stepped off the stage and all three girls were handed microphones. The DJ began playing the track music to CeCe Winans's "Always Sisters." The girls began singing while everyone looked on and danced to the song. Brenda had been shocked when Danielle had come up with the idea to sing for Lauren at her party. Brenda wasn't the best singer in the world, but her ability to carry a tune was used against her when she tried to get out of doing the selection. They'd practiced all last week, behind Lauren's back, and the look of surprise and pleasure on Lauren's face let Brenda know it was all worth it.

When they finished, the girls collectively said, "Happy birthday, Lauren. We love you, girl."

Lauren was in tears as she ran on stage and hugged each of her friends before they joined in a group hug.

The girls came off the stage and the DJ announced that they were now going to slow down the music for the father-daughter dance.

Brenda watched as Lauren danced with her father while Beyoncé's "Daddy" blared throughout the building. Though this was Lauren's party, she had personally chosen this song as a tribute to her father, who'd put up with her spoiled attitude and smart mouth for the last eighteen years and still loved her like a father should. Brenda thought it was a nice gesture and wished she could share a moment like that with her own father.

Once the dance ended, the DJ began playing more slow songs. Knowing that Ken was clearly aware she had returned from the restroom, Brenda made her way toward him, hoping that Zane would go back to hanging with his friends.

"Hey." Ken smiled as she approached him. "I though you might've left me out here to dance by myself."

Brenda laughed. "I would never do that to you," she whispered in his ear as they began dancing again.

"Bre, I wanted to talk to you about us," Ken stated.

Brenda inhaled deeply and prepared herself to hear him out.

"I know you don't want a commitment, but I really feel like we belong together. And I think if you just give us a chance, you'll see that I would never hurt you."

She looked up at him and noticed the sincerity in his eyes. She liked him a lot, but could she give her heart to him and not be afraid of getting hurt? And what about Zane? He wanted the same thing Ken did. A commitment. The word alone made Brenda shudder, but she knew in her heart that she wanted a guy to love and care for her just as much as she loved and cared for him.

Ken placed a soft kiss on her lips, and then said, "Don't say anything now. Think about it and be sure of your answer before you tell me your decision."

Brenda nodded and they resumed dancing to the slow jams that were being played over the loud speakers. She didn't know what she had gotten herself into. She was falling hard for Ken; that had not been a part of her plan. As Ken held on to her, Brenda wondered what it felt like to be in love. She began to wonder if experiencing that emotion was worth compromising her beliefs in men and risking heartbreak. Maybe it was.

Suddenly, Brenda felt someone tapping on her shoulder, breaking her out of her thoughts. She slowly raised her head from Ken's chest and turned toward the person who'd intruded on their dance. It was Zane, standing before her, looking extremely upset. Brenda looked back at Ken, who looked confused as he gazed into a familiar face.

"Wassup, Zane?" Ken greeted his acquaintance.

"Nothin' but you being all hugged up wit' my girl," Zane pointed out as he looked down at Brenda. "What's up, Bre? I thought you were here with me."

"Well, I—" Brenda started to explain.

"I'm sorry, bruh, but I think you're confused. Me and Brenda are here together," Ken cut her off. "Tell him, Bre," he urged as he looked down at his date.

Her gaze shifted between two guys and she became speechless.

"Oh, I see," Zane said as he backed off. "Is this why you didn't want to be with me?" he asked as he pointed to Ken.

"No, I—" Brenda tried to speak again.

"No, it's all good," he told her. "I thought you were different. Guess I was completely wrong." He walked off dejectedly.

Brenda watched him walk away and her heart became heavy.

"You know what?" Ken spoke up, causing Brenda to realize that he was still standing behind her waiting for an explanation. "I'm not even believing this, Brenda. I was honest and straightforward and you didn't even have the decency to return the favor. You talked about being afraid of commitment because you didn't want to get your heart broken and I understood that. But I don't understand this situation at all. If you didn't want to be with me, all you had to do was say so," he said before walking away.

Brenda fought off tears as she stood on the dance floor alone. She had been trying to protect her heart, but in the process she broke those of two guys she truly cared about. That had not been a factor in her plan either.

Lauren

Lauren had just finished her fifth slow dance with one of her guy friends. She had been dancing all night and she was starting to become tired, but she wasn't tired enough to forget that Sterling had promised her a dance. It was eleven o'clock and her parents had promised to leave by ten-thirty, so they weren't around to keep a watchful eye on her. Many of the chaperons who had been recruited to watch over the partying teens were too busy indulging themselves in drinks and gossip at the bar in the hotel to be doing their jobs. Even Nira wasn't as on edge as she had been when the party first began; she was now walking around with a champagne glass full of sparkling cider in her hand, though she was still speaking into her earpiece, making sure everything was in order. Lauren decided to look for Sterling to make sure that he would make good on his promise. She walked off and found him standing by the punch bowl, apparently a post he had assigned himself. She smiled as he looked up in her direction.

"Would you like something to drink? I'm sure you've worked up a thirst." He smiled.

"And you've been working too much," Lauren told him. "You promised me a dance."

Sterling looked around nervously. "Lauren, I don't think this is a good idea at all."

"Why not? It's just a dance."

"A dance that could go too far."

"Only if you want it to," she teased. His guarded look remained and Lauren pouted playfully. "Please, it's my birthday."

Sterling sighed heavily. "I know and I've been enjoying the party, but—"

"Please," she begged again with doe-like eyes looking up at him. "Please. Just one dance."

He sighed again and gave in. Lauren took his hand and led him to the middle of the dance floor, where any watching adults couldn't see them. As soon as they began dancing, the DJ began playing another slow jam. Sterling hesitated when he saw Lauren reaching up to wrap her arms around his neck. Lauren stepped closer to him and felt his body tense as she placed her hands on his broad shoulders. She laughed softly as he stood rigidly with his arms dangling by his sides. She took his arms and placed them around her waist, and then replaced her hands on his shoulders. She laid her head on his chest and felt his heart pounding. She could tell that he was afraid, but there was no need to be. She loved him and she would protect him. No one would be able to judge them. Lauren knew that this was right. Gradually, she felt his body loosen up and she smiled as he hugged her closer. With her head resting on his chest, Lauren fell into the mixture of emotions she was feeling. She had hoped for this moment all night long, and she knew just what to do to make it last.

She pulled away from him and looked up into his eyes. "I have something for you," she said softly. "If you want to use it, you can. If you don't . . . no hard feelings, okay?"

Sterling gave her a confused look as she slipped her hand into the small silver clutch purse she'd been carrying all night. Slowly, she pulled out a hotel room key. She had asked her parents for the room for her and her friends, but had decided to use it for another purpose. She held it discreetly against her palm as she placed her palm against his chest. She knew that without seeing the item in her hand, Sterling knew exactly what she held.

"Lauren, I—"

"Shhh." Lauren shook her head. "You can use it or just leave it at the door so I can return it in the morning. It's up to you."

She slid the key into his pants pocket and continued dancing with him. Sterling resumed holding her and Lauren let herself fall deeper into the embrace. She hoped with all her might that he would come to her room tonight. Being with him would be the best present she could receive for her birthday.

Chapter 19

Jayda

Jayda had enjoyed the evening with Evan. He had been the perfect gentleman all night. As she drove Brenda home, she talked about the party and her wonderful *boyfriend*.

"I can't believe he asked me . . . *finally*." Jayda's heart was in overdrive. "He was so sweet. He was singing to me and everything. He didn't sound all that good, but *ohmigosh,* I think I'm in love. No, I'm not in love, but I'm getting there."

Jayda was talking so much—which was way out of her character—that she didn't even notice how quiet Brenda had gotten. Soon, Jayda realized that Brenda was inattentively listening to her babble on and on about Evan while gazing out of the window and watching the scenery of the city as they passed by.

"I'm sorry, Bre. I've been talking so much about my *boo* that I haven't even asked you about your night. How'd you juggle Ken and Zane all through the night?" Jayda glanced at her for a response.

Brenda shook her head and sat in silence.

Glancing in her direction again, Jayda immediately noticed the tears that were settling in the corners of her eyes. "Brenda, what's wrong?"

"They dumped me. Both of them," Brenda answered tearfully.

Jayda sighed as she watched Brenda cover her face with her hands. "I'm sorry, Bre." She did feel sorry for her friend, but for some reason, Jayda wasn't surprised at the news.

"Me too." Brenda sniffed as she pulled herself together. "But I did keep my promise to myself. I didn't get my heart broken."

"So you don't think that you broke your heart by breaking theirs?" Jayda asked.

Brenda shrugged. "I don't know. I *do* know that I feel horrible."

Jayda pulled into Brenda's driveway and parked her car before facing her friend. "Maybe you should call them, tell them how sorry you are."

"No, I can't do that," Brenda said. "I'm too embarrassed to do that right now."

"Well, you should at least set things straight. You weren't exclusive with either of them, were you?"

"No, but they had both proposed that option."

Jayda looked surprised. "Zane wanted a commitment? Wow, you musta really put something on him." Not that Jayda thought Brenda would carelessly be intimate with Zane while dating Ken, but sex was the only reason Zane stayed with any girl for any length of time.

"It wasn't even like that," Brenda stated. "He didn't try to get with me or nothing. He was really sweet and so was Ken. I just hate I couldn't let either of them go because I like both of them."

"Well, I still think you should explain why you did what you did."

"I guess." Brenda opened her door to exit the car. "Thanks for the ride. See you Monday."

"Bye," Jayda said as she watched Brenda get out of the car and close the door.

As Jayda watched Brenda enter her house, she hoped her friend would be okay. Though Brenda said she wasn't heartbroken, Jayda could tell this was having a major effect on her and it would continue to weigh on her heart until she made things right.

Danielle

Danielle smiled as she and A.J. stood on her front porch. The party had lasted until a little after one in the morning and she was worn out. A.J. had been Danielle's dance partner all night, regardless of the fact that several girls and guys had intruded, asking him or her to dance, respectively. Danielle had a blast and hated the night had to end.

"I had a great time, Danni. You are a great dancer," A.J. said.

"So are you."

"Danielle, do you remember when we first met and I told you that there was something familiar about you?"

Danielle paused for a moment of thought as she let her mind travel back to the day she'd met A.J. in the mall. She smiled as she recalled his statement. "Yeah. What? Have you've seen me before and are just realizing it?"

A.J. laughed. "Something like that. You remind me of this girl I used to be friends with back in high school. Her name was Carmen. We were really close."

She raised an eyebrow and her smile widened. "Really?"

He nodded. "We were best friends. A lot of people thought we were dating, but we were nothing more than friends."

Danielle's face went stiff. "Really?" she said in a deflated tone. She wondered what he was getting at.

A.J.'s smile slowly disappeared. "She died last year from cancer."

"Oh, I'm so sorry," she responded.

"Thank you, but you don't have to be because, although I miss her, I know she's in a better place." A.J. took Danielle's hands and squeezed them. "I said you remind me of her because she had such a friendly nature about herself. She was also a Christian who, with my help, was able to fully give her life to Christ."

Danielle was beginning to understand why A.J. was telling her this. He knew she was struggling where her faith was concerned. She hadn't known that she was being so transparent with him. Maybe that was a good thing.

"I think you're having trouble giving yourself fully to God." His eyes questioned her, but she remained silent. "Maybe I can help. I would love to take you and Kennedi with me to church sometime."

Danielle searched his eyes and tried, once again, to figure out if he was trying to judge her. From what she could tell, he was being genuine. "Let me think about it," she answered.

"Okay, that's fine. You let me know whenever you want to go and I'll come get you." He leaned forward and planted a light kiss on her forehead.

Danielle smiled as she unlocked her door and went inside of her house. She watched as A.J. drove away. She finally knew why he had been brought into her life. In just the few weeks that she'd known him, he'd done nothing less than encourage and uplift her. God had given her a friend she would surely hold on to for years to come.

Lauren

Lauren waited nervously on the king-sized bed. The party had been over for an hour, and after Nira had her assistants transport all of her gifts to her company vehicle and made sure that the decorating team would begin cleaning the ballroom, Lauren felt free to go to the hotel room she'd purchased for the night to wait for her ultimate birthday gift. There was only one problem: she had been waiting for Sterling for forty-five minutes.

She looked down at the black lace bra and panties, which were barely covered by a black silk robe that stopped midway her thigh. The CD that had been playing in the stereo was on its last song and the candles were burning their wax rapidly.

She got up with a sigh, turned off the music, and blew out the candles, leaving the room barely dim. She would spend the night alone, much to her dismay. Apparently Sterling was a man of ethics and morals, and part of Lauren admired that. She loved him, though, and she had been anticipating this night for a long time. Sleep would definitely be hard to come by tonight.

The sudden jiggling of the doorknob frightened her. She watched as the door slowly opened and there stood her dream. He smiled awkwardly as he stepped over the threshold.

"I . . . I didn't think you were going to show," Lauren said nervously.

"I almost didn't, but I knew you would be expecting me." He repeated the statement he'd said earlier that night. "I didn't want to let you down." Sterling closed the door behind him as he gazed at Lauren's attire through the darkness.

She smiled. "I'm glad you didn't." She walked toward him and took his arm. "Would you like to dance with me?" she asked as she turned the music back on.

He took a deep breath. "I'd love to."

They slowly rocked back and forth. Lauren pulled back and looked into Sterling's eyes. As if in slow motion, he leaned toward her and pressed his lips firmly against hers.

She savored the taste of his kiss before he pulled back and gazed lovingly at her.

"Happy birthday, Ms. Hopewell."

Chapter 20

Danielle

Danielle couldn't believe that she was actually sitting in Olivia Benson's living room. It had taken all of thirty minutes to find the woman's phone number and address and another five days for her to actually make the call. Surprisingly, Olivia asked for Danielle to immediately come to her home. She had also asked for her to bring Kennedi, but Danielle had decided that treat would have to be saved for a later date. She and Olivia had too much too discuss and a lot of it couldn't be said in front of a four-year-old.

Olivia came back into the living room with two cups of tea. She handed one to Danielle before taking a seat in the armchair across from her. They sat in silence for several long minutes. Danielle didn't know where to start; she had so much to say, so much to get off of her chest. She wanted to be straightforward and honest, but cordial at the same time.

"I know you have many questions," Olivia stated softly.

Danielle nodded, still unable to find a place to start. "I think it would help . . . if you explain your role in everything. I think that will help me . . . figure out what I want to ask you."

Olivia nodded as she sat on the edge of her seat. She placed her teacup on a coaster that rested on the coffee table. "First, I would like to apologize for what we did to you. I know it couldn't have been easy for you in the past four years and I know there is no way any of us can repay you for what we did. I guess I played my role in the whole incident because, like any other mother would, I wanted to protect my son. Every mother who has a son can attest to this: there is never a girl good enough for him, and the younger they are, the more trouble they cause. That was my conclusion. It's not that I never liked you." Her gaze shifted between Danielle and her hands that rested in her lap. "You were a really sweet girl, but when you became pregnant, I felt like you were trying to take my son away from me by trapping him in a relationship. Part of me actually believed that you got pregnant intentionally and that the child wasn't even Keenan's. I didn't know what to do. Keenan was only *thirteen,* just a baby . . . *my* baby." She had tears in her eyes. "He wanted to get away from you and the baby. He was so afraid and I was too. So his father agreed to take him in, and though it was extremely hard, I let my baby boy go."

Danielle gazed at Olivia and noticed that she looked much older than her actual age. Though in her early forties, stress had certainly taken effect on her physically. She was still an attractive woman though, and as Danielle looked into the older woman's eyes, she saw Keenan's face . . . Kennedi's face.

"Well, I guess that pretty much answers my questions of why you all left me hanging, even though part of me doesn't understand it completely. But I do accept your apology," Danielle finally spoke. "I cared for Keenan and I would have never tried to trap him. And if I did, I don't think I would have done that by deliberately getting pregnant. I've had some pretty bad thoughts and words about you and Keenan and even his father, who I don't even know, but I've never said a word of it to Kennedi. I would never want her to think that her father doesn't love her.

"I've had a pretty hard time with Kennedi, but it's been an experience I wouldn't trade for anything in the world. She is so precious and I love her so much." Her voice cracked, showing signs that tears were fast approaching. "I will do anything for her. Lately, she's been asking about her father and I've been as honest as I can *without* making Keenan seem like a deadbeat dad. She wants to know him so bad and before now I didn't think that would be possible. If it were up to me, I would continue to be her mother and father, but her heart is yearning for his affection . . . and that is something I can't give her on my own." She paused and wondered if she was in way over her head. Olivia seemed very sincere and caring, but would she offer to help Danielle bring Kennedi and Keenan together? She decided that she'd come too far to turn back. Kennedi wanted to meet her father and Danielle would do everything in her power to make that possible.

"I would like for them to meet," Danielle finally stated. "I want Kennedi to get to know her father and I want Keenan to get to know her. I don't know how often you get to see him, but if it is at all possible for you to help me . . ." She could barely finish the statement before tears began streaming down her face.

Olivia had tears in her eyes also. "I will." She offered Danielle a tissue and took a few for herself. "I get to see Keenan during Thanksgiving and Christmas and for a few weeks during the summer, but to speed up this process I'm sure I can convince him to come for spring break."

Danielle wiped her eyes. "Thank you. This means a lot to Kennedi . . . and me."

Olivia rose from her seat and opened her arms to Danielle. Danielle received the loving embrace.

"You've grown so much," Olivia whispered. "I can see that God's been working with you and through you as He has been with me. I know it took a lot for you to come way out here to see me, but I'm glad you did."

"Me too," Danielle said tearfully.

Lauren

I wonder if I made a mistake. I'm praying that I didn't, but I can't help but to feel like I did. My party was on Saturday and it was the best night of my life. I danced and had fun with my friends. I even received tons of gifts, none of which I'm thinking of returning.

My most cherished gift was from Sterling. He gave me everything I had wanted and longed for. He loved me tenderly and took his time, making sure he didn't hurt me. We spent the whole night together and afterward he held me close and made me feel protected. After we left each other, I was sure that our relationship would only progress. I was looking forward to seeing him on Monday to discuss us, but he never showed up at school. As a matter of fact, he has been absent all week. My best bet is that he called in sick. What do I do now?

I love him, in all honesty, I do. Many people will say that I'm only eighteen, barely old enough to know when I'm in love, but I know what I feel in my heart. I know Sterling feels the same way; he's just too afraid to admit it. I know he has a lot riding on the line. His job and his credibility. But what about me? I gave him something that no one else has ever had. My innocence. Of course, I didn't tell him that, but the fact still remains. I haven't cried yet and I'm not going to until I know what's really going on with him. I hope that he is okay and he will be willing to talk about us.

Lauren sighed as she closed her journal and placed it in her nightstand drawer. She was so confused right now and she didn't know what to do. Each day that passed, her heart grew heavier and heavier. She hoped that she could set everything straight before her heart completely fell and burst into a million pieces. She wanted Sterling to tell her that everything was all right and that he wasn't regretting anything that happened between them, but his absences had made her believe that he did. That notion alone made her heart sink another inch.

Her mother appeared at her doorway, slightly startling her out of her thoughts. Cathy's face was aglow with excitement and Lauren hoped that her mother couldn't sense her discontentment.

"What's up, Ma?"

"Come downstairs, your father and I have a surprise for you," Cathy said. She walked away from the door, giving Lauren no chance to protest.

Lauren dragged herself from her bed and took her time going down the stairs. Her mother was already outside, standing on the sidewalk as if she was waiting for someone. Lauren was standing by the doorway. Though it was only seven o'clock in the evening, she had already showered and slipped into a pair of flannel pajama pants and a tank top. She did not want to be outside for her neighbors to see her so unkempt.

"Lauren, get yourself over here. Ain't nobody out here," Cathy said.

Lauren smacked her teeth; she could clearly see several guys from her school standing on the corner, laughing with each other about something. She noticed that one of them was Jarred. She looked at him and he barely glanced at her before turning back toward his friends. *That was strange,* Lauren thought as she stood next to her mother. As a matter of fact, she had hardly seen Jarred all week. Usually, she could barely go one day without him popping up in her face. She pushed the matter out of her mind; she had been asking to be rid of him, now she was. *Good riddance.*

"Mom, what's this all about?" Lauren asked as they stood on the side of the road. "I'm tired. I just want to go to bed and sleep."

Cathy said nothing; she only kept looking up the street. Suddenly, a royal blue Volkswagen Jetta sped by their house. Lauren took a few steps back and watched disgustedly as the car continued down the street.

"Mom, I'm really tired. Whoever's coming over can visit me *inside* the house."

Just as Lauren was about to turn and go into the house, the car came barreling back up the street. It came to a screeching halt right in front of her house. She looked at the driver and didn't believe her eyes.

"Daddy!" she screamed. "Are you crazy? Driving like that through a neighborhood? And whose car is that? I'm sure they don't know you're out here tearing up the streets with it."

Reuben turned off the engine and climbed out of the vehicle. Lauren noticed that both of her parents were laughing as she stood looking at them with her hands on her hips. She felt like she was the parent and they were the careless teenagers.

"What is so funny?" Lauren demanded.

Reuben held the keys up in front of her face. "Do you want the car or not?"

Lauren's face dropped. "This is mine?" she asked quietly.

"Yes, sweetie," Cathy said.

"For real, this is *my* car?"

"Yes, girl." Reuben was still laughing.

Lauren stood staring at the car. She didn't deserve this. Surely, her parents would have rethought giving her this gift if they were aware of the night she spent with Sterling. She felt guilty because they had too much trust and belief in her and, though they didn't know it, she had demolished all faith they had in her.

"Lauren, you don't like the car?" Reuben asked. "I can return it, but I'm not getting another."

Lauren turned toward her father with tears in her eyes. "No, I love it, Daddy." She hugged him tight, needing to feel his protective arms around her. "Thank you so much. I love you."

"I love you too," Reuben responded.

Lauren knew he had no idea of the real reason behind her tears. He probably believed they were due to her feeling overjoyed by the gift they'd just presented to her; she wouldn't tell him otherwise. She embraced her mother also. When she looked back up the street where Jarred was hanging with his friends, she noticed they were all looking at her car. Jarred glared at her angrily and shook his head. He quickly said good-bye to his boys and left without giving Lauren a second glance.

Lauren wondered what was up with him. What had she done to him to make him so bitter and angry? Besides the fact that she'd ignored, embarrassed, and mocked him, she couldn't figure out what the sudden change in his demeanor had resulted from.

Chapter 21

Brenda

Brenda's phone hadn't rung all weekend, and, though she'd hoped that at least one of the guys would call, she hadn't been very optimistic. She hated herself so much for breaking their hearts, but mostly for breaking her own heart in the process. Jayda was right; it had taken a night's sleep for Brenda to realize that her heart was torn almost as much as, if not more than, Ken's and Zane's.

The past week at school had been terrible. Being so close to Ken and Zane and not being able to speak to them was torture. It was even harder when she had a class with each of them. Passing back papers to Zane was no longer as enticing as it used to be. He avoided looking at her even if she continued to look in his direction for attention. The same thing went for Ken, only it seemed as if her heart longed for his attention more than it did for Zane's. Ken avoided all contact with her and she didn't know what else to do. If neither of the guys would hear her out, how could she explain things to them?

Thinking about this for the past week had given Brenda a massive headache that had yet to go away. The music blasting from down the hall did little to settle her pounding temples. Her mother was out running errands and David and Maya were with their father, so the music had to be coming from Taylor's room. Brenda got up and walked to her sister's closed door.

"Tay," she yelled as she banged on the door. "Taylor!"

Brenda heard fumbling around and her brow furrowed in suspicion. *What is she doing in there?* "Taylor, come open this door right now before I call Mama," Brenda threatened.

The door cracked open and Taylor stood before Brenda, looking extremely disoriented.

"What do you want?" Taylor asked.

Brenda searched her sister's eyes. "I need for you to turn down your music. I have a major headache."

"Okay," Taylor said.

Brenda watched her sister's eyes and noticed that they weren't their natural white color. "Are you okay? You look high."

Taylor laughed. "I'm fine."

Brenda pushed her way through her sister's room despite Taylor's attempts to keep her out. The room was a mess; clothes were thrown everywhere, CDs lay around without the protective covering of their cases, the bed sheets were hanging off the bed, and the room smelled of cheap perfume and marijuana. Brenda noticed the window was open and she knew exactly why.

She spun around toward Taylor and pointed an accusing finger in her direction. "I know you haven't been up here smoking weed."

Taylor folded her arms across her chest. "No," she lied forcefully.

Brenda began turning over piles of clothes and looking behind dressers.

"What are you doing?" Taylor screamed.

Brenda ignored her sister as she looked under the bed before pulling up the mattress. She found just was she was looking for. She shook her head as she picked up the Ziploc bag half filled with marijuana. She held it up for her sister to see what she had found.

"So what? Are you gonna tell Mom now?" Taylor questioned defensively.

"Why are you doing this to yourself?" Brenda demanded. Taylor immediately began crying as she fell onto her bed.

"Do you know what this stuff can do to you?" Brenda continued to interrogate her.

"And? It's not like you care," Taylor yelled back.

"Taylor, how can you say something like that?" Brenda asked through a whisper.

"Because it's the truth," her younger sister responded in a high-pitched scream.

Brenda's face showed her surprise. All sorts of questions were going through her mind. How long had Taylor been doing this? Who had she gotten it from? How was she paying for it? Why did she believe that no one cared about her? Brenda sat next to her sister with the marijuana still in her hands. She allowed the silence to envelope them so she could sort out her thoughts before saying something she would surely regret.

"Tay." Brenda sighed. "Why do you do things that are so . . . Why are you so . . ." She couldn't find the perfect way to ask the question but Taylor already knew the perfect answer.

"Stupid. Crazy. Out of the ordinary," Taylor said as she cried. "I want attention, Bre."

Brenda refused to look at her sister for fear of crying herself. "Tay, you get plenty of attention."

"No, I don't, Brenda. Everybody in this house is wrapped up in their own little worlds and has their own thing going on. You're the pretty one, so you go out with your friends and get a lot of attention from guys. Chase is the successful one, so he gets all of Mom's praises.

David and Maya are the youngest and the most naïve, and they get plenty of attention from their father. Me, I'm stuck in the middle; I'm the rebel who does things like dye my hair and get my belly button and my tongue pierced just so I can come home and hopefully get yelled at by my mother, but does she notice? No!"

Brenda looked at Taylor. "You got what pierced?"

Taylor lifted her shirt and stuck out her tongue for her sister to see the two silver objects shoved into her flesh. At that moment, Brenda knew Taylor was right. The notion that Taylor barely opened her mouth when she spoke and that she suddenly carried a slight lisp should have tipped them all off as soon as she got the piercing. A vague memory of Taylor refusing dinner and eating applesauce instead a few weeks ago resurfaced in Brenda's hindsight. How had she missed all the clues? She couldn't even say she didn't know. She just never paid them any attention.

"I can't believe you did that."

"It was just so Mom would wake up out of her little fantasy world and pay more attention to her kids, namely me."

Brenda looked down at the drugs in her hands. "Are you addicted to this stuff?"

"I don't think so. I've only smoked it a few times. Plus my friends said you can't get addicted. Regardless, this is still the first pack and I got it almost a month and a half ago." Taylor looked up at Brenda with tears in her eyes. "I want you to tell."

"What?" Brenda asked disbelievingly.

"Please, Bre. I want Mama to know what's going on. I need her to stop running after these men and realize that no one in this house is happy. Bre, I know you're not happy, and Maya and David are always with their dad, so they can't be too comfortable when they're here."

"You're right, but Mama's not going to listen to me. I've been trying to tell her this for a long time and she's still running after these guys." Brenda shrugged.

Taylor took the marijuana from her sister and stood in her bedroom doorway. "Bre, I promise that if you at least say you're going to try—and I trust your word alone—I will go flush this crap right down the toilet."

Brenda saw Taylor's eyes begging for her to say yes. Apparently, she really wanted things to improve so that they could all feel better. Brenda couldn't deny her sister the one thing that could save her from destruction. She had to help her . . . and everyone else in this house.

Jayda

Jayda hadn't heard from her father in almost a month and her mother was not offering any information concerning the separation, so she didn't know if they were even trying to work things out. Candice and Cameron had come to Jayda asking the same questions that she had been asking their mother: What's going on? Are they going to get a divorce or try to resolve their issues? Why won't anyone tell us what happened? Where is Daddy?

Jayda, of course, didn't have any answers to their questions, but she was their big sister and they had come to her. She had to find out some information. So for the past hour, Jayda had been begging her mother for something that would help her understand all of this.

"Jayda, please, stop asking me these questions," Heather cried. "Please."

"But, Mama, the twins wanna know . . . I wanna know . . . just *something* that will give us a clue."

Heather took out a sheet of paper and scribbled on it before handing it to her daughter.

"Is this where he is?" Jayda asked, looking at the paper and noticing a local address written on it. She was familiar with the neighborhood, but didn't know anyone who lived in that area, so she wondered why her father would move there.

Heather nodded tearfully. "Just please don't ask me anything else. Whatever you find when you get there, don't bring it back here. I don't want to hear a word."

"Should I take the twins?" Jayda asked nervously.

"That's up to you and them, but if they don't go with you they're not going to find out from me."

"Thank you, Mama," Jayda said solemnly before leaving the master suite.

Jayda went upstairs and told her siblings about the information she'd just received. The twins agreed to take the trip with her and assured her that they were prepared for anything they might find. They piled into Jayda's car and drove for about thirty minutes until they reached a pleasantly quiet neighborhood. Jayda drove slowly through the streets, looking for the right house.

"There it is," Candice screamed, causing Jayda to hit the breaks hard. "That's his car, right there."

Jayda looked at the sheet of paper in her hand and noticed that the address on the brick mailbox matched the handwritten one on the paper. She took a deep breath and prepared herself for the encounter. Her nerves were out of control and she felt as if she couldn't breath. She held firmly on to the steering wheel and quickly parked the car, afraid that she would accidentally press the gas pedal that would send them crashing into a large SUV parked against the curb.

"Jay, what are you waiting for?" Cameron asked. He was obviously ready for a confrontation.

"N . . . n . . . nothing," Jayda said as she shakily took off her seat beat. "Let's go."

They got out of the car and walked up the driveway toward the house. Jayda was hesitant to knock on the door for fear of what might be on the other side, but Cameron was running out of patience. He rang the doorbell once and, rapidly, knocked on the door three times.

Jayda's heart was nearly pounding out of her chest with each thump. Several scenarios played in her mind, but she had no idea what to expect. When the door was finally answered, she couldn't believe her eyes.

"Jayda?" the man asked cautiously, as if he weren't sure if he knew it was her.

"Mr. Murphy?" Jayda questioned. All of the nervousness and anxiety quickly fled Jayda's body as confusion and anger took their place.

Simon Murphy was one of her father's running buddies. Preston would usually leave early in the mornings before work or even sometimes on Saturdays to go jogging with the man. Simon was a very elite business man who went through a very messy divorce last year, leaving his wife to care for their four children, one of whom had recently graduated from Jayda's school. She'd heard rumors about Simon fooling around with other men, but she was certain they were just rumors. This man couldn't be the reason her parents were separated.

"What are you doing here?" Simon asked.

Jayda was starting to boil and if she could only clear her thoughts, maybe she would ask the right questions that would help her figure everything out. She pushed her way into the house and looked around for her father.

"Mr. Murphy, I'm not sure exactly what's going on here, but you have exactly one second to tell me that my dad isn't here or else I'm about to ransack this house," Jayda threatened.

Simon looked from Jayda, who had her fists balled up at her sides, to Cameron and Candice, who both had their arms crossed over their chest. "Umm, baby . . . I mean, hon . . . Preston, I think you need to get out here," Simon spoke nervously as Jayda's body began to shake.

"Si, what's going on out here?"

Jayda spun around to face the voice that was booming from down the hallway that surely led to a bedroom. When she saw her father pause midway down the hall at the sight of her, Jayda lost all control. She ran toward him full speed and began hitting him on his bare chest as hard as she could.

"How could you . . . you . . . sorry excuse for a . . . You make me . . ." Jayda could barely finish one thought before another rushed out of her mouth as she released all of her anger while Preston tried his hardest to calm her down.

He picked her up into his arms as she kicked, hit, and screamed, and carried her into the living room. At the sight of their father, Candice fell onto the floor in tears and Cameron's stare became piercing and cold as angry tears filled his eyes, but never fell.

"Daddy, why?" Candice cried as she hit the floor repeatedly.

Jayda had pulled away from his embrace and began cursing violently. Soon, her anger was directed toward Simon, who had been too shocked to move.

"I thought the rumors about you weren't true," Jayda cried. "I defended you and your daughter when people at school started talking mess about you."

"Jayda, please. I am—"

"No," Jayda cut off his excuse. "You're nasty and . . . and . . . disgusting. How could you ruin my family like this?"

"Jay, baby, just lis—"

Jayda turned toward her father so quickly with a stare so piercing, Preston probably thought she would literally kill him if he uttered another word. "And you . . . Oh my God, I can't even stand the sight of you right now. Don't ever speak to me again. I hate you!"

Jayda walked over to her sister and picked her up off the floor, and she practically had to drag Cameron out of the house. She moved them quickly toward the car, ignoring Preston's constant calls for her to come back so they could talk this out.

After helping a frail Candice into the car, Jayda turned toward her father, who was standing in his doorway, apparently not sorry enough to come all the way outside and approach his daughter. "You know what," she yelled, refusing to go back toward the house, regardless of the fact that she was screaming loud enough for the neighbors to hear. "I'm glad you left. I'm glad that my mother is finally rid of you. For the longest, you have been like this poisonous creature sucking every bit of happiness that she had left in her and now that you're gone, the twins and I are going to do everything we can to help her regain her happiness. I hope you're happy with *Mr. Murphy,* but enjoy him while you can because I'm sure he won't be around too much longer. Oh, but when he leaves, please save yourself the trouble of trying to come back to our family because as of today, you have been dismissed. Have a nice life." Jayda turned around and got into her car. She drove off without even looking back to see that her father was still standing in his doorway.

Candice cried the entire drive home and Jayda tried to fight her own tears. Cameron's tears had yet to fall and Jayda knew that he wished he would've said or done something that would've made his father feel worse for his actions toward them. Jayda just couldn't believe that her father had left his family to be with another man. She was still struggling to make sense of all of this.

Jayda heard her parents argue one day about her father being unfaithful, and his excuse was that he'd been molested as a child. She'd never understood what that had to do with him cheating, but now it was all coming together. Jayda never thought that her father would become involved with a man. She was prepared to see another woman behind the oak wood door, but *a man?* And how long had this been going on? Had there been more than just Simon? *Ugh!* All these thoughts were making Jayda sick.

She pulled into the driveway of her home and put the car in park. "You guys go on inside and don't say a word to Mama about what happened. She already knows what's going on and I promised her that when we found out we wouldn't bring any of it back to this house." Jayda's voice was even and held no emotion.

Candice sniffed.

"Candi, you have to stop crying, and, Cam, please soften up your face," Jayda instructed them. "We need to be strong for Mama because if she sees you two crying, she's gonna break down. Now, go in the house."

"Where are you going?" Cameron asked harshly.

Jayda knew that his anger was not directed toward her, so she calmly replied, "I need to clear my head. I'm going for a drive."

"I wanna . . . go," Candice pleaded with red eyes.

"No, Candi. I'm going alone. Now dry your faces and get in the house," she ordered them.

Unhurriedly, they did as she asked, and once they entered the house, she pulled out of the driveway. As Jayda drove, tears began to cloud her vision. She felt so hopeless and helpless. She needed to feel loved and protected . . . like her father used to make her feel. She wanted to be comforted and she knew just where to go. She made a left turn into a neighborhood where several people were hanging outside regardless of the fact that the sky had grown dark. She dodged a few guys and girls who stood in the middle of the road, and soon pulled into the driveway of a two-story townhouse.

She could barely walk once she'd climbed out of her car. But she didn't have to go too far because, as if he could sense her presence and knew she needed him, Evan came out of his house and pulled Jayda into his arms, allowing her to cry on his chest.

Chapter 22

Lauren

Monday morning, the sun was shining and the warm temperatures were gradually revealing themselves, but Lauren and her girls looked and felt exhausted. She could tell that they were all struggling with their own problems but she was too tired from dealing with all of her drama to even ask about what was going on in their lives.

They climbed out of Jayda's car and headed toward the school building. Her walk to her locker lacked its usual sass and sophistication, and she barely checked her makeup before shutting the metal door and heading to her first-period class.

Lauren was surprised to see Sterling sitting at his desk when she and Jayda walked into his classroom, but she wasn't too shocked when he didn't raise his head to greet them as he usually did. Jayda gave Lauren a confused glance but she simply shrugged. Jayda didn't ask any questions and Lauren knew that she was definitely dealing with something personal as well.

The class filled up quickly and the late bell rang, signaling that class was about to start. Lauren watched Sterling avoid eye contact with her as he began teaching the lesson. She knew that he was well aware of the fact that she was waiting for an explanation and she hoped that he felt he owed her one. Hopefully, he would give it to her soon, because she was tired of wallowing in her depression.

By the end of the period, she had decided to approach Sterling and figure out what was going on with him. She told Jayda to go ahead without her and waited for everyone to leave before confronting him.

"Sterling, we need to talk," she stated evenly from her desk, not even trying to give him the respect of referring to him with the title "Mr." as she'd done in the past, especially when they were in school.

Sterling looked up at her and sighed. "We do," he agreed solemnly.

Lauren got up and walked toward him. "I was hoping to talk to you *last* Monday . . . about us."

"I figured you would," he replied.

"And yet, you weren't here all last week."

He shrugged. "I needed time to think."

She nodded in understanding. "I did a lot of that too."

Sterling stood up and scratched his head. "Lauren, I—"

"Please don't say you made a mistake," she pleaded.

"If I said that I didn't I would be lying," he confessed.

Lauren's heart was breaking by the second, but she was determined not to cry. "But I gave you my . . . my virginity," she whispered.

Sterling shut his eyes and ran his hand over his face. "Please don't tell me that." He took a deep breath. "Lauren, this is not going to work."

"But I love you," she confessed tearfully. She hoped that would change his mind.

"Don't say that," he begged. "Lauren, you don't love me."

"Yes, I do," she forcefully declared. "I love you with all of my heart. Don't you feel the same way?"

"I care a lot about you," Sterling said.

Lauren gazed at him sorrowfully. She couldn't believe that she had given Sterling her all and he was standing here telling her that he didn't want to be with her. This couldn't be happening. What she hated most was that she still loved him regardless of what he thought.

Lauren walked toward him and placed her hands on his face. She placed a delicate kiss on his lips and stepped back as she searched his eyes. "Please tell me you felt something."

Sterling took her hands in his. "Lauren, if this was a different situation or environment, I would love to have you as my lady, but it's not."

Lauren gazed at him and snatched her hands away angrily. "Why didn't you say that before you slept with me?" She picked up her books and turned toward the door, but was shocked to find Jarred standing in the doorway with a mixture of disbelief and anger in his eyes.

Sterling sighed as he sank into his seat with his head in his hands.

Lauren mustered up enough dignity to walk past Jarred and toward the girls' restroom to cry her eyes out.

Brenda

"I would just like to tell everyone how proud I am of you. Eighty percent of the class made a B or higher on last week's test. I can tell that improvements were made. Brenda, could you please pass these back out?"

Brenda took the papers that her calculus teacher, Mrs. Saunders, held in her hand. She walked around the classroom and returned each paper to its owner. When she got to Zane's test, she moved it to the bottom of the stack so that his would be the last one she'd give out.

When she'd handed out all of the papers and moved to give him his paper, she held it out at a distance. She wanted Zane to look up into her eyes and see how sorry she was. She needed to look into his eyes and determine his feelings. But she barely received a glance when he looked up only long enough to snatch the paper out of her hand.

Brenda sighed as she took her seat. She didn't know what to do about this situation with Zane and Ken. They weren't discreetly trying to avoid her. They had made it clear that they wanted no dealings with her. They didn't care to hear her excuses or apologies. They just wanted to move on with their lives and forget all about her. Brenda couldn't let that happen.

As she dwelled on her problem with Zane and Ken, the troubles at home eased into her mind. She hadn't gotten around to telling her mother about Taylor's drug abuse yet. Brenda was afraid of her mother shrugging the situation off as if there were no problem. Eileen was known to do that.

Brenda had come to realize that her mother was just trying to avoid the problems in her home by pretending as if nothing were wrong. Everything that her children went through was considered a "stage." The issues within their home had been labeled a "stage." Brenda had to find a way to get her mother to see that many of these "stages" could last for a lifetime. Their family was in trouble and Eileen had to face reality soon.

Brenda's thoughts consumed her mind, so much that she was having a hard time focusing on what Mrs. Saunders was saying. When the bell rang, Brenda was snapped out of her thoughts. She knew she'd have to review the chapter or else she was going to fail the chapter test tomorrow.

As she gathered her things, Brenda watched Zane leave the classroom without even tossing a glance in her direction. She tried to hurry so she could go after him, but her teacher's voice stopped her.

"I wanted to discuss the grade you received on your test last week," Mrs. Saunders informed her.

Brenda nodded. "Oh." She looked through her notebook and couldn't find the paper.

"I have it right here, Brenda. I purposely didn't give it to you because I wanted to wait until the end of the period so that we could discuss it."

Brenda had been so caught up in her own thoughts that she hadn't even realized she hadn't received her test back. Mrs. Saunders handed the paper to Brenda. When Brenda looked at the red number displayed at the top of her page, she nearly fainted.

"*A seventy-nine?*" Brenda questioned. "This can't be right."

"That was my exact thought," her teacher admitted. "I checked your paper several times to make sure that *I* wasn't making a mistake, but your grade remained."

Tears began to fill Brenda's eyes. She had never gotten a C in her life. Getting B's was hardly acceptable for her. All she'd expected were A's—*high* A's.

"You made very simple and careless mistakes on this test. Now, I know it's not my business, but this isn't common for you, Brenda. Are you having any personal problems at home or otherwise?"

"Why would you ask that?" Brenda questioned tearfully.

Mrs. Saunders shrugged. "Like I said, a grade like this is not common for you. A personal problem is the only thing that I can think of that could hinder you from doing your best."

Brenda thought about confiding in Mrs. Saunders, but the nearly fifty-year-old teacher couldn't possibly relate to what Brenda was going through. "No, there's no problem. I'll just study harder next time."

Before her teacher could say any more Brenda rushed out of the classroom toward her next class. Zane, Ken, Taylor, Eileen, a C. All of her problems flooded her mind and they were affecting her academic standing. As she walked down the hall, Brenda realized that she had allowed her worst nightmare to come true.

Chapter 23

Jayda

Jayda pulled her car into an empty parking place near the baseball field. She had just taken Danielle and Kennedi home and was coming back up to the school for cheerleading practice, but she needed to see Evan first.

She ran out to the field and stood against the fence that surrounded the sports ground. She watched Evan practice for a few minutes and enjoyed the view. He was a great baseball player and would be drafted for sure. Jayda hoped she'd be around to see his dream come to pass of becoming one of the greatest players in Major League Baseball.

When the team took a break, Evan turned toward Jayda and smiled. She was sure that her entire face was as bright as the afternoon sun as she watched him walk toward her.

He kissed her lips softly before greeting her. "Hi. What are you doing here?"

Jayda shrugged. "I just wanted to see you before I go to practice. I also wanted to thank you again for Saturday night. You were there when I really needed you. I appreciate that."

"Well, that's what I'm here for. It's good to see you smiling."

Jayda couldn't keep her grin from spreading wider. Though her problem still hung over her head, being around Evan gave her peace.

When she had gone to his house on Saturday night, he had taken great care of her. They stood in his driveway for nearly a half hour before Jayda had calmed down enough to allow him to help her into his house. His parents had been kind enough to greet her before permitting Evan to take her up to his room, where Jayda cried herself to sleep. When she woke up an hour later, Evan had still been sitting by her side, like he had been before she dozed off. Then, he had spent the next half hour consoling her without prying for information. He'd prayed that whatever was bothering her would soon pass and her heart would be healed and, although Jayda felt talking to God was useless at that point, she had felt slightly better after he'd taken her problem to his Heavenly Father.

The loud shriek of a whistle brought Jayda back to the present. She and Evan looked toward the baseball field and found the team screaming for Evan to return to the field so that they could finish their practice.

Sterling had his hands placed on his hips. "Ms. Henderson, can we please have our star player back?"

"Sorry," Jayda yelled back. She looked up at Evan. "I have to get to practice anyway." She fixed the baseball cap on his head so that the bill would be facing forward.

Evan leaned forward and gave her a lingering, tongue-free kiss. Sterling blew his whistle again and Jayda pulled away.

"You better go before they bench you next game."

Evan laughed. "Only if they want to lose."

She gave him a soft hit against his chest. "That's not nice," she said, though she laughed with him. "I'm going to go. I'll see you later." Slowly, she eased from his embrace and walked away, knowing that he and more than half of the team would be watching her. A smile graced her lips at the thought.

By the time she'd reached the locker room, she had two minutes to change into her practice gear. When she went out into the commons area, she noticed that she was the last girl lining up. As they began practicing, Jayda saw Lauren in the front helping the coach direct the dance the girls were learning. Lauren had been discontent all day long and she still looked slightly perturbed. Jayda had been so wrapped up in her own problems that she hadn't even questioned her best friend's unhappiness.

Jayda recounted the day's events in her mind and realized that Lauren hadn't mentioned Sterling all day long. Not one word. She had stayed after class during first-period, but even after that, she had not spoken of Sterling. Jayda was certain that their teacher had something to do with whatever was wrong with Lauren.

"Lauren, what's up? You've been acting weird," Jayda pointed out as she drove Lauren home that afternoon. Lauren didn't feel the need to purchase a parking pass for the same price it would have been for the whole semester since they only had two months left in school, so she continued to ride with her friend.

Lauren shook her head. "Nothing. I'm fine. Practice always works my nerves, especially the underclassmen who act like they can't get the routine."

"No, I'm not talking about practice," Jayda explained. "You've been out of it all day long. What's goin' on?"

"Nothing, Jayda."

Jayda refused to take that as her final answer. "Well, does it have anything to do with Mr. Sterling? Because you didn't even greet him this morning."

Lauren was silent and Jayda knew she'd hit a nerve.

"So what's going on with you two?" Jayda continued to pry.

Lauren remained quiet as she turned her gaze toward the cars riding along with them on the street.

Jayda tossed a quick glance at her friend. Lauren was ignoring her for sure. Jayda was usually good at reading her friend and so far, just from the solemn look on her face, Jayda knew that something had occurred between Lauren and Sterling. But what?

Jayda turned into Lauren's neighborhood and pulled up into her driveway.

"Thanks for the ride," Lauren said, but before she could climb out of the vehicle, Jayda grabbed her arm.

"Lauren, I'm your best friend. Tell me what's going on."

Lauren looked at Jayda, but couldn't gaze directly into her eyes. "I've decided that I don't want Sterling anymore."

"What?" Jayda asked in disbelief. "What brought on this change?"

"I just changed my mind." Lauren shrugged nonchalantly, but Jayda could see something in her eyes that said she'd been hurt.

Not wanting to pressure her any further, Jayda released her grip on Lauren's arm and allowed her to exit the car.

As she drove home, Jayda tried to figure out what might have happened between Lauren and Sterling that would cause Lauren to give up on Sterling ever becoming the main man in her life. The last time she'd seen them together was at Lauren's party. Sterling had shown up and Jayda knew that had been the highlight of Lauren's night. *Maybe something had happened later on in the evening that could've put out the fire between the two. Maybe she tried to seduce him,* Jayda thought. The thought quickly fled from her mind. *She's not that crazy.* But the more Jayda thought about it, the more she realized that Lauren had been willing to do *anything* to get her claws into Sterling. Maybe her friend had gone too far.

Chapter 24

Danielle

"Eight, nine, ten. Ready or not, here I come."

Danielle tried to stifle her laughter from her hiding space in the hall closet as she imagined Kennedi opening her eyes and looking around the house for her mother and uncle. She knew her brother was in the shower, where he'd been hiding since they began playing the game. Jackson was allowing Kennedi to find him, but Danielle had moved from behind the curtains in the den to the space between the living room sofa and wall. She liked giving her daughter the opportunity to use all of her brainpower to figure out where she could be hiding.

"Giving her the chance to actually search for you stimulates her mind," Danielle had explained to her brother when he'd asked her why she kept moving from one hiding space to another. "Plus, that's the object of the game. You're not supposed to *let* her find you."

Danielle shook her head when she heard Kennedi scream, "I found you, Uncle Jack." The girl had just begun looking for the hiders and had already found Jackson. Danielle knew that Kennedi would go looking in the den and living room for her just because those were the places she'd hid before. Hopefully, Jackson wouldn't ruin the game by telling Kennedi where she was hiding.

"Kennedi, she's not under the sofa. *You* can't even fit under the sofa." Danielle heard Jackson laugh.

It had been about five minutes and Danielle could tell that Kennedi was getting worried.

"She's not here," Kennedi said. "I'll ask Grandma."

Danielle laughed as she heard Kennedi knocking on Beverly's room door. She couldn't hear the conversation, but she could imagine what was coming out of Kennedi's mouth: "Mommy's lost. We were playing hide 'n' seek and I lost her. She's gonna be mad at me."

Danielle could hear Jackson's hearty laugh and knew that her daughter had said something close to what she'd imagined. Part of her wanted to stay in the closet and continue with the game, but another part of her could see Kennedi soon becoming afraid and she didn't want to worry her daughter to tears. So, quietly, she emerged from the closet and moved toward the stairs. She could now hear Jackson and Beverly trying to tell Kennedi that her mother was somewhere in the house; she just needed to look harder.

Danielle walked down the stairs and slowly made her way down the hall that led to her mother's bedroom. She stood behind Jackson and tapped him on the shoulder, but signaled for him to be silent. She then made the same motion to her mother, who'd seen her come into the room. Danielle eased her way up to Kennedi with a wide smile on her face. She grabbed her daughter by the waist and picked her up.

"I win!" Danielle shouted as Kennedi giggled.

Kennedi grabbed her mother's neck and hugged her hard. "I thought you got lost."

"No, I'm just a good hider." Danielle laughed as she placed Kennedi back on the floor.

"Okay, Kennedi, since you won the first two games, what do you think your prize should be?" Jackson asked.

Kennedi wasted no time pondering over an answer. She jumped up and down as she shouted, "Ice cream!"

Danielle smiled as she grabbed Kennedi's hand. "Ma, do you wanna come with us?"

Beverly looked up and Danielle could tell her smile was forced. "No, you guys go ahead."

Danielle suppressed the heavy sigh that tempted her lips. She had made several attempts to resolve things with her mother since the dinner fiasco weeks ago, but apparently Beverly hadn't taken notice, because she continued to make curt comments when speaking to Danielle, especially when it had something to do with Kennedi.

As Jackson drove to a nearby Dairy Queen, he commented on the tension in the household. "How long have you and Mama been like this?"

Danielle shrugged. "Since Kennedi was born. Mama thinks I don't know what I'm doing when it comes to Kennedi, but apparently I'm doing fine."

"Well, maybe Mama doesn't think so," Jackson suggested. "She seems to comment on everything you do when it concerns Kennedi. Like last night, she nearly had a fit when she saw Kennedi scooting down the steps on her behind."

"I know," Danielle said, remembering how her mother had called her from the kitchen and had started a fifteen-minute argument about Kennedi roaming around the house without someone supervising her. "But last week she was getting on me because I was carrying Kennedi down the stairs like she was a baby. Maybe we just need to move to a single-level house."

Jackson gave a small laugh in response as he pulled up to the drive-thru window of the fast food restaurant. After ordering their desserts, Jackson asked Danielle if there was anywhere she wanted to go.

"I don't know. It's nice to get out of the house, so wherever you wanna go is cool. Just don't take my baby and me anywhere where there is a bunch of fast girls, obnoxious guys, or loud conversation or music. I have a headache." Danielle flashed Jackson a quick smile when he sighed.

"Well, I guess that means the only place we can go to is a park," Jackson said mockingly.

Kennedi's cheers signified that that suggestion pleased her. Danielle laughed when Jackson shook his head. She knew he was used to parties and hanging out late, but when he decided to hang out with his sister and niece, those were not options.

When they reached the park, Kennedi ran toward the swings and Jackson followed close behind. Danielle decided to rest on a bench and hoped to get some quiet time alone. As she sipped on her chocolate shake, she watched as Jackson pushed Kennedi on the swings and remembered when her father used to do the same with her. Neil Brookes tried his hardest to always be there for his kids, even with his hectic work schedule. Business meetings and trips kept him away for long periods of time, but when he was home, he spent every free moment he had with his children.

Danielle and Jackson never had to fight for his attention because he gave it to them equally. Danielle loved spending time with her dad. He always kept a smile on her face. He was funny, loving, and generous. He tried his best to make a happy home for her and the rest of her family. He'd tried even harder to hide the fact that there was a problem between him and his wife, but things kept in the dark could only be hidden for so long.

Even after the divorce, Neil remained faithful to his kids. He tried relentlessly to keep their bond strong. He'd take them out every weekend—movies, bowling, skating, shopping. Anywhere Danielle and Jackson wanted to go or anything they wanted to do, Neil had it covered.

He'd continued to show his love even hundreds of miles away. But Danielle slowly began to feel as if she weren't as close to her father as she used to be. At first she began chalking it up to the distance between them. How could he take her out or spend time with her when he was so far away? But when she had to be the one to call him just for a few minutes of conversation, Danielle knew she'd lost that special bond with her father.

Maybe he was too busy trying to grow closer to Neil Jr. Danielle tried not to think about the brother she'd never known, but it was a difficult task. She had been waiting for her father to call. She had expected for him to offer an explanation. She had figured that he would just want to know that his eldest son had made it to the other end of the country okay. But Neil's voice hadn't graced their telephone lines in nearly three months. The last time Danielle had talked to Neil, he had cut their conversation short because he was headed to lunch with a business partner. She hadn't heard from him since.

Maybe he's just afraid. Danielle was sure that he was apprehensive to contact them. She was sure that he was afraid of what may be said to him in response to his actions. Danielle didn't even know what she would say to her father if he called. She was sure that there would be no pleasure or understanding in her tone.

Kennedi's laugh brought her attention back to the present. Jackson was pushing her a little high, but unlike her mother, who would've had a fit by now, Danielle was sure her brother was being careful.

She wished she could show her mother that she was being responsible when it came to Kennedi. Sure she made mistakes, but she was only seventeen for goodness' sake. Danielle thought she deserved a break. She was raising a nearly five-year-old toddler on a single check and felt that she was doing pretty well. She had given up all of extracurricular activities, such as Honor Chorus and softball, and many material things just so that her daughter wouldn't go without life's most essential necessities.

Danielle felt that there was something deeper to Beverly's overprotective nature. It had nothing to do with Kennedi or how Danielle raised her . . . or maybe it did, but Danielle felt as if the problem had more to do with Beverly than it did with her and her daughter.

The sky had gone from a horizon painted in pink and purple to a dark canvas enhanced by a full moon. It was time to get Kennedi home and in bed. Danielle had to get up for school tomorrow and was getting a little sleepy herself. So she yelled to Jackson that it was time to head back home.

Chapter 25

Brenda

Brenda heard her mother enter the house through the garage. Eileen was late. She usually clocked out of work at seven o'clock and would be home by seven-thirty. But it was nearly ten o'clock at night. Brenda had cooked for and fed her siblings. Maya and David were already in bed. Even Taylor was taking her shower and preparing to turn in for the night.

Brenda knew her mother had been at her husband's house again, which Brenda found to be ridiculous. Eileen's divorce would be final in a few days, but she couldn't seem to completely rid herself of her lazy husband.

She looked down at her calculus book and decided that she'd studied enough for the past three hours. It was time to talk to her mother. Hopefully, Eileen would be open to listening to Brenda's plea for her to stop ruining their family in order to satisfy her desires.

When she went downstairs, Brenda found her mother in her bedroom, kicking off her high-heeled shoes and humming a sweet melody. Eileen was dressed in a mini skirt and a halter top. The lime green shirt looked very familiar to Brenda and she knew that her mother had been in her closet again. She had to admit, though, that her nearly fifty-year-old mother looked good in the outfit. *That doesn't mean she should wear it,* Brenda thought before walking into the room.

"Mom, can we talk?" Brenda requested as she watched her mother slip out of the skirt.

Eileen smiled toward her daughter. "As soon as I get into my pajamas."

Brenda waited patiently on the queen-sized bed as Eileen finished undressing and preparing herself for bed.

"So what's up?" Eileen asked when she finally joined her daughter.

Brenda looked for a way to tell her mother what was going on with her thirteen-year-old daughter. She didn't want to just begin blaming Eileen for all the problems she and her siblings were going through, but she didn't want her mother to just assume that another "stage" was in process.

Taking a deep breath, Brenda settled for saying, "Mama, there's a lot going on in this house that you don't know about."

Brenda watched as her mother's eyes revealed her interest to know more.

"Tay is going through a lot right now."

"Oh, Bre, Taylor is always going through something," Eileen stated, using her hand to casually wave off her daughter's concern.

"No, Mama," Brenda objected. "She's really going through something. And it's not just her. So are Maya and David." She hesitated before adding, "And me. You just don't see it because you're out running the streets with that loser husband of yours."

"Now, wait a minute, Brenda—"

"No, just please let me talk. Taylor is smoking weed. She's getting high in order to get away from the problems that have become the sixth member in our household. She's had metal shoved into her skin so that she could come home and hear you yell at her for being so stupid. She's changed her hair color from brown to black to red to blue and green so that you'll show her that you care about her by punishing her. Maya and David don't even like being here, Mama. You see that they're always with their dad. And me, well, I'm just following in your footsteps. Flirting with any guy who'll give me attention and in the process I've hurt not only myself, but two wonderful guys who actually cared about me." Brenda's face was red and her eyes were beginning to water. She watched her mother's facial expression and noticed that it had not changed.

"I'm not trying to blame you for any of our mess," Brenda continued. "I'm telling you this so that you'll stop worrying about where your next husband is coming from and begin to pay more attention to your suffering kids. You don't need those men to make you happy, Mama. You have five children who love you, but you don't see that."

Brenda gently grabbed her mother's hands. "I love you so much. I'm so afraid that I'm going to lose you to some guy on the streets and I'll be left to take care of the rest of us. Mom, we need you here with us."

Brenda studied her mother's face. Eileen's expression was so impassive that Brenda began to wonder if her mother had been listening to her at all. Eileen was known to ignore someone if they were telling her something she didn't want to hear, but Brenda's eyes pleaded with her mother to show some compassion. All Eileen had to do was acknowledge that their family was headed down a dangerous road and Brenda would be able to tell if she'd gotten somewhere with this conversation.

"Look, Brenda," Eileen began after a long silence. "I'm not going to deny that we have a problem, but all families have problems. All teenagers at some point go through a stage where they want to experience rebellion. Taylor's just acting out. She'll soon move past it. Maya and David are still little and they don't understand anything other that the fact that I'm not home all day, like some of their friends' parents are, but they'll soon get over that. And you . . . Brenda, you're a beautiful girl. Guys are going to come and go in your life. It's a blessing and a curse at the same time. As for me, you of all people should know that I'm going to live my life. I'm not going to let my children hold me back from my happiness. I'm not going to change who I am because you guys want to play victim." She paused and looked into her daughter's eyes. "I love you guys, but—"

Brenda's eyes had grown cold and angry. "But not enough to stop acting loose and wild out in the streets."

She stood and marched out of the room, ignoring her mother's plea for her to come back. Brenda wiped her tears as she went into her room. She couldn't believe that her mother was not going to stop making a fool of herself for the sake of her kids. She often heard Lauren say that her parents would do just about anything to keep her happy. Brenda wished she knew what that felt like.

Lauren

Lauren was laying in a fetal position in her bed that night. Her body shivered as if she were cold, but her forehead was spotted with beads of sweat as if she were hot. She bit down on her bottom lip to keep herself from bursting into tears again. She'd cried for hours now, but she couldn't cry herself into sleep, though she was tired. All she could do was think of Sterling and how he had rejected her.

If she hadn't really been sure that she loved him before, Lauren was positive she did now because she felt as if her heart were torn into pieces. She felt as if her fairy tale dream had turned into her worst nightmare. The love she had for Sterling had been rooted deep within her heart. She knew it would be hard to get over him.

She had been thinking about not going to school tomorrow, the next day, or the next. She had thought about dropping Sterling's class. She had even thought about asking her parents to allow her to transfer schools. But with only two months left before she graduated, Lauren knew that none of those thoughts could become actions.

She couldn't imagine walking into Sterling's class tomorrow morning as if everything were all right. She knew that he wouldn't be able to do the same either. The tension would be obvious to everyone in the class.

And what about Jarred? Would he turn Sterling in? With all Lauren had done to him in the past, she couldn't blame him if he did. She had called him names, embarrassed him in front of many people, belittled his character, and tainted his ego. He had every right to do the same to her.

The last thing she wanted was for Sterling to be fired and his credibility to be scarred, but then again, he had used and abused her. If he was so adamant in his stance about them not crossing the student-teacher line, then he should not have come to her hotel room. Lauren had given Sterling something that she'd been saving for a long time. He'd received her most treasured gift. He used her vulnerability to temporarily satisfy himself. He had taken her virginity, and then acted as if she didn't matter anymore.

"Lauren," Cathy called as she knocked on her daughter's closed door.

Lauren tried to answer, but all she could muster was a soft moan.

Cathy opened the door and walked into the dark room. "Baby, are you okay? It's nearly midnight and you haven't eaten, taken a bath, or anything." When she noticed that Lauren was rocking back and forth, Cathy approached her bed.

"Cold," Lauren muttered through chattering teeth.

Cathy leaned forward and rested the back of her hand against her daughter's forehead. "Oh, Lauren, baby, you're burning up."

"Oh, God," Lauren moaned.

She held her body closer as the room seemed to grow cold, but her body hotter. She felt sick. She was sick. Now, she had an excuse not to go to school.

Chapter 26

Jayda

"I think something happened between Lauren and Mr. Sterling," Jayda confessed. "I don't know what, but something's happened."

Evan sat across from her at the lunch table. "Why would you think that?"

Jayda rolled her eyes. "Come on, Evan. I know you knew something was up with them before."

He shrugged. "Yeah, Lauren would come to practice all the time and Coach's whole attitude would change."

"And now they act like the other doesn't exist," she added. "Before Lauren's party, she and Mr. Sterling were close to crossing *that* line. Now they have so much space between them, they seem to be on two different planets."

Evan was silent and Jayda watched as his eyebrows rose at a passing thought. "You don't think that they slept together?" he suggested in a lowered voice.

"No!" Jayda screamed, drawing attention from nearby students enjoying their lunch.

Evan gave her a look that said he knew that she had thought about it.

"Okay, maybe I toyed with that idea, but I don't think Lauren would be that desperate. She's smarter than that. She wouldn't do something like that knowing the consequences. She's not that naïve. She would know that Mr. Sterling wouldn't take their relationship that far and if he did, he probably . . ."

"Would miss a week of school because he'd be too afraid to face Lauren, and then when he did confront her, he would tell her that they would not be able to see each other anymore. With that in mind, Lauren would be hurt and her emotions would be so haywire that she'd miss a couple of days of school." Evan tilted his head and gazed at Jayda.

Jayda stared blankly at Evan and knew that he was right. Lauren had slept with Sterling. "So what do I say? What am I supposed to do now?"

"*You* aren't supposed to do anything," Evan told her as he continued to eat his chicken sandwich.

"But . . . but I have to do something. Lauren is hurt. Mr. Sterling's . . . a dog—"

"Hold on now," he cut in. "Coach did not act alone. Now, I'm definitely not saying that he doesn't deserve to suffer consequences like Lauren is, but you can't blame him for being a man."

Jayda narrowed her eyes and glared at her boyfriend. "So you're telling me that if you were my teacher and I was your student and I approached you about compromising your credibility just to spend one night with me, you'd give in because you're a *man?*"

"No, because I'm a Christian man. I know how to handle temptation on a spiritual level. But Coach is not very spiritual, so he allowed his hormones to overpower his judgment. Lauren was very determined and obviously very persuasive when it came to getting what she wanted. So what I'm saying is that you can't just blame Coach. Lauren was wrong too."

Jayda knew that. She had been trying to tell her friend that going too far with Sterling wasn't a wise choice. But as Jayda had predicted, Lauren had done what she wanted to do. "So what am I supposed to do?"

Evan gazed into her eyes and softly said, "You be there for your friend if she comes to you."

"But Ev, she's not going to come to me. She wouldn't even tell me what was up when I *didn't* know what was going on."

"She can only carry the burden alone for so long." He placed his hand over hers. "She'll come to you."

Jayda silently prayed that Lauren would come to her. But as close as she and her girlfriends were to one another, one thing they were known to do was keep the most troubling situations from each other. While she hoped Lauren would at least confide in her, she also prayed that she would be able to help Lauren as much as she could with this dilemma. Jayda had always been good at giving advice, but this seemed way out of her league. She'd need some assistance on this one.

"So, what's going on with you?"

"Huh?" Jayda confusedly looked up at Evan.

"You've been so worried about Lauren. I'm asking you what's up with you and your family. How's everything going?"

Jayda sighed. "It's kinda dreary. It's worse than when my parents used to argue. Candice looks terrible. She's cried every night since we found out the truth. And Cameron is still livid about Daddy's sexuality. I actually think he's more ashamed than anything else; he doesn't want to talk to anyone."

"And what about you?" Evan questioned.

She hunched her shoulders. "What about me?" Her voice was suddenly soft. "I'm okay." She lowered her eyes so that he wouldn't be able to tell she was lying.

He leaned forward so that he could gain eye contact with her. "Really? You're no longer angry or hurt?"

She shook her head. "I'm just tryin'a be there for my family."

He sat back in his chair and shook his head. "Well, if I caught my father with another man, I know I would be upset."

Jayda lifted her eyes so that Evan could see her anger. "Are *you* serious? You *did not* just say that."

She began placing her trash on her tray before getting up and throwing away her half-eaten lunch. Before she could disappear into the nearest restroom, Evan had caught up with her. He gently grabbed her by the waist and turned her toward him so that he could look into her eyes.

"I'm sorry. I didn't mean anything by that," he said. "I was just tryin'a get you to stop lying to yourself."

Tears began to fill Jayda's eyes. "I am angry," she admitted. "I just couldn't believe it when I saw Mr. Murphy in that house. Just to know that my dad tore our family apart for some *man* . . ."

Evan hugged her as she cried. "It's okay. Everything is gonna be fine. God's will shall be done."

Jayda pulled away from him. "I never thought I'd be with someone so spiritual."

He pretended to be offended. "Why not? Is something wrong with me being like this?"

She shook her head with a slight smile gracing her lips. "No, I love who you are. I've always known something was different about you, especially when it came to how you treated others and how you carried yourself, but I just never thought that all of that was because you were a Christian. And I never grew up in a household where God was the topic of discussion at dinner, so being with you has been a really different experience for me."

"Well, when you carry Christ with you, it changes how people see you and how they interact with you, whether they understand the difference between a person who walks with God and another who doesn't."

"I wish I had what you have," Jayda whispered as she laid her head against his chest. "Maybe my life wouldn't be so full of crap."

"Whether you walk with God or not, your life is always gonna be full of trying times," Evan explained as he used a strong hand to rub her back. "But walking with God changes the way you handle those situations. You can always have what I have, Jayda. It's just a matter of asking God for it."

Jayda didn't answer. For the moment she just took comfort in the arms of the one who, in the last few weeks, had shown her how different a person's heart could be when God resided in it.

Chapter 27

Danielle

Danielle laughed as Kennedi showed her the dance that her teacher had taught her class today. She watched as Kennedi placed her hands on her hips and wiggled, then turned around and jumped up and down, and finally she clapped her hands and stomped her feet before jumping up with her hands in the air as if she were a cheerleader.

"All right!" Danielle sang as she applauded her daughter. "That was great, Kennedi. Can you teach me that dance?"

"Yeah," Kennedi said gladly.

Before Kennedi could begin the dance lesson, Danielle heard her cell phone ringing from downstairs, where she'd left it earlier. Danielle told Kennedi to keep doing the dance so that she would be able to teach it to her once she came back.

She ran downstairs and grabbed her phone off of the sofa. She glanced at the caller ID and noticed that it was Olivia Benson calling. "Hello?" she answered the phone right before the last ring that would send it to voice mail.

"Hello. May I please speak to Danielle Brookes?"

"Hi, Ms. Benson. This is Danielle."

"Hi, how are you?"

Danielle could hear the smile in the woman's voice. "I'm great. And you?"

"Terrific. I have great news," Olivia said jovially. "I talked to Keenan last night and I convinced him to come down here for spring break."

Danielle's heart fluttered because she knew that soon all of her daughter's dreams would come true. "That's wonderful, Ms. Benson. You sure he doesn't mind spending his break down here instead of on the beach somewhere?"

"No, he said he had been thinking about coming down here for a few days anyway," Olivia informed her. "So it works out just fine."

Danielle released a subtle laugh. "Thank you so much for all you're doing, Ms. Benson."

"Well, don't thank me yet. He's coming down, but I didn't tell him about Kennedi."

Suddenly, Danielle's smile fell. "Oh. Well, why not?"

"I wasn't sure if it would change his mind if I did," Olivia explained in a calm tone.

"Well, not to be ungrateful, but I would have preferred if you had told him why you wanted him to come. I don't want to have to trick him into seeing his own daughter. Ms. Benson, maybe this isn't a good idea."

"Oh, Danielle, don't worry about anything. I know my son. Of course he's not perfect, but he has grown over the last several years. Something is telling me that he's going to want to see Kennedi, but my apprehensive nature is telling me that part of him would be nervous about meeting her, so I just asked him to come. I'll let him in on the surprise once he gets here."

"And what if he comes all the way down here and doesn't want to see her?" Danielle questioned, not trying to hide the edginess in her voice.

She could hear Olivia sigh softly through the earpiece. "All I can tell you, Danielle, is that if it's God's desire for this to come to pass, then it will come to pass. The fact that he was planning to visit anyway shows there's something right about this."

Danielle's anxiety waned slightly and she agreed that once Keenan came into town, Olivia would give her the okay for her to meet with him before bringing him face to face with Kennedi.

Just as Danielle ended the call, Jackson came through the door, with A.J. following him. Danielle greeted them before going upstairs to check on Kennedi, who had gotten tired of waiting for her mother and had began coloring in her coloring book.

Danielle could hear A.J.'s and Jackson's muffled voices in the kitchen. She wondered why her brother had brought A.J. over to their home. Danielle was sure he was supposed to be at work or at least at home studying for a class.

Since the night of Lauren's party, Danielle hadn't talked to A.J. much. She was sure that he was still waiting for her to accept his invitation to church. It wasn't that she didn't want to go to church; the thought just made her a little anxious.

She hadn't been an avid churchgoer since her father had moved to New York. Her mother would usually wake her up early Sunday morning and make her get herself and Kennedi ready for the nine o'clock service, but, bit by bit, Danielle pulled away from the church. She would tell her mother she was too tired from taking care of Kennedi or she would purposely apply to work Sunday morning, so that her mother, along with Kennedi, would leave for church without even trying to persuade her daughter to excuse herself from work so she could attend the worship service.

That had been the beginning of the growing distance between Danielle and God. Her mother eventually caught on, but didn't force her daughter to do anything she didn't want to do. Beverly had always said that God would work on Danielle's heart. Now that He was, Danielle was becoming afraid.

She'd asked God to keep her parents together, but that prayer was never granted. She'd prayed that Keenan would stand by her side throughout and after her pregnancy, but that never came to pass. Then when her father announced that he was moving to the northern end of the country, Danielle had prayed that, if God wouldn't keep her family under the same roof, He would at least keep them in the same city. That prayer was never granted either.

God had let her down so many times, but part of Danielle still wanted a relationship with Him. She was just afraid of being hurt again. With all that was going on within her family, she knew she could use a good Christian friend. But if she asked God to heal the broken ties within her family, would He disappoint her again? Part of her didn't want to find out. But maybe A.J. could help her. She decided to go back downstairs to see what the guys were up to.

"Hey, Kennedi. A.J.'s here," Danielle said and smiled when her daughter jumped up and ran toward the stairs.

Danielle helped Kennedi down the stairs and they found the boys in the kitchen making sandwiches.

"Hi, A.J.," Kennedi shouted as she hugged his leg.

A.J. smiled down at the little girl. "Hi, Kennedi. How was school today?"

"Fun. We learned a dance."

Jackson turned toward his niece. "Well, why don't you come into the den and show it to us."

"Okay. Let's go." She ran out of the kitchen and into the den.

The guys followed her and sat on the sofa, while Danielle stood in the archway that separated the den from the living room. She watched as Kennedi began the dance. Her little girl seemed to be dancing with more energy than she had before when she'd just been dancing for her mother. Danielle knew that Kennedi was still striving to impress A.J. Silently, she prayed that Keenan would see his daughter so that Danielle wouldn't have to continue telling Kennedi that her father couldn't make time to visit her.

"Mommy, come dance with me," Kennedi requested.

Danielle shook her head. "No. I don't know that dance, Kennedi."

Kennedi playfully rolled her eyes. "It's easy." She began doing the dance again, explaining the moves as she went along. "Now, you do it."

Danielle looked at her brother, who was laughing, apparently, at the thought of his sister doing the childish dance. She narrowed her eyes and pointed a sturdy finger in his direction, silently telling him not to mock her.

"Danielle?" A.J. called.

Danielle looked at him. "What?"

He laughed. "We're waiting for you to dance."

"Oh, you guys are really enjoying this." She walked over to her daughter and began to dance.

Danielle laughed as she wiggled and turned and jumped. She was much too old to be doing this, but she was enjoying it because she was with her daughter. The wide smile plastered across Kennedi's face let Danielle know that she'd made her baby girl very happy.

"You did good, Mama," Kennedi said as they sat on the floor.

Danielle planted a kiss on Kennedi's cheek. "So did you." She looked up at A.J. "So what are you doing hanging out with my loser brother?"

Jackson tossed her a warning look.

A.J. laughed as he watched the siblings stare each other down. "Well, actually, I'm on my break. I just came over here to see you."

Danielle couldn't control the grin that spread across her face. "You came over here to see me?"

He nodded as he bit into his sandwich. "I came to see how 'Operation K and K United' was coming along."

She blinked her eyes a few times and allowed her confused gaze to tell A.J. that she had no idea what he was talking about.

"You know. The *reunion event*." He nodded in Kennedi's direction.

"Oh," Danielle said in realization. "Umm. I talked to the . . . *coordinator* today and she said that our *special guest* is coming, but he doesn't know what's going down when he gets here."

Jackson looked between the two and asked, "What in the world are y'all talking about? Y'all sound like y'all are working for the CIA or something with all these code words."

"You didn't tell him?" A.J. asked Danielle.

"Of course not," Danielle answered. "You know Jackson doesn't like him."

"Who don't I like?" Jackson's back stiffened as he sat straight up in his seat so his sister would know that he didn't take too kindly to being left in the dark.

Danielle hadn't planned on telling Jackson so soon, but she knew he wouldn't let her get away with keeping this from him. She just hoped that he wouldn't get so upset that he would try to hinder the progress that was being made.

She prayed silently as she said aloud, "Someone's coming to see *her* during spring break," Danielle said, pointing toward Kennedi's back so that her daughter couldn't see that they were talking about her.

Jackson crossed his arms, letting Danielle know that he could tell where she was headed. "*Who's* coming to see her?"

Danielle shrugged. "Someone who hasn't seen her in a *long, long* time."

"Like how long?"

"Like never," she said softly.

Jackson shook his head. "I can't believe this."

"Jackson, she deserves to get to know him especially now that she's getting older and is going around adopting other guys in order to take his place." Danielle cast a glance at A.J. "Now, he's coming for spring break and I'm going to talk to him just like I talked to his mother a few weeks ago. Then if he wants to see her, I'm going to introduce them."

Jackson shrugged. "Whatever. You do what you do, but I'm going with you when you go see him. I have a few words for the brotha."

Danielle didn't even bother objecting because she knew her brother was firm in that decision. Besides, she'd need someone to take her to Olivia's house and she didn't want to put A.J. out of the way by asking him to accompany her. She just prayed that Jackson wouldn't embarrass her. She knew God would work it out for everyone's good. She just had to trust in Him.

With that thought she turned toward A.J. and asked, "So do you have room for two for Sunday morning service?"

A.J. smiled. "Most definitely. I've got room for three if Jackson wants to come."

Jackson gave A.J. a skeptical look. "Are you talking about church? I don't know, man."

"Déjà's coming," A.J. added.

Jackson's smile was wide. "I guess I'll check it out."

"A.J., you shouldn't use girls to persuade my brother into going to church," Danielle said. "He'll only be going to see your sister."

A.J. shrugged. "I gotta get 'em how I can. By any means necessary."

"All right, *Malcolm X*." She laughed. "But he needs to come with the right purpose in mind."

He shook his head. "My job is to just get him there. God will handle the rest."

Danielle had to agree. God had been handling a lot of things lately. If He could get both her and Jackson to come to Him, and then allow Keenan and Kennedi's meeting to be a success, her prayers would be answered.

Chapter 28

Jayda

Saturday, the girls met for brunch. Jayda had come up with the idea, knowing that each of her friends was going through their own problems. She had noticed that none of them, including herself, had gone to one another for comfort or advice. They were at a point in their lives where they were soon going to be separating and going off to their respective colleges and this was a time when they should really stick together.

Jayda had picked up Danielle, who'd left Kennedi with Jackson, and they were sitting in the restaurant waiting for Lauren and Brenda. When the girls finally arrived, they decided to order before getting down to business. After that was done, Jayda wasted no time in getting to the point of this meeting.

"So what's going on with everybody?" she questioned. "We look like we all have baggage hanging off our shoulders, but as far as I know none of us have gone to one another to talk about it. That's unusual for us. Now, I'm not tryin'a get in nobody's business, but if something's bothering any one of you, you know you can come talk to me."

"If that's the case, Jayda, then why haven't you come to one of us with whatever's holding you down?" Brenda questioned with a slight attitude.

Jayda shrugged. "Well, that's why I wanted us to meet up today. I think we should all put our problems on the table. Starting with me, of course." She took a deep breath before continuing, "I went to see my father last weekend. I had been begging my mother for the longest to tell me what was going on and when she finally gave me his address, I took the twins and went to find out what was going on. When we got there, I was so scared of what I might find, but when I saw who my father had left our family for, I went crazy."

"Don't tell me he's with a man," Danielle pleaded, her eyes showing the fear she felt from the possibility.

Jayda nodded her head as tears filled her eyes. "He is."

"What?" Lauren asked in disbelief. "Like he's sleeping with a man?"

"Not just any man. Simon Murphy," Jayda answered solemnly.

"Sariah's dad?" Brenda questioned, mentioning their schoolmate who'd recently graduated.

Jayda nodded again. "I cussed my daddy out so bad. Then I told him that I hated him. After I took Candi and Cam home, I couldn't face my mom, so I went to Evan's and stayed there for a couple of hours. I still can't talk to my mom about it." She shook her head. "I still can't believe it."

"I don't believe it, either," Brenda said, "but I don't see why you're avoiding your mom. Leaving was your father's decision. Hooking up with that man was your father's decision. You didn't make him do any of those things."

"I know that," Jayda acknowledged. "Evan's been tryin'a help me get over it, but it's hard. He's making me go to church with him tomorrow. He says I need to stop looking for physical answers and look toward God for spiritual answers. So I guess tomorrow I'm gonna find out what those answers are."

Danielle's broad grin caught Jayda's attention and she asked, "What are you so happy about?"

"Nothing exciting really. It's just that A.J.'s taking Kennedi, Jackson, and me to church tomorrow too. He's been trying to help me also," Danielle said. "I have a couple of things going on that I haven't shared with you guys. I never told you all why Jackie had come home. He found out that my dad has a son." Shock spread across her friends' faces. "Yeah, I was surprised too. The boy's about ten years old and his name is Neil Jr. It's a long story, but basically, my dad's affair produced Junior. Since his mother died a few months ago, my dad's been keeping him. One day Jackson heard Junior call my father 'dad.' He went ballistic and left."

The conversation came to a pause when the waiter arrived with their orders. As soon as he left, they continued.

"So what about you?" Jayda questioned Danielle. "How do you feel?"

Danielle shrugged. "I'm upset of course. I was really upset with my mom because she knew about it this whole time and didn't tell me a thing. Right now we're kinda like you and your mother, Jayda. And I've been waiting to hear from my father. I figured he would've called by now, but he hasn't. At least I don't think he has; knowing my mother, she'd probably hide that from me, too."

She took a deep breath. "But I haven't been too consumed with that because I have something more serious taking place." Danielle placed her palms together and inhaled once more. "Keenan is coming down for spring break."

"What?" Lauren and Brenda shrieked at the same time.

"Is this something you wanted?" Jayda questioned.

Danielle held a small smile as she nodded. "Yes. After that dinner disaster with A.J. and Déjà, I had to do something. So with a little help from A.J., I got up enough nerve to call Ms. Benson, Keenan's mother, and we straightened mostly everything out. She talked Keenan into coming up for the break. He doesn't know it's to see me or Kennedi, but we'll work through all of that once the time comes."

"Wow!" Brenda exhaled as if she'd been holding her breath. "That's good. I'm happy for you. I know you're nervous though."

"Yeah." Danielle laughed. "I've been trying so hard not to tell Kennedi that she might be able to finally meet her father. You know how I am with surprises. I'm just trying to get through it. I hope he'll be willing to see her."

"Well, I'm sure he will," Jayda said. "And as far as the situation with your father, take it from someone who knows, if you really want to find out what's going on, do what you have to do in order to get the information. Since you already know the truth, you won't be in for any major surprises, but be prepared for anything your father might say. And try to be cool. Try not to say anything you'll regret," she advised. "I wish I would've been calm because now I regret a lot of the things I said. I never would've thought some of those words would come out of my mouth."

Danielle nodded. "Thanks. I don't know if I'll be able to call him, because I'm still upset, but I'm hoping for a message tomorrow at church."

"Me too, girl," Jayda agreed.

Brenda cleared her throat. "Well, I guess I don't mind going next. Just like Danni, I have a few issues on my plate. For starters you guys know about Ken and Zane. I've been trying to talk to them since the party and they won't speak to me. I've tried calling them. I've left a message on each of their voice mails. I don't know what else to do. Maybe it's better this way; I don't really know. I just wish I could explain myself. I've never felt so bad before in my life." She paused before continuing, "And I don't know what it is, but I really miss Ken. It's like . . . I'm sorry that I hurt Zane because I know he really liked me, but with Ken this whole situation is different. I feel like I was unfaithful to him. Even before I got caught at the party with both of them, I felt like I was cheating on Ken when I would be with Zane. When I would kiss Zane, I would pretend that it was Ken. When I was with Zane, I would imagine that I was with Ken. I don't know how to describe my feelings . . . but I know that I feel different when I'm with Ken."

"I call it love," Jayda interceded. "That's exactly what it is. I don't even have to explain it to you because sometimes love can be unexplainable."

"Since when are you an expert?" Brenda questioned with a smile at Jayda's revelation.

Jayda waved her hand around in the air. "I just know," she said with a smile. "Continue . . ." she instructed Brenda.

Brenda shook her head. "Well, there's the situation with Ken and Zane, and then there's this thing at home with my mom. She refuses to stop chasing after her bum of a husband."

"Have you tried talking to her?" Danielle asked. "Maybe she just needs to hear how you feel."

Brenda gave a dry chuckle. "Danni, I waited up for my mother for nearly three hours the other night just so I could talk to her. I told her everything from me completely disapproving of her lifestyle to Taylor getting high to get attention."

"Oh my goodness," Danielle spoke softly. "Taylor was doing drugs?"

Brenda nodded. "And when I found out, she practically begged for me to tell because she wanted Mama to know what was going on. But did Eileen care? No. She blatantly stated that she was not going to allow her kids to hold her back from living her life. So I just let it go. I've decided that I'm gonna take care of my family until my mother opens her eyes. I've been talking to Maya and David and they said that once I graduate they want to move in with their father. He's about to get married and his fiancée has treated them better than Mom has. Since they'll be leaving soon, I'm gonna find a way to keep Taylor."

"Does your mother know she's about to lose her kids?" Lauren asked.

Brenda shook her head. "She wouldn't care if she did. If she doesn't want to do what she needs to do to keep us at home, then she has to suffer the consequences."

"No disrespect to your mother, but I sort of agree," Danielle said. "I can see that whatever has been going on has been having a major effect on you. I thought it might've just been the thing with Ken and Zane, but the situation at home seems more serious."

"It is," Brenda responded as she pulled at her hair. "I don't want to hurt my mother, but she's leaving me no choice. I don't want to leave my sister there to kill herself because my mom's not paying any attention. I've got to do what I feel is best. I've already started looking for a job that would pay for an apartment so that I can prove I have a stable home for Taylor to move into."

"So what you're saying is that if you have to you're gonna take this to court," Jayda surmised.

Brenda shrugged. "I don't know. I guess I will if it comes to that. By the time I start college I want Taylor to be with me."

"That's a lot to take on when you're just starting college," Jayda said. "Are you sure you're gonna be able to handle it?"

"I'm gonna try." Brenda sighed.

The table grew silent. It was Lauren's turn to share and the girls knew that whatever she was going through was serious. Jayda hoped that she wouldn't have to drag any information out of her friend. She'd pulled them all together so it would be easier for them, Lauren especially, to confide in each other. Apparently, the pressure was too much for Lauren because before she could utter a word, she burst into tears.

Jayda began to pray silently. *Lord, please help my friend. She needs you right now. Show her what you've been slowly revealing to me. You are here for us . . . all of us. You know our problems and our situations. You can help us if no one else can. You love us more than we love ourselves. Just please keep us.*

As the words spilled out of her heart, Jayda heard Danielle's soft voice saying everything she was thinking. As Danielle prayed aloud, Jayda continued to plead silently with the Father.

"Father, we don't know what may be going on," Danielle said as Lauren's soft sobs continued, and they both placed their free arms around Lauren's shoulders. "But we know that you do. Give her the strength to be able to let us in and, if not, allow her to let you in. Give her peace and let her know that you love her no matter what. We pray that her heart will be healed. In your name, we all pray. Amen."

The girls looked up and all had tears in their eyes. Lauren's cries had softened, but she still had tears flowing down her face like a river. When she tried to dry them, another batch would break out. They rested in silence as they allowed Lauren to cry. None of them pushed for her to tell them what was going on, but, instead, they waited until her tears subsided.

"I slept with Sterling," Lauren finally said softly.

Jayda exhaled as if she were relieved to hear the truth come from Lauren's mouth.

"It happened the night of my party," Lauren continued. "I had my parents pay for a hotel room. Initially, it was meant for all of us to spend the night there, but I decided to use it for Sterling and me. When I gave him the key, I wasn't sure if he'd show up, but he did and we had sex. At the moment it was wonderful. He was even there when I woke up the next morning. I looked forward to seeing him on the following Monday so we could talk about us, but he didn't show up all that week. When I finally did get a chance to talk to him, he told me that he'd made a mistake and that we could no longer see each other. Of course I stupidly told him that I loved him; then I admitted that I'd given him my virginity. All he could say was that he was sorry, but I was still upset." She wiped more tears. "Then, to top it all off, Jarred heard the whole thing. He was coming in for Sterling's next class, and he was standing at the door when I told Sterling that if he wasn't gonna change his mind about us then he shouldn't have slept with me."

"Oh, Lauren," Danielle moaned. "I'm so sorry."

Lauren shook her head. "Please don't feel sorry for me, because I knew better. Jayda tried to tell me not to get caught up, but I did and I ended up with a broken heart."

"So you didn't come to school on Tuesday and Wednesday because you didn't want to face Mr. Sterling?" Brenda questioned.

"Well, sort of. I'd been thinking about not coming to school, but I was actually sick. I had a fever of about a hundred and one, so my mom made me stay home. By Thursday, I was still a little sick, but my temperature had gone back to normal and my mom didn't want me to miss any more days. So I came to school, but I tried to keep a great deal of distance between me and Sterling."

"So that's why on Thursday you came in nearly fifteen minutes before the bell rang to end the class period and yesterday, you came, but said you had to go the bathroom and never came back?"

Lauren gave Jayda a guilty glance. "I just couldn't take being so close to him. It's not just about me still having feelings for him. It's the fact that I gave myself to him and now I have to pretend like nothing's happened."

"So what about Jarred? Do you think he'll tell?" Brenda pointed out the other factor in the situation. "You know how much he liked you. Do you think he'll do something like that just to get back at you?"

Lauren shrugged. "I don't know. I hope not. I don't want Sterling to lose his job." She looked up at her friends with a sense of urgency. "You guys *have* to promise you won't tell *anybody*. There are enough people at school who probably knew something was going on between Sterling and me anyway, but I don't want to give them any more to talk about. If they see that we're no longer speaking to each other, maybe the rumors will subside."

Jayda took Lauren's hand. "Don't worry, girl. This information won't go outside of this restaurant."

Danielle and Brenda nodded in agreement.

"I kinda feel a little better," Lauren said as she took a deep breath. "Getting all of that off of my chest feels like a weight has been lifted."

Danielle agreed. "Yeah. Jayda, thanks for bringing us all together."

"Yeah, I know how we all tend to get when we have really serious stuff going on. While our personalities are completely different, we are similar in one way: we will hold the deepest, darkest stuff in until we're about to burst and it's just not healthy," Jayda stated with her friends nodding and chuckling in agreement.

"Plus, this was only one part of my plan," Jayda admitted with a sly smile. "I wanted to see if you guys wanted to come to church with me and Evan tomorrow. I guess I can exclude Danni since she's already made a commitment to someone else, but if you guys want to come, I'm sure Evan wouldn't mind making a few more stops."

Lauren pursed her lips before replying, "I don't know, Jayda. I'm not really a religious kinda person."

"Me either," Brenda said. "Besides, from what I could tell, both sets of my grandparents are Catholic, but my mom doesn't really practice any specific religion. I'm not even sure what I'm supposed to believe in."

"Well, I'm not gonna force you," Jayda told them. "But I would really feel better if I had some company. I'm not very religious either, and even Evan says that he's not a religious person. He's spiritual . . . I don't really know the difference, but if it works for him, I'd like to see what it's all about."

"Maybe another time, Jay," Lauren said after a few moments of silence.

"Yeah, I'll think about it for sure," Brenda agreed. "But I don't think I'll feel comfortable going to church."

"That's fine." Jayda looked at Danielle. "I wish A.J. and Evan attended the same church."

"What church does Evan go to?" Danielle asked.

Jayda shrugged. "Westlake Chapel of Church of God in Christ?"

"That's A.J.'s church," Danielle confirmed with a smile. "So I guess I'll be seeing you tomorrow."

Jayda looked up toward the ceiling of the restaurant. "Thank you, Jesus," she spoke exaggeratedly, causing the girls to all burst into laughter.

Chapter 29

Jayda

"Come on you guys," Jayda yelled up the stairs to her siblings. "Evan will be here in a few minutes."

She walked into the living room and looked at the mirror positioned high on the wall. She used her index finger to push a stray hair back into place, and then stood back and looked down at her black pinstriped skirt set, making sure that every button on her jacket was fastened. Finally, she tightened the straps on her black T-strap pumps. She heard heavy footsteps coming down the stairs and she knew that it was Cameron. Her brother and sister had only agreed to come to church with her because they'd both been excited about spending time with Evan—of course, for very different reasons. Jayda couldn't care less about their reasons for going, though; she was just happy that they were getting out of the house.

She walked out into the foyer and gave her brother a once-over. "Cameron, where is the jacket to your suit?" she asked as if she were his mother.

"Hey, nobody said anything about a jacket. You lucky I ain't come down here in jeans and a white tee." Cameron pulled at his black slacks.

Jayda shook her head, knowing she wouldn't be able to get him into the jacket. "Well, at least go take off those Reeboks and put on your dress shoes."

He made a loud grunt as he ran back upstairs. "I don't know why you trippin'. It's just church," he mumbled.

Jayda rolled her eyes. She knew she was giving her brother a hard time, but she didn't want to go into church looking as if they were just going to hang out at the park. Evan had told her that she didn't have to overdress, but he'd said he would be wearing a suit, so she definitely didn't want to feel out of place.

"You guys, come on," Jayda yelled again.

She had been ready for the last half hour and having free time on her hands was rattling her nerves. She knew she was really nervous about going to church because she hadn't been in a while. Her family was never one to attend church religiously. They might even be what some would call a CME family: one who went to church only on Christmas, Mother's Day, and Easter. But Jayda knew that if church had made Evan who he was, then it couldn't be all that bad.

The doorbell rang, and just as she was about to yell for her siblings to hurry up, Cameron came downstairs with Candice right behind him.

Jayda's eyes opened wide at her sister's attire. "Candi! You better have a jacket."

Candice rolled her eyes as she held up the black waist-length jacket that would cover what her ruffle halter dress left bare.

"Put it on," Jayda whispered harshly as she went to open the door.

Evan stood before her, dressed in a typical black Sunday suit, but, to Jayda, he looked as if he were wearing a formal tuxedo. He smiled as she moved aside to let him into the house.

"Good morning," he greeted her with a light kiss to her cheek. "You look lovely."

Jayda blushed as he took her hand.

"So do you, Candice," he said, to the thirteen-year-old's delight. "And, Cameron, you look . . . almost like me." Evan pulled at the left lapel of his suit jacket.

Cameron looked down at his jacketless suit.

"So, are you guys ready to go?" Evan asked them.

"Wait. Not yet," Cameron said as he ran upstairs.

Jayda took the time to tell her mother that they were about to leave for service. She had tried to get her mother to come with them, but Heather wasn't up for it just yet. Jayda understood, but hoped her mother would come around.

When she returned to the foyer where Evan and Candice waited, Cameron was rushing back downstairs, pulling on his suit jacket at the same time. Jayda shook her head and looked up at Evan. A wide smile graced his lips. Apparently, her little brother was trying to impress her boyfriend. *Who could be a better role model?* she thought as Evan took her hand and led her and her siblings out to his car.

Danielle

Déjà pulled her SUV into the church's parking lot and turned off the engine. Jackson nearly jumped out of the truck so that he could rush to the driver's side to assist her out of the vehicle.

Déjà smiled as she took his hand and stepped out onto the concrete ground. "Thank you," she said appreciatively.

Danielle laughed at her brother's antics as A.J. helped her out of the truck. "He's trying so hard," she whispered to A.J.

A.J. shrugged and gave her a serious look. "But he's rackin' up major points with my sister. Trust me, she likes it."

Danielle was surprised and allowed her face to show it. She'd thought that because Déjà was slightly older than her brother she wouldn't be interested in him, but apparently she was taking notice.

"Mommy, don't forget me," Kennedi said from her car seat.

"I haven't forgotten my precious angel," Danielle said as she unbuckled the belt that secured Kennedi in the seat and helped her out of the car.

When Danielle placed Kennedi's feet on the ground, Danielle straightened out her daughter's blouse and skirt. Then she brushed her hands over her own pink V-neck tunic, which she wore over a pair of black slacks. Danielle took her daughter's hand and the group followed A.J. into the church, already full of worshippers. An usher led them to a row with enough empty seats to sit everyone.

Danielle looked around the building for Jayda. The church seemed to cater to at least a few hundred members, many of whom had already arrived. However, she was able to spot her friend sitting with her siblings, Evan, and his parents in the section to the right of where she was sitting. Catching Jayda's eye, Danielle waved. Jayda nudged Evan and pointed toward where Danielle was sitting. The couple waved and then Danielle watched as Evan looked beyond her and nodded toward A.J. The guys exchanged silent greetings before focusing their attention on the man who'd called the church to order with an opening prayer. She would have never guessed that A.J. and Evan knew each other, but then again, with this being their home church, they had to have come across each other at least once during their time here.

After the prayer, the choir began to lead the church in a series of praise and worship songs. Danielle joined in, singing the songs she was most familiar with. She noticed the smile on A.J.'s face and knew he was enjoying the sound of her voice in his ear. The last time he'd heard her sing had been at Lauren's birthday party. Then, she had been singing a song about friendship, now she was singing about lifting up the Lord and she knew that she sounded just as heavenly.

By the end of the worship service, Danielle was preparing herself for the Word that would come forth, hoping that it would speak to her heart. She watched as a woman, dressed in a pastel blue two-piece skirt suit, approached the pulpit. From the photo and information on her program she concluded that the lady was the pastor of the church—Pastor Tina Browne.

She opened her sermon with a worship song, "Welcome into This Place," and then she said a word of prayer: "Father God, we come before your throne this morning, thanking you for waking us up and bringing us out to worship you. We ask that you open our ears so that we may not just listen, but take heed to the Word that will come forth today. Let it touch the hearts of those who need it. In your most magnificent name, we pray. Amen."

Pastor Browne looked out into the faces of the congregation. "For the last several Sundays we've been discussing relationships with God. We are going to continue with this series, so if you will, please open your Bibles to Jeremiah, chapter nine, verses twenty-three and twenty-four. I will be reading from the New International Version."

Danielle smiled as A.J. positioned his Bible between them so they could share.

"Thus says the Lord: 'Let not the wise man glory in his wisdom, let not the mighty man glory in his might, nor let the rich man glory in his riches; but let him who glories glory in this, that he understands and knows Me, that I am the Lord, exercising loving kindness, judgment, and righteousness in the heart. For in these I delight,' says the Lord."

Several members could be heard mumbling in response to the scripture.

Pastor Browne smiled. "This scripture has the potential to convict the hearts of many people who claim to have a good relationship with Jesus Christ. Many of us, including myself, can find ourselves indulged in our riches or our intelligence, but what God wants is for us to indulge ourselves in Him. Because when He comes back He's not going to go around asking each of us if we were satisfied with the money we made on our jobs, or if we were ecstatic about excelling in school, or if we were pleased with ourselves just because we were good to our friends. He's going to judge us by our ability to be happy in our relationship with Him."

Amens came from the members who agreed.

"It's nice to rejoice when we get a new car, house, or just simply are able to pay our bills, but we need to do the same when it comes to having God in our lives. He's the most important thing," Pastor Browne continued. "Listen to this. Revelation, chapter two, verses four and five say, 'Nevertheless I have this against you, that you have left your first love. Remember therefore from where you have fallen; repent and do the first works, or else I will come to you quickly and remove your lamp stand from its place—unless you repent.'

"Usually when our relationship with God is new, we're happy and excited. I've heard people who've just given their lives to God say things like, 'Oh, I can't wait to spend some time alone with God. I can't wait to see what He has in store for me.' Well, that euphoria lasts for only a while. Soon after, I see the same people com-

plaining about all they've done with God, but they still
feel empty. That's because you're not doing what you
have to do to keep your relationship with Him fresh!"
she exclaimed with her hands on her hips.

"It's just like when a couple first falls in love. They'll
put all they've got into their relationship to keep the
passion and the love flowing, but as soon as that new-
ness wears off and they get *used* to each other, they
stop trying."

Those who related to the analogy shouted out in
agreement as understanding chuckles filled the sanctu-
ary.

Pastor Browne continued, "And you'll see 'em walking around with their heads hanging down and their
feet dragging the floor because they feel like their
spouse has let the fire die down, when in all honesty,
they are just as much to blame. If you want to keep
a hot and heavy relationship, you have to *work!*" she
shouted again.

Agreements flooded the building once again.

"The same goes for a relationship with God. You
can't just go to church and read your Bible for a few
months and expect for things to just be happily ever
after because you *think* you've done what you're supposed to do. You have to continue talking to God and
worshiping Him and getting to know Him in order to
keep things going. Just as you would in a marriage or
when you're dating.

"Anyone who has a relationship with Jesus right
now is dating Him." She nodded to show that she'd
meant exactly what she'd said. "You're getting to know
Him. He's getting to know you. You are spending time
together. It's a spiritual relationship. And when Jesus comes back, guess what's going to happen?" She
paused as if waiting for a response. "There's going to

be a wedding. Yes, you're going to marry Jesus. The church is His bride. We are who He's coming back for in the end. So we have to be ready. We have to go back to doing what we used to do when we first started dating Jesus, so that our fire for Him will be burning bright when He comes back for us."

Danielle took in everything Pastor Browne was saying, but she felt a little lost. The pastor seemed to be speaking to those who had relationships with Jesus. Danielle had been saved at one point in time, but that had been before she'd had Kennedi. Everything that had occurred after her daughter's birth had gradually pulled her away from her relationship with God. How was she supposed to get that back?

"In the book of Revelation, God says that He wants us to be either hot or cold for Him," the pastor continued with her message. "Anyone who is lukewarm will be spewed out of His mouth. That means that you're either with Him or you're not. You're either in the world or out of the world. You can't go hang with your boys and get high on Saturday, and then come to church and lead devotion on Sunday, acting as if you weren't doing anything wrong the night before. God does not like that. He's going to throw you up. Like I said before, if you want your relationship to remain hot, then do what you have to do to keep it hot. If you wanna be cold, be cold. But the only thing that's going to get you into heaven is being hot for Christ.

"If you were hot for Christ once and now you're lukewarm or cold, you need to get back to where you used to be. God is a God of second chances. All you have to do is ask Him to give you that little bit of oxygen that will allow your flame for Him to burn brighter than before. Romans ten, and nine, say that if you confess with your mouth that Jesus is Lord and you believe

He died on the cross and God resurrected Him three days later, then you will be saved. It's really that easy, and once you ask God to become your Lord and Savior, He's there for a lifetime. It's just a matter of putting the heat back into your relationship with Him."

Danielle listened as Pastor Browne continued with her message. She felt the tug on her heart. She'd been going through so much lately and she needed someone to carry her burdens to. Of course she had A.J., Jackson, and her girlfriends, but they couldn't solve all of her problems. She knew that God could.

Danielle didn't think twice when Pastor Browne held an altar call. She took Kennedi's hand and led her to the front of the church. She was a little disappointed when her brother didn't make the same move. Her happiness returned, though, when she felt someone grab her right hand. She smiled at Jayda as she released her hand and placed her arm around Jayda's waist.

As Pastor Browne prayed over them, Danielle and Jayda felt a spiritual connection develop between them. This had been the breakthrough that they, along with Lauren and Brenda, had needed. Now that the two of them had received it, it was only fair to share it with their girls.

Chapter 30

Lauren

Monday morning, Lauren rushed out of her second-period class toward her locker, hoping to find at least one of her girlfriends. She pushed through crowds of students and shoved people aside to get to where she needed to be. When she reached the senior hallway, she found Jayda walking with Evan. The couple looked so happy being in each other's company that she hated to break into their conversation, but her issue was more pressing.

"Jayda!" Lauren called from a few feet away.

Jayda spun around and saw her friend nearly tripping over her own feet trying to get to her. "Lauren, what's wrong?"

Lauren subconsciously gripped Jayda's arm and pulled her away from her boyfriend. "Please, tell me that you did not say anything to anybody about what we talked about on Saturday." Her eyes were nearly bulging out of their sockets.

"I promise I didn't."

"Not even to Evan?"

Jayda was silent for a moment.

"Jayda, you promised!"

"No, Lauren. He already knew before you even told us. I swear I didn't tell him a thing."

By this time, Danielle and Brenda had joined them.

Lauren looked wildly at them. "Did you guys say anything?"

"Lauren, just calm down," Danielle said when she noticed that students were starting to stare at them.

"No, I will not calm down! I had Fabian Swatters come up to me last period and ask me if I would sleep with him since I slept with—"

"Lauren!" Brenda covered her friend's mouth before she could say any more. "None of us said anything. We gave you our word." She dropped her hand, giving Lauren control over her lips.

"Well, how did he find out?" Lauren asked with tears in her eyes. She looked around and noticed several people glancing toward her. When she looked farther down the hall, she saw Jarred standing around with the same group of guys she usually saw walking down her street. She pushed through her friends and marched right up to him. "I need to talk to you." She grabbed Jarred's arm and dragged him out of the building.

"Lauren, you need to check yourself," Jarred said as he snatched his arm out of her grasp. "What's your problem?"

"You." Lauren pointed a slim finger in his face. "*You* are my problem. Why did you do it? Because I wouldn't go out with you? Was it because I was so mean and hateful toward you? What? Did you want to get back at me for all I'd done to you?" She hit him against his chest. "Why did you do it, Jarred?" she screamed.

Jarred took a few steps back, placing distance between him and Lauren. "First of all, *don't* put your hands on me. Second, I don't know what you're talking about."

She lowered her voice. "You told about what happened between me and Sterling."

He rolled his eyes heavenward and gave a loud sigh. "I don't know where you're getting your information from, but I didn't say anything about you to anybody. I do have better things to do with my time. Now, if you'll excuse me, I have to get to class."

Before he could walk away, Lauren grabbed his arm. "Don't lie to me, Jarred. You were the only person who knew and you're the only person who had motive. It had to be you."

Jarred chuckled menacingly and shook his arm out of Lauren's grip once again. "Girl, you are so full of yourself. Trust me, I'm not the only person in this school who has motive to ruin your precious reputation. You may be popular, but it's not 'cause people like you," he snidely informed her. "Now, what *you* need to do is watch how you handle your business around school."

"What?" Lauren asked in confusion.

"*I* wasn't the only person standing at the door that day when you and Mr. Sterling decided to put all your business on Front Street by handling it during school. I was just the only one you saw when you walked out of the room. There were plenty of people standing outside of Mr. Sterling's classroom and it wasn't to hear your little secret. He did have another class to teach that day. You aren't the center of the world, Lauren."

Lauren watched as he walked back into the school building. Seconds later, Jayda, Brenda, and Danielle rushed out to her. They bombarded her with questions, wanting to know if Jarred had been the one to reveal her secret. All Lauren could do was cry. She knew that her reputation was ruined. Sterling would lose his job. And she would have to apologize to Jarred.

Brenda

Brenda sat down at her regular lunch table and began to eat. She couldn't believe that Lauren's secret was out. The rumor had been circulating around school since second-period. Apparently, Fabian couldn't keep the gossip to himself. Sometimes guys were as bad as girls when it came to running their mouths. Brenda knew that by the end of the day, Sterling would be called into the principal's office and repercussions were inevitable.

If Sterling admitted that the rumors were true, he'd probably be fired on the spot. But if he denied them, he'd be placed on paid leave until the school could schedule a hearing. That would cause Lauren to have to miss a few days of school so that she would be able to testify. By the time the whole situation came to a close, Sterling's and Lauren's names would have been dragged through the gutter and back.

"So is it all true?" Traci asked as she sat down at the table along with Daphne.

Brenda sighed. "Is what all true?"

Daphne stretched her neck out dramatically as she rolled her eyes. "Girl, stop playin'. You know what we're talking about."

"Yeah, we know you got the dirt. What's up with Lauren and Mr. Sterling?"

Brenda pretended to play along as a wide smile spread across her face. "Ooh, I've been waiting *all day* to tell somebody this." She moved to the edge of her seat as if she were about to reveal a top-secret plan, and was amused when the two girls leaned in also. "What's going on is . . ." She dramatically paused before saying, "Really *none* of *your* business," she snapped.

The girls sucked their teeth and moved back into their seats. Brenda knew they were upset, not because she'd caught an attitude with them, but because she hadn't revealed the information they were so desperately seeking.

"Whatever," Daphne said. "Everybody knows anyway."

"Apparently, you don't," Brenda said. "If you did, you wouldn't be asking me."

"It's 'bout time somebody got something out on Lauren." Traci laughed as she spoke to Daphne. "She acts like she's such a goody-goody. I knew she was just like everybody else."

"No, that's where you're wrong," Brenda cut in. "Lauren is not like everybody else. She doesn't talk about her friends behind their back. She doesn't act like she likes somebody just to get something from them, then turn around and say that she never liked them."

"I didn't say I never liked her," Traci stated evenly.

"And what makes you think I'm talking about you?" Brenda asked curtly. "Maybe it's because you know you're wrong." She stood and placed her tray into the trash can before leaving the cafeteria and heading toward the library: the only other place administrators allowed students to go if they didn't want to eat during their lunchtime.

When Brenda walked into the massive room, she headed toward the computers. They were nearly full, but she found an empty one right next to Ken. *Ken?* Brenda's heart fluttered involuntarily at the sight of him. She had been dwelling on her problems with him since Saturday, when she'd revealed to her friends her true feelings about the situation. Having to see him in her class every day didn't help matters either. She decided to take the empty seat next to him, hoping she could get him to talk to her.

"Hi," she said softly as she sat down and signed on to the desktop.

Ken barely glanced at her before returning his gaze to his computer screen.

"Working on the anatomy assignment?" she asked, noticing that the title of his paper dealt with what they'd been studying in their science class.

This time he didn't even look her way as his fingers continued to race over the keyboard. Brenda gave up and decided to use the time to work on the assignment her human anatomy teacher had given the class. But with her unsolved problems with Ken on her mind, she couldn't concentrate on the work. She decided to use the Internet to e-mail him, knowing that, just like every other student who used the computers in the library, he would be logged on to his e-mail.

After signing on, she looked up Ken's e-mail in her address book and began to pour her heart out on to the screen.

Ken,
I know you don't want to talk to me and you don't have to. You don't even have to respond to this e-mail. All I want to say is that I'm sorry for hurting you. I led you on and that was not right. You were honest with me about your feelings and I wasn't.

Well, I'd like to be honest now. When I first began seeing you and Zane at the same time, I didn't think anything was wrong with it. I figured that I was not in an exclusive relationship with either of you, so I had the right to see whomever I chose to.

It wasn't until you asked for an exclusive relationship that I began to feel bad. I had already begun developing feelings for you, but I didn't want to let you know that because I was afraid of getting hurt. There's so much behind that statement that's hard to explain right now, but I guess I can just use the phrase "Like mother, like daughter." I'll leave the interpretation of that up to you.

I realized I was in trouble when a few days later, Zane asked me to be his girl also. I was already in too deep. It wasn't planned, but I had already allowed my feelings for you to grow a little too much. I didn't want to choose between the two of you because I felt that if I allowed my heart to lead me, I'd choose you and I knew that that would only lead to more trouble. Not that I felt you would break my heart, but I was not used to feeling what I felt for you. So I kept you hanging on to the possibility that I'd be committed to you, when in reality, I was terrified of, but a little pleased with, where our relationship was headed.

I just hope that you can find it in your heart to forgive me. I know there's not a possibility of our relationship going back to how it used to be and I wouldn't want it to. Right now, I need to focus on what's important and that's my schoolwork. I do hope that we can be friends, though. You were a really good one.

Always,

Brenda

She gazed at the length of her letter and felt that she'd written too much, but she quickly clicked the send button before she lost her nerve. As she waited for Ken to receive the e-mail, she resumed working on her assignment. Ten minutes later, she received a new message. She quickly opened it when she realized it was from Ken.

Apology accepted. Friends are good.

Brenda closed the message just as the bell, ending her lunch period, sounded, and then she logged off the computer. She and Ken arose from their seats at the same time. He turned toward her and gave her a small smile before walking out of the library. Brenda knew things were looking up. *One down, one more to go.*

Chapter 31

Danielle

"So what do you think is gonna happen?" Danielle asked Jayda as they headed toward Kennedi's school that afternoon.

Jayda shrugged, not taking her eyes off of the road ahead. "Mr. Sterling is probably gonna get fired. His class had a substitute last period because he had been called to the office."

"I can't believe this is happening." Danielle sighed. "And Lauren is so devastated."

"She had her dad come pick her up after third-period. She couldn't take it anymore. She probably won't come for the rest of the week."

"I don't think she should hide from her problems." Danielle leaned her elbow against the passenger side door and rested her head against her fist. "Ever since Sunday I've been praying for all of us and I just get this feeling that everything is gonna be all right. But in order for that to happen we have to put all of our problems in God's hands."

Jayda glanced at Danielle and smiled. "I've been feeling the same way. We really need to be sharing this with Bre and Lauren. They could really use us, especially now. After church on Sunday, Evan told me that now that you and I have something that Lauren and Bre don't, it's our job to make sure they get it. So as we grow and learn more about this new thing we have going on with Jesus, we should share it with them."

"You know, that man of yours is something else," Danielle said as she gazed at Jayda. "He's a good influence to have in your life. A.J.'s the same way. I mean, just look how much of an impact they've had on us."

"I know," Jayda agreed. "Evan is even gonna hang out with Cameron sometime. He says that he thinks my brother is at a critical point in his life when he needs a good male role model. So, he's gonna try to be that for him. Cameron loved the thought of hanging out with Evan. I think it's just because he sees how popular Evan is, especially with girls. But, hopefully, Cam will get more out of it than just popularity."

"Speaking of a male role model," Danielle said, "have you talked to your dad?"

"Have you talked to yours?" Jayda questioned.

"No."

"Ditto."

Danielle chuckled. "This is so stupid. We can't hold grudges forever."

"I'm not holding a grudge. I just don't want to speak to him for fear of what may come out of my mouth again. You know I have to work on this tongue because, as I'm sure my dad learned that day, if I'm pushed to my limits, there's no leash on this thing."

Danielle's laughter filled the car. "You are so crazy. I don't curse, but I've had a problem telling people off before and I know that if I call my dad, I may slip."

"Exactly, so why even test the waters?"

"Because regardless of what my dad did, I still love him. Just like you still love your dad. And love doesn't keep a record of wrongs."

Jayda's silence allowed them to momentarily enjoy the soulful sounds of Adele. Then she said, "Well, I'd still have to wait until I know I won't go off before I can call him."

"In the meantime, we can pray that God will work on our hearts," Danielle suggested.

"Not a bad idea." Jayda pulled into the parking lot of the elementary school.

They got out of the car, entered the building, and greeted the secretary before going into the aftercare classroom to pick up Kennedi. When Danielle walked into the classroom, she was surprised when Kennedi's teacher approached her instead of her jubilant daughter.

"Hi, Ms. Hollis," Danielle greeted the woman.

"Hi, Danielle. Can I have a word with you please?"

Danielle looked worriedly at Jayda before consenting. Ms. Hollis led Danielle to a corner in the room for privacy. Danielle wondered what could have happened today. Had Kennedi been troublesome? The four-year-old was known for playing victim when she was not able to get her way, but usually Kennedi was a well-mannered toddler, so Danielle didn't know what to expect.

"Ms. Hollis, what's going on?" Danielle asked nervously.

The teacher took a deep breath before answering, "Today, I let the kids sit down and talk about their families. And a lot of the kids here have parents who are quite a bit older than you, so several of them were talking about how they have a mother *and* a father at home."

"Oh goodness," Danielle whispered as she covered her mouth with her hand.

"I guess the conversation was too much for Kennedi to handle because when I asked her about her family she burst into tears," Ms. Hollis informed her. "I just thought you should know because she's been out of it all day. She hardly ate lunch and she wouldn't sleep during naptime. She's just been really solemn."

"Thank you, Ms. Hollis. I guess I can tell you that I am in the process of bringing Kennedi's father into her life, but it's a surprise so I haven't shared that with her."

Ms. Hollis gave her a reassuring smile. "Well, I do hope things work out. Kennedi is a delight and I love having her in my class. I like seeing her happy and it's apparent that you're trying to do everything you can to make sure that happens. I'll go get Kennedi from the art room."

As the woman walked off, Danielle rejoined Jayda at the entrance of the classroom. "Girl, I can't wait for Keenan to come here next week. Kennedi really needs him in her life."

"What happened?" Jayda asked.

"The same thing that's been happening for the past year or so: Kennedi wants her daddy."

"Hi, Mommy." Kennedi ran out to her mother with a smile on her face.

Danielle noticed that Kennedi's smile was not its widest. "Hi, sweetie."

"Look at my picture." Kennedi held up a sheet of paper in her hand.

Danielle took the picture and examined it. She noticed two figures holding hands.

"Is that what my daddy looks like?" Kennedi asked.

Danielle inhaled as she tried to hold back her tears. She looked over at Jayda and then at Kennedi's teacher; they both held compassionate gazes. She tried to smile when she answered, "Your daddy looks just like you. Are you ready to go home?"

"Yes," Kennedi said, apparently satisfied with the answer. She took Danielle's hand and waved to her friends and teacher as they walked out of the building.

By the time they got home, Kennedi had fallen asleep in the back seat of the car. Jayda decided to help Danielle carry her books, while Danielle carried her sedated daughter into the house.

After Jayda left, Danielle carried Kennedi into her room and laid her on her bed before going into her own bedroom and doing the same. She was extremely tired. So much had happened in one day. Lauren, Sterling, and Kennedi. All of their problems swam around in her head and she knew that, though everything was stressing her and her friends out, God had everything in control.

Brenda

"Come in," Brenda said in response to the light rapping on her door. She smiled as her little sister, Maya, entered her room. "What's up, li'l bit."

Maya placed her hands on her hips and said, "Don't you think I'm getting a little too old for that name? I'm almost ten."

Brenda laughed. "But you're about as tall as an eight-year-old. Even David is catching up to you."

Maya sat on the edge of Brenda's bed. "It ain't my fault my dad's short for a man." She laughed. "Anyway, I was coming to tell you that my dad said that he wants to keep me and David."

Brenda's wide smile matched her sister's as they embraced happily. "Your dad's a good man, Maya. You and David deserve him."

"Daddy says the same about us." Maya laughed before her face turned serious. "Have you told Mom yet?"

Brenda shook her head. "I'm a little scared. I don't want her to be upset with me, but I can't leave you guys here with her out running the streets."

"Tay is so happy that you want to take her with you when you leave. She really likes being around you." Maya giggled. "I think it's just because you're pretty."

Brenda blushed. "Well, she's pretty too. And so are you."

"Hey, don't you think I'm pretty?"

The girls turned toward the voice and noticed David standing in the doorway of his sister's room, with his arms folded across his chest and his lips pursed as if he were angry that he had not been referred to as pretty.

Brenda laughed as she opened her arms out to her brother. David ran into her embrace. "Davie, you're not pretty. You're handsome just like your daddy."

David jumped up and down. "Oh, did Maya tell you that Daddy wants us."

"Yes, she did," Brenda replied, pinching the tip of his nose.

"Do you think Mommy will be mad at me?" David asked, his big brown eyes pleading for his oldest sister to tell him that their mother wouldn't hold anything against him.

Brenda held her brother's head to her chest. "I don't know, Davie, but you know what I've learned since I've been on this earth?"

David looked up at her. "What?"

"You should do whatever makes you happy. And if moving in with your daddy makes you happy, then you should do it."

"Hey, guys, what's going on?" Taylor's voice piped in.

"Dang, is my room the hangout spot tonight?" Brenda laughed as she motioned for her sister to enter.

"So what's up?" Taylor sat on top of Brenda's dresser.

"Bre was telling us to do what makes us happy," Maya stated proudly as if she was going to live by that advice for the rest of her life.

"Well, you know what would make me happy?" Taylor said, looking at her older sister. "You telling Mom that I'm moving in with you this summer."

"*This summer*," Brenda repeated disbelievingly. "Tay, I have to get a job and make some money before I can even start looking for an apartment. It's gonna take awhile."

"Well, I'm not staying here by myself after you leave."

"You won't be by yourself. Maya and David will still be here," Brenda informed her.

"Uh-uh. Daddy said he's gonna ask Mommy for us when we get out of school," David corrected her.

The room grew silent. Brenda was terrified of her mother finding out that she would not only be losing one daughter, due to her leaving for college, but she would be losing all of her children once Brenda left. Eileen was sure to have a fit once she heard this. There would be no easy way to break the news to her. Brenda definitely was not going to try to persuade her siblings to stay if they didn't want to. She had just told her brother to do what made him happy. She couldn't renege on that statement now.

"Well," Brenda breathed as she looked at Taylor, "I'ma try to work something out. I don't want to leave you here by yourself."

"And just where are you going?"

The kids nearly jumped at the sound of their mother's voice. Eileen's gaze darted around the room in bewilderment.

"What's wrong with you guys?" she asked. "You act like I just walked in on some surprise plan."

If only you knew, Brenda thought as she tried to calm her racing heart.

Eileen's motherly instinct immediately kicked in and she demanded, "What's going on in here? Why is everybody in Brenda's room?"

Brenda looked down at her brother, who'd been sitting in her lap, and his eyes were already filling with tears. She noticed that Maya had drawn closer to her also. Even Taylor looked slightly intimidated.

Eileen noticed the fear in her children's eyes also. "What is going on?"

Brenda had just told her friends on Saturday about her plans to take care of her family so she wasn't prepared to tell her mother so soon, but knew that now was as good a time as any to reveal the truth. "Mom, you know that we would never intentionally try to hurt you, right?"

Eileen didn't respond. She only placed her hands on her hips and glared at her daughter, waiting for her to continue.

"I've tried to tell you how your behavior is affecting everyone in this house, but you didn't want to listen," Brenda spoke as tears began to threaten her own eyes. "When I leave for college, I'm taking Taylor with me."

"What?" Eileen screamed hoarsely.

"And Maya and David are gonna move in with their father," Brenda continued.

"What?" her mother repeated. She placed the palm of her hand over her chest.

Brenda could see Eileen's chest rising and falling rapidly as if she were losing her breath. "I'm sorry, Mom, but we can't live in this house anymore. Taylor was gonna kill herself by using drugs and you didn't even care. Why should I leave her here just for you to continue ignoring her and for her to carry out her plans?"

"How . . . How . . . Why are you doing this to me?" Eileen breathed gruffly.

Brenda narrowed her flooded eyes and tears began to trickle out onto her cheeks. "You did this to yourself, Mom. I told you what was going on, but you didn't want to listen. I'm sorry."

Eileen let her eyes wander from her youngest child to her eldest, letting them see the hurt she felt in her heart. Her eyes stayed on Brenda the longest as she allowed her stare to pierce her oldest daughter's heart. Then, she left without another word.

David and Maya fell against Brenda as they wept. Taylor was also shedding a few tears. Brenda beckoned for Taylor to join the rest of her siblings and she allowed them to cry wherever their tears found comfort.

Brenda wanted to tell them that everything would be fine. Their mother wouldn't be hurt for long. Eileen would soon realize that this was for the best. But she couldn't say anything. She felt her mother's pain and wished that she hadn't been the cause of it. Without any comforting words, Brenda lowered her head and allowed her cries to mingle with those of her brother and sisters.

Chapter 32

Jayda

Jayda knocked on her mother's room door before opening it slightly. "Mom?"

Heather's moan came from under her sheets.

Jayda sighed, knowing her mother wouldn't be up for a conversation, but they needed to have this talk.

After returning home from church on Sunday, Jayda had shared with her mother the salvation she'd received during the service. She had also shared with Heather the guilt she'd been feeling about how she'd been avoiding her since finding out about her father's sexuality. Heather told Jayda that she understood why she'd been so distant, knowing that news like that wasn't something that was easy to discuss. But she assured Jayda that she had nothing to feel guilty about. Just like Brenda had told her, leaving their family for someone else was a decision Preston had made on his own.

Jayda walked into her mother's room and lay down next to her. "Mom," she spoke softly as she slowly pulled the covers from over Heather's head.

She could tell her mother had been crying again. Heather's eyes were red and her hair was mattled. Jayda could see that her mascara had been ruined by the flow of her tears. "Mom, I don't wanna be mad at Daddy anymore," Jayda said. "I don't want you to be mad at him anymore either. I'm not saying that I want him to come back home, but I do want to forgive him. Evan said that if I stay mad at Daddy, I won't be able to move on with my life and I'm guessing that goes for anyone who's holding a grudge against someone else. So that means that you shouldn't hold what he did against him, either. He was wrong, no doubt, but I don't want to waste years of my life being upset with him." She gently smoothed her mother's hair down with her hand. "So, I'm going to call Daddy and let him know that I forgive him. Eventually, I hope you can do the same." She kissed her mother's cheek before climbing off of the bed.

Before walking out of her mother's room, Jayda grabbed the cordless phone that sat on Heather's nightstand. She went upstairs to her bedroom and sat cross-legged on her bed. Inwardly, she thanked God for sending Evan into her life. He had been so supportive during this time in her life. She would have never gotten through her father's infidelity if it had not been for Evan's wisdom, which, of course, he'd said had come from God. Last night, when Jayda had asked him how he'd gotten so smart, he told her that he'd asked God to give him wisdom and understanding so that he would be able to get through the toughest of times.

"All you have to do is ask, if you want it," Evan had said in the parking lot of his church after the Wednesday Bible Study service.

"That's it?" Jayda had asked as if she didn't believe it could be that easy.

He had shrugged. "That's how God works, babe."

Jayda smiled as she asked, for the millionth time in the last twenty-four hours, "God, please give me wisdom and peace that surpasses all understanding." Then she decided to add, "And please, please don't let me go off on my dad again."

She dialed her father's cell phone number and was sure that Preston had seen the house's number on his caller ID because he answered before the phone could ring a second time.

"Hello?" Preston seemed to have urgency in his voice.

Jayda only hesitated a moment before she spoke softly, "Hi, Daddy. It's Jayda."

She could hear him exhale as if he'd been holding his breath. "Hey, Jay baby. How's it going?"

"Everything's going fine." Her voice was shaky, almost matching the nervousness she heard in his. "How . . . are you?"

"I'm fine."

The line was silent and Jayda almost wanted to say, "I was just calling to see how you were doing. I have to go now. Bye." But she heard Evan's voice speak: *Babe, you've got to let this go before it runs your life.*

"Daddy, I just wanted to call you and let you know that I'm sorry for cursing at you and I don't really hate you at all. I love you a lot. I was just so hurt to see you with Mr. Murphy, not just because he's a man, but because you left our family for him. I just don't understand it at all. What is it that he gives you that Mom and your kids don't?" She felt herself getting heated again, so she paused and collected herself. "Never mind; please don't answer that. You don't have to explain yourself. I don't even want to talk about that. I just wanted you to know that I've changed in the last couple of weeks."

She thought twice before saying, "I have a boyfriend, now. His name is Evan and he's really nice. He's a Christian and the twins and I went to church with him last Sunday. Danielle was there, too, and we both got saved." She began to cry, though she didn't know the reason behind her tears. "Evan's been trying to get me to call you for weeks, but it wasn't until I accepted Christ that I understood why he was so adamant about it. He said that because I love you I should forgive you just like God loves the people on earth so He sent Jesus to die for us so that we may be forgiven of our sins." *Am I witnessing?* she asked herself. She really wasn't sure, but she did know that everything that was leaving her mouth was coming from deep within her heart, so she continued, "So I forgive you, Dad, because my love for you overpowers anything you could do to our family. I hope you can forgive me for what I did the other week."

"Oh, Jayda," Preston finally spoke when he realized that his daughter was finished speaking. "I should be the one asking you to forgive me. I'm sorry for hurting you all. I don't have any excuse for leaving, but I just wasn't happy at home anymore. I just couldn't be happy hiding who I truly was," he confessed. "I don't know how long things are going to be like this, but I don't want our relationship to change. Because you love me so much to put aside all of your hurt and anger and forgive me, I know I can do the same. I love you, sweetheart."

"I love you too, Daddy," Jayda answered with a small smile. "I guess I'll let you go now."

"I want to see you and the twins. I would like to see how your mother is doing, too, but I'm sure that's not a good idea just yet."

"No, it's not. I'm not sure about the twins, either. Candice is still upset about everything and Cameron doesn't want to talk about it at all." Jayda paused. "I guess I would be up for an afternoon out with my dad."

"That's great. I'll see when I have a full day off and I'll call you about it."

Jayda could hear the excitement in her father's voice. "Okay, I'll talk to you later."

After hanging up, Jayda felt much better than she had in days. Though she wasn't completely over this situation with her father, she knew it would only be a matter of time before she would be.

Chapter 33

Lauren

Friday morning, Lauren and Jayda walked into Sterling's classroom to find a gracefully aging woman sitting at his desk. They looked at each other knowingly and took their usual seats. By the time the late bell rang most of the students had entered the classroom.

Immediately, the woman stood and introduced herself. "Good morning, students. My name is Mrs. Jefferson and I will be your instructor for the remainder of the year."

At her statement, students began to whisper in dissatisfaction. Lauren refused to look at anyone, knowing that they would only see her and know she was to blame for Sterling's termination.

"Okay," Mrs. Jefferson interrupted the class's chatter. "Let's get right into today's lesson. We're going to go over chapter twenty-six. Please take notes because there will be a quiz tomorrow."

The class showed their displeasure by groaning and moaning.

Brenda

Mrs. Saunders handed last week's tests back to her students. She smiled when she reached Brenda's desk.

She handed Brenda her test and smiled. "Welcome back, Ms. Killian."

Brenda was nearly jumping out of her seat in joy when she saw the big red 120 at the top of her paper. Every one of her answers had a small red check next to it. She had even gotten the extra credit questions correct. *Thank you, God!*

Brenda became baffled. *Did I just thank God for something?* She knew that Danielle and Jayda had been having major effects on her lately. Brenda didn't know if they were intentionally planting the seed into her soul, but they were. Ever since returning from church with their respective male friends, Jayda and Danielle had talked about their salvation to no end. They had intrigued Brenda with their talk of peace and forgiveness. This morning, when Jayda had told Brenda that she'd settled the tension that had been between her and her father, Brenda knew Jayda had been changed. In the past, Jayda wouldn't so easily let something like what her father did roll off of her shoulders. But now, she seemed to have no animosity toward him.

"Maybe you guys are on to something," Brenda had told Jayda this morning as they walked off toward their separate classes. She had seen the smile form on Jayda's lips just before they departed. She wasn't sure what had changed her friends, but she wouldn't mind finding out.

She thought about how she and Ken had begun picking up the pieces of their relationship and wondered if Zane would be willing to do the same. If Ken could forgive her, maybe Zane could too. Brenda tore a sheet of paper from her notebook and began to write, hoping Zane would receive her humble apology and allow her to be his friend once again.

Zane,
I am so sorry for hurting you. I hate having you so upset with me, but I don't blame you. I acted as if I was

only interested in you when really I was also interested in someone else. I know I should've been honest like you were with me. Can you please forgive me? I would like to be your friend again.

Brenda

She realized how much more brief her letter to Zane was than the one she'd given to Ken, and she was well aware of the reason behind that. The feelings that she'd developed for Ken went far beyond what she felt for Zane and her apologies to both guys seemed to reflect that. Without hesitation, she folded the note in half and discreetly passed it back to him. She waited patiently for him to read it and hoped that he would respond. She felt him tap on her shoulder and she turned slightly to retrieve the note from him.

Brenda, I guess I can be nice and accept your apology, but about us being friends—I'm not so sure. I have to trust my friends and right now I don't have too much trust in you.

Brenda took a deep breath and exhaled. *At least he's forgiven me,* she thought. Now she knew she could move forward with her life.

Lauren

"Nice goin', Lauren," a female student snarled on her way out of the classroom.

Lauren glared at the girl as she gathered her books and stood to leave. She looked at Jayda. "I can't believe this."

"What? The fact that Mr. Sterling got fired or the fact that everyone's blaming you?"

Lauren sighed. "I don't know. I just wish that all of this drama would go away."

As they walked out of the room, they ran into Jarred, who barely gave Lauren a fleeting look.

"Jarred," Lauren called after him.

After seconds of reluctance, Jarred turned to face Lauren.

Her eyes were full of regret when she said, "I'm sorry for what I said to you on Monday."

"Look, Lauren, I don't want your apologies, okay?" Jarred shrugged. "I'd much rather you go back to ignoring me." He turned and walked into the classroom.

Lauren sighed as she and Jayda resumed walking.

"Man, that boy is really angry with you," Jayda stated. "I've never seen him act like that before."

"Me either. He's been like that since the week after my party. I just thought he might've been mad because he didn't get an invitation, but now I don't know what the problem could be."

Jayda glanced at her friend. "You don't think he might've known about you and Mr. Sterling before it got out into the open?"

"You mean before that day Sterling came back to school?"

Jayda nodded. "It's possible. Evan figured it out when you didn't come to school on Tuesday and Wednesday last week. Maybe Jarred did the same, only sooner."

"I don't know what to think. I just want to make everything right."

They walked into their second-period class as Jayda said, "Well, we have early release day today and as soon as this class is over, spring break officially begins. I want you to have fun, so you need to handle your business ASAP."

Lauren released a heavy sigh as the bell rang, indicating the beginning of the next class period. She wanted to have fun during the break, but with her troubles still on her mind, she knew she wouldn't be able to. She had to find a way to fix things.

Chapter 34

Brenda

Just as Brenda entered her house, the phone began to ring. She picked it up and glanced at the caller ID. The number was unfamiliar to her so she placed the phone back in its hook, figuring that the caller was either a bill collector or someone who had the wrong number.

She had just gotten into her bedroom when the phone began to ring again. She ran back downstairs to retrieve it. She noticed that it was the same number and figured that somebody was trying to reach someone at her home, so she answered it.

"Hello?" Brenda sang into the receiver.

"Dang, girl, why I got to call the house twice for you to answer the phone?"

Brenda was caught off guard by the male's aggressive tone. "Excuse me? I think you have the wrong number." She quickly hung up while shaking her head in disgust. "I don't know who he's tryin'a call, but it can't be anybody at this house, especially if he doesn't have the decency to offer a greeting," Brenda spoke aloud to herself.

Not a full minute later, the phone began to ring again. This time the caller was really going to get a taste of Brenda's sharp tongue.

"Hello? Who is this?" she snapped, ready to go into full attitude mode.

"Brenda, this is your *brother,* Chase."

Brenda screamed out in hilarity, knowing she'd almost made a fool of herself. She hadn't heard from her bother in months, so having him call and just speak to her any kind of way wasn't something she was used to. "Boy, don't ever call here and don't say 'hello,' 'how you doing,' or something. You were about to get told off." She laughed. "What's up?"

"Nothing really." Chase laughed along with his sister. "I'm getting some time off the base and wanted to come see you guys. Is it all right?"

Brenda shrugged. "I guess. It's a little tense around here, though."

"What do you mean?" Chase inquired.

She proceeded to tell her brother all that had occurred in the last couple of months, including her plans to take Taylor once she left for college and David and Maya's decision to move in with their father.

"Man, how y'all just gonna leave Mom all alone like that?" Chase questioned in disbelief.

"I'm sorry. Come again?"

"That's wrong, Bre," he told her.

"How is wanting to be safe and happy wrong?" Brenda asked, not believing that her brother wouldn't take her side on this. "Taylor was about to kill herself!"

"I understand that, but think about what may happen to Mom if y'all leave. She's gonna be alone and she's gonna get depressed. She may not eat, she might not sleep, and all of that could lead to one thing."

"So what you're tryin'a say is, if we all leave, we're gonna send Mama into her grave?" Brenda placed her free hand on her hip.

"Look, let's talk about this later on tonight," Chase said. "I'm at the airport and I'll be at the house within the hour."

She smacked her lips in mock disgust. "And what if I would've told you that you couldn't come over here? What were you gonna do? Sleep at the airport?"

He laughed. "Between you and Mama, neither of you know how to say no to me. Now, have me a nice plate of spaghetti ready when I get there, please."

Brenda sucked her teeth. "Sure, I'll have all the ingredients on the counter so you can make it yourself."

"C'mon, Bre," Chase pleaded. "I haven't been home in almost two years. Can't I get my favorite meal?"

"Chase, you were just here for Christmas," she argued, remembering that her brother was known for his melodramatic attitude.

"Just have my food ready, girl."

"Yeah, whatever," she said before hanging up.

Brenda couldn't keep the smile off of her face as she went into the kitchen to begin making her brother a nice welcome-home meal. Chase knew she would do as he'd requested just because she loved him that much.

Though he had just been home for the holidays a few months ago, Brenda was glad her brother was coming up to spend spring break with her. She needed him now more than ever. Maybe he could be of some assistance and help them figure out what could be done about the problems in her household.

Lauren

"Mama, can I please go out for a drive?" Lauren asked as she watched her parents cuddle in their king-sized bed.

Cathy looked up at her daughter. "Lauren, it's pouring down outside. Where are you trying to go?"

Lauren looked out of the window and shrugged. "I just want to go for a drive." She couldn't tell her parents where she was headed, knowing they would immediately start asking questions.

Reuben kissed his wife's cheek and said, "Baby girl, you can go. Your mother and I could use some alone time." He placed a tender kiss on Cathy's lips.

Lauren shook her head. "Thanks, Daddy. I'll be back shortly, so handle your business quick."

"Girl, get out of here," Cathy commanded with a laugh. "And be careful."

Lauren walked out of the room and closed the door behind her. Her car was parked in the driveway, so she placed the hood of her jacket over her head and walked out of the front door. As she started her car, she took a deep breath, praying that she was doing the right thing.

She pulled out of her driveway and moved toward the entrance of her neighborhood. As she drove, her heart was racing and she had to force herself to decrease the pressure she was putting on the gas pedal. The rain was pounding against her windshield and the windshield wipers didn't seem to be doing their job quick enough. She tried to slow down so she could be cautious of her surroundings. She squinted as she studied the street signs at each intersection. When she reached the correct street, Lauren made a left turn into the neighborhood.

She hadn't been in this neighborhood in a while, but she remembered it vividly. She, along with the rest of the cheer squad, had come here last year for a fellow cheerleader's birthday cookout. Lauren smiled faintly as she passed the girl's house. She was sitting on the porch along with Jayda that late summer afternoon when she first saw Sterling. He had been running down the street in basketball shorts and a muscle shirt, which had been clinging to his body as a result from the sweat that had accumulated on his torso. Lauren had been mesmerized by the way he'd smiled briefly in her direction as he passed by them. She recalled asking her friend if Sterling lived in the neighborhood and the girl had pointed out his house, which was located in the center of the cul-de-sac. She remember thinking at one point that the entire encounter had just been a figment of her imagination, especially when she started visiting the neighborhood in hopes of catching a glimpse of the sun-kissed beauty, but never did. However, she had been pleasantly surprised when she approached her first class on the first day of her senior year and Sterling had been standing at the door, greeting the students who were entering his classroom. That day, Lauren had been determined to claim Sterling for herself. She had been unwavering in her belief that it was only destined that they become an item.

And look where that got me, she thought as she pulled her car into Sterling's driveway. *I'm here begging for this man's forgiveness when he's the one who hurt me.*

Silently, she hoped that Jayda and Danielle were right. Her friends had told her that if she wanted to make everything go away, she needed to start where the problem was rooted. She had to resolve things with Sterling and ask him for his forgiveness, so that she could move on with her life and begin to put the pieces of her heart back together.

Unsteadily, Lauren turned off her car, unlatched her seat belt, and opened her door. She tried to firmly place her feet on the ground and take sturdy steps toward the front door. She stood on his front porch, allowing the rain to saturate her clothes.

After a few more deep breaths, her shaky finger reached up and pressed down firmly on the doorbell. She could hear its chime and part of her hoped that Sterling was not home, so she wouldn't have to go through with this. If he wasn't home, she would have more time to prepare herself for her apology and his response. Maybe she could make a run for it before the door was answered. She could always do this on another day, preferably one that was sunny. There was no rush. Without a second thought, Lauren turned around and headed back to her car. Just as she was about to open the driver's side door, she heard the front door open.

"Excuse me, can I help you?" she heard Sterling's voice call out.

She knew he had no clue as to who she was because her hood was pulled up over her head and concealing part of her face. *Might as well get it over with,* she thought as she slowly turned to find him standing in his doorway, looking as gorgeous as ever in his gray sweatpants and black T-shirt. She walked toward him and had to steady her heartbeat when she found herself standing directly in front of him. She could tell by his demeanor that he was surprised to see her, especially under the present circumstances.

"May I come in?" she asked softly.

He refused to make eye contact with her. "I don't think that's a good idea."

"Please," she requested emotionally. "I only want to talk."

Sterling sighed and hesitantly stepped aside, allowing her to enter.

Lauren pulled her hood off of her head and studied his living quarters. She noted that he had great taste in furniture. She decided that she would stand by the door so that she wouldn't soak his navy carpet with the water dripping from her clothes. She watched as Sterling moved toward his den and turned off the basketball game he'd been watching. He looked at Lauren and watched as she played with her car keys, keeping her eyes lowered.

"If you take your shoes off, you can have a seat on the couch," he offered.

Lauren looked at his leather sofa and then up at him, apprehensively.

"It's fine," he assured her. "I'll just wipe it down later."

She slipped out of her American Eagle slides and walked, barefoot, over to where he sat on the couch. She moved as close to the end of the sofa as she could, so she wouldn't allow herself to be tempted to do anything she hadn't come to do.

"So what are you doing here?" Sterling asked her.

Lauren kept her eyes glued to her red-painted toenails. "I'm sorry for getting you fired. It wasn't intentional. I hope you know that. I'm also sorry for pushing you to do something you had told me you didn't want to do. When you said that our relationship should remain professional, I should've stopped with my pursuit there, but I didn't and I hope you forgive me." Her words were so rushed, she was sure that Sterling hadn't understood a thing she'd just said.

Only a few seconds ticked by before he spoke, "Lauren, you don't have to apologize to me. You didn't make me do anything that I didn't want to do. I'm a grown man with a mind of my own, and though you were very persuasive, I made the decision to sleep with you *on my own*. And that decision is what got me fired. Not you."

"Everybody at school is so mad at me. They've been talking about me so bad."

"Take it as a compliment," he said nonchalantly.

"What?" She finally looked up at him. "Do you know what they've been calling me? Everybody thinks I'm such a whore. Girls are trippin' out on me and the guys just think that they can come up to me any kind of way now. How can I consider *that* a compliment?"

Sterling shook his head and looked her directly in her eyes. "Don't take their words or gossip as a compliment. Take the fact that they spend their time talking about you as a compliment. Apparently, you're so fascinating to them that they can't keep you off of their minds. Of course it's not so great to be given a disgraceful label, but you don't have to live up to it."

Lauren chuckled dryly and said softly, "I slept with my teacher. I think I've lived that label to the fullest."

Sterling was quiet as he allowed his eyes to travel to his television. Lauren watched as he blankly stared at the dark sixty-four-inch flat screen. She could tell he was uncomfortable being so close to her and discussing this matter. She almost wanted to tell him that she'd come and done what she had to do; now it was time for her to go. But she felt as if there was still unsettled business between them.

"I don't want you to think that I used you," Sterling suddenly stated.

His voice was so gentle and quiet that Lauren almost thought she'd heard the words in her mind.

"I truly did want to be with you that night," he continued. "I'd thought about it many times. I still think about it and sometimes I think that it was worth being fired."

"Then why did you tell me that you didn't want to be with me anymore?" she asked, trying to contain her composure. "I thought that our relationship would continue from that point. I felt like since we'd connected on so many levels, we would continue to see each other. But you avoided me, and then broke my heart."

His eyes reconnected with hers. "After that night, I couldn't sleep. That whole week, I was out of school, I was restless. All I could think about was that night and I knew it had been a mistake. And one reason it was a mistake was because you were still my student. If that had not been the case, we wouldn't even be having this conversation."

"So you only think it was a mistake because I was your student?" Lauren questioned hoarsely.

Sterling shook his head. "There's one other reason."

Lauren's eyes questioned him.

"I knew you loved me. I figured it out as we were dancing at your party. I could see it in your eyes and it scared the crap out of me. I didn't want to hurt you, but I knew I didn't love you like you loved me."

"You didn't love me like I loved you," she reiterated quietly. "How do you love me? Or do you even have love for me at all?"

He inhaled and released the breath before answering, "I think the best way to describe my love for you is how one loves his friend. I knew that if our surroundings were different I could grow to love you as a man loves his girlfriend or wife, but because we acted before the time was right, that could never happen."

Lauren knew what he was saying was true. Even now that Sterling had been fired and she was legal, they still could not have a relationship with each other. Too much had happened between them. Lauren's heart was too fragile and Sterling was sure to find another woman to take her place. She was not naïve. Sterling probably had a date with a beautiful woman tomorrow night. She couldn't and wouldn't expect for him to put his life on hold for her. He was a decent man who would make a woman very happy someday. He deserved that. And she deserved a man who would love her like she loved him.

"Again, I'm sorry if I hurt you," Sterling repeated.

Lauren sighed heavily. "You did, but I'm sure I'll bounce back."

He nodded.

"Thank you for seeing me. I don't know if everything is settled, but as long as you've accepted my apology, I know that my reason for being here has been handled."

Sterling smiled slightly. "Seeing as how you don't really have a reason to apologize to me, I don't feel comfortable saying that I forgive you . . ." He chuckled when Lauren rolled her eyes heavenward and shook her head. "But since you're being so stubborn about it, I accept your apology. I hope that you, too, can find it in your heart to forgive me for playing a part in all of this mess."

Lauren nodded as she stood. "Of course. Well, I have to get going. I told my parents I wouldn't be gone long and I don't want them to worry about me."

"Speaking of your parents," Sterling said, standing to his feet, "please tell them I'm sorry for any trouble I caused."

Lauren's eyes darted around the room as she nervously fumbled around with her keys.

"You didn't tell them, did you?" Sterling questioned suspiciously.

She shook her head. "I thought the school would call and inform them, but I guess they've left that part up to me."

Sterling's brow furrowed in confusion. "That doesn't make any sense. I'm sure the protocol is for the school to call your parents in a situation like this."

"Well they haven't. My parents haven't said anything to me about it," Lauren explained. "I am so afraid that they're gonna be disappointed in me. How would you take hearing that your daughter had sex with her teacher?"

He shrugged. "I'm not sure. I really don't want to offer an opinion since I am the teacher in this situation.

But I can tell you that they're gonna love you no matter what."

She smiled and slipped into her shoes. "Thank you. I guess I'll see you around."

Silently, he nodded. He opened the front door for her and watched as she rushed to her car in order to evade the rain.

Driving away, Lauren felt a bit at peace. She was proud of herself for confronting Sterling like an adult. Her mother always told her that conquering life's trials helped a person to mature. They became stronger and wiser. Soon, they would be able to handle anything with confidence. Lauren felt as if she was well on her way.

Chapter 35

Danielle

"What a way to start the break," Danielle said as she gazed out at the rain pounding against the concrete parking lot in front of her job.

Selena laughed. "I know, but at least it's not as bad as it was yesterday. So what are you planning to do during spring break?"

Danielle shook her head. "Hopefully, get some rest. Well, maybe not since Kennedi's not going to school all next week, so I guess I'll be home with her. Maybe Jackson will take us somewhere." A self-conscious smile spread across her face. "Kennedi may get to meet her father sometime next week."

Selena clapped her hands excitedly. "Danielle, that's so great." She gave her a hug.

"I talked to his mother last night and she said he was coming into town on Monday, so I'm gonna meet with him on Tuesday or Wednesday, depending on when his mother tells him that I want to see him. Then, based on how our conversation goes, Kennedi should get to meet him by the end of the week, before he goes back home." Danielle exhaled as if she'd said all of that in one breath. "I hope everything goes well."

"Oh it will," Selena assured her, her voice still very optimistic. "Keenan's about your age now, right?"

Danielle nodded.

"He's probably changed so much."

"Doubt that," Danielle said, mostly to herself. "The Keenan I remember is a self-centered, immature, and egotistical mama's boy who runs away from his responsibilities."

"But the Keenan you remember was also thirteen years old, so, of course, at that age he's going to be negligent of his responsibilities," Selena pointed out. "He can't be the same unless there's mentally something wrong with him. A thirteen-year-old and a seventeen-year-old think on very different levels."

"Okay, say that you're right," Danielle supposed as she propped her elbow onto the countertop. "Keenan is mature and thinks of others, *but* he's still not ready to be a father to his daughter. What then?"

"You continue to be the best single parent you can be," Selena answered without hesitation. "You've been doing a great job for nearly five years. You're a strong young woman, Danielle. You can handle life's tests like nobody I've ever known. Like you told me weeks ago: God will never put more on you than you can bear."

Danielle smiled. "Yeah, I know." She glanced down at the gold watch resting on her wrist. "My brother will be here any minute to pick me up. So I'ma go ahead and clock out."

Selena nodded. "I'm leaving in about thirty minutes. Today is my last day working because I'm gonna be checked into the hospital on Monday."

"So it's time for Mr. Man to enter the world?" Danielle asked.

"Yeah, like two days ago, so they're going to induce my labor next week."

"Are you ready to become a mother?"

Selena pondered over the question before shrugging. "I'm not sure, but I'm not worried about all of that. I'm just gonna do the best that I can and hope that my baby won't hold any of my shortcomings against me." She laughed.

Danielle's face was serious when she said, "He won't. I worried about Kennedi doing the same for the first two years, but once she was old enough to tell me that she loved me and that I was a 'good mommy,' I stopped stressing over it."

"Danielle, you've been such a good friend to me, especially in the last few months. Thank you so much." Selena embraced her.

Danielle squeezed her firmly. "You're welcome. Just promise me that you'll never give up on motherhood. Trust me, there'll be times when you want to, but when you start to feel that way just look into your baby's eyes and you'll want to keep on going just for him."

Selena pulled back. "I promise." She looked toward the store's entrance. "Well, it looks like your brother's here."

Danielle looked outside and noticed that Jackson had just pulled into the parking lot. "Make sure you or someone else calls me once you have your little one. I would love to come by and see him and check on you." She grabbed her jacket and umbrella.

"I will," Selena promised.

Jackson walked into the store and greeted Selena before leading his sister to the car. "Man, Selena looks like she's long overdue," he noted as he pulled out of the parking lot.

"Yeah, she was due earlier this week, but that's normal. She'll be induced in a couple of days," Danielle informed him. "Did you stay at home all day?" she asked.

Jackson shook his head. "I spent most of the day with Déjà visiting CAU's campus. It was real nice before it started raining again. I spoke to a couple of students and a few professors and I was told that if my application was sent in early I could enroll this summer." He peered over at his sister and noticed her wide smile. "What's up?" he asked her in confusion.

Danielle looked at him, her smile still in place. "You spent the whole day with Déjà?"

He nodded. "Yeah. Is that a problem?"

"Nope," she said. "Y'all are just getting really close, that's all."

"Just like you and A.J. are close," he pointed out.

"But I'm not tryin'a get with A.J. I still like him—a lot—but I feel like we're just supposed to be friends . . . at least for now." Danielle nodded her head in his direction. "You, on the other hand, have been sprung over Déjà since the first day you met her."

"Well, I like her and after spending so much time with her that feeling has only grown. I don't know if she feels the same way. She probably thinks I'm just a kid, but I guess I'll have to prove her wrong."

Danielle decided against telling her brother that he didn't have to stress himself out in order to show Déjà that he was mature, because she had already taken notice of that. Danielle figured that if Déjà wanted Jackson to know what she thought of him, she would tell him when she was good and ready. In the meantime, it would be fun watching Jackson vie for Déjà's affection.

When they arrived home, Danielle noticed an unfamiliar BMW parked in their driveway.

"Who's car is this?" she asked her brother.

Jackson shrugged. "It wasn't here when Déjà dropped me off earlier. It's a rental though," he surmised, gazing at the license plate. "Guess we have dinner guests." He got out of the car and headed toward the front door.

Danielle followed him as he went into the house. They could hear voices coming from the family room down the hall.

"I don't think this is a good idea," Danielle could hear her mother saying.

"Look, Beverly, I'm not going to let another day go by with things being like this," an authoritative male voice spoke persistently.

Danielle immediately recognized the voice. She looked up at her brother and shook her head. "It can't be . . ."

Jackson's face was fixed and Danielle could tell he was getting upset. "It better not be," he said as he stomped down the hall with his sister on his tail.

When they reached the family room, they found their mother sitting in the wingback chair in the corner of the room and their father sitting adjacent from her on the sofa. Both adults looked up when their children walked into the room.

"What are you doing here?" Jackson commanded of his father.

Danielle placed her hand on his forearm to try to remind him to be calm, but Jackson wasn't trying to take the hint. He moved out of his sister's grasp and stepped closer to his father.

Neil stood, towering over his son by about four inches. "Jackson, please lower your voice. And you might want to change that tone of yours as well."

Jackson glared at his father as if Neil had no right to tell him what to do. "Mama, why you let this man in your house?"

"Jackson," Neil said once more in a firmer tone.

"Jackie." Beverly rushed to her son's side. "Please calm down, baby. I know you're upset and you have every right to be, but you need to respect your father." She looked between Jackson and Danielle. "Now, both of you come sit down so that we can work this out."

Danielle hadn't taken her eyes off of her father since she'd entered the room. Inwardly, all she wanted to do was wrap her arms around him and never let go. She hadn't seen Neil in two years and, though he was here for a disheartening reason, Danielle couldn't fight the love she felt for her father. But, because she was still upset with him for keeping his son a secret, Danielle resisted the urge to rush to Neil's side.

"I need to go check on Kennedi." Danielle turned to leave the room.

"Danni, Kennedi's fine," Beverly said as she moved toward her daughter to guide her back into the room. "She's upstairs with . . ." She stopped short and paused before saying, "She's fine."

Danielle tossed her mother a suspicious glance and then she turned to her father, who was shaking his head.

"It's all right, Beverly," Neil stated as he moved his gaze to Danielle. "Kennedi's upstairs playing with Junior."

Danielle's heart began to race at the fact that the little brother she'd never met was upstairs with her daughter. She subconsciously lowered herself onto the loveseat that sat against the wall. She had been putting off contacting her father, even though she'd been urging the rest of her friends to deal with their problems head-on. Part of Danielle felt like such a hypocrite; but another part of her knew that she hadn't made a move toward reconciliation because she was afraid of the outcome the encounter with her father would have. Now, she would find out.

Jackson reluctantly took a seat next to his sister and acted as if he didn't want to hear a word his father had to say, but Danielle knew that he wanted closure just as much as she did.

"Danielle, Jackson, Beverly," Neil began after everyone was settled. "I apologize for lying and cheating."

"Neil, don't apologize to me. I've heard enough of your excuses," Beverly interrupted. "The kids are the ones you should be speaking to."

"Beverly, could I please just do this without you making it harder than it already is?" her ex-husband asked with an edge in his voice.

Danielle shook her head. Even after five years of divorce, her parents still couldn't get along. She would've thought that by now they would've learned to be cordial to each other, but their relationship hadn't changed a bit. She watched as her mother rolled her eyes and sat back in her chair with her arms folded over her chest.

"Like I was saying," Neil continued snidely, keeping his eyes on his children, "I'm sorry for hurting you guys. I also apologize for keeping you in the dark about Junior, but I didn't want to complicate things any more than they already were."

Danielle began to speak as if her voice had a mind of its own. "Daddy, that is such a lame excuse."

Everyone in the room seemed surprised by her outburst, even Jackson. Danielle felt as if that statement had come from deep within and she knew there was more, so she allowed her heart to continue.

"Every adult who gets into hot water uses that excuse. How will the truth complicate a situation? If anything, it should make things easier to deal with. If you had just told us that you and Mama were divorcing because you had a son by another woman, we would have understood why our family was being broken apart. We would've been upset, but at least we wouldn't have been left in the dark."

She looked toward Beverly. "The same thing goes for you, Mama. When we talked about this, you used the excuse that I was depressed about my own situation and that you didn't want to make me feel even worse and all of that nonsense. I would've been able to take the fact that I had a brother who was not my mother's son. Stuff like this happens every day. I'm not saying that I would've been cool with it, but just think if you guys would have just told us the truth in the beginning. Jackson wouldn't be so heated. *Junior* wouldn't have had to lie to everyone about who he was. And I surely wouldn't be sitting here, talking to my parents like they are two little children.

"Now, personally, I don't need to hear any excuses about the affair, the lies, or Junior. I don't care to hear the details. All I've ever wanted was the truth. My parents are no longer together because my father has a son by another woman. Plain and simple." She looked at her father. "Daddy, I forgive you for lying, for cheating, and for hiding the truth." She then moved her gaze to her mother. "Mama, I forgive you for hiding the truth also. I love you guys and I'm not going to hold this over your heads for the rest of my life. I do have better things to do." Danielle settled back into her seat and waited for someone to respond.

The room became blanketed with a thick sheet of silence. No one seemed to know how to react to her outburst. Maybe it was because they all still had more to say, but as far as Danielle was concerned, the conversation was over. Wasting time talking about something that couldn't be changed was not something she wanted to do at this point. It was only important to her that she relieve herself of the burden she'd been carrying by forgiving those who had wronged her. With that done, she could move on and so could everyone else.

"Well." Jackson finally breathed as if he'd been holding his breath, afraid that his parents may spew out a strong argument in response to Danielle's tirade. "I guess I'm with Danni on this one. Although I am still very upset about the situation, I know the best thing to do is to get over it and move on. I guess I should also apologize for hitting you, Dad. It was an irrational decision and I hope you forgive me." He gazed at his father for a response.

Neil seemed to still be in shock by his daughter's rant, but he managed a weak smile and an, "Of course I do, son." He then looked at Danielle and shook his head, but his smile stayed in place. "Girl, you got a mouth on you," he said, to her amusement. "Must come from your mother, 'cause if I would've ever said what you just said to my parents, back in the day, *you* wouldn't be here today." He gazed at her lovingly. "But you are right. No more excuses. Thank you for forgiving me." He stood with outstretched arms and Danielle immediately received his embrace.

Danielle remained standing as she looked at her mother. Beverly was trying hard to keep a stern face, but Danielle could see the faint smile tugging at her lips. Without another word, she walked toward her mother and hugged her tight.

Danielle felt a release from Beverly's body as if she'd been holding something inside much heavier than their issue at hand. Beverly's next words would cause Danielle to understand that her outburst had made her mother come to realize that Danielle was more than able to care for herself.

"You've become a very mature young lady," Beverly whispered in her daughter's ear. "I'm sorry for riding you so hard, but I've finally realized that you are now a responsible young adult and a very capable mother."

Danielle smiled and complimented her: "I learned from the best."

She was still unsure of the reason behind her mother's apprehension toward her ability to care for herself and her daughter, but that was no longer an issue in Danielle's mind. She was just glad that her mother had finally loosened the hold she'd had on Danielle, now allowing her to live her life.

Chapter 36

Brenda

"Brenda. Brenda!"

With the sounds of Miguel blasting in her ears, Brenda briefly glanced up from the magazine she was reading to find her little brother standing in her doorway with his hands waving wildly in the air. She looked at him in concern as she removed the earphones from her ears.

"What?" she questioned him.

"You should turn down your music so you can hear when I call your name," David said as he leaned against her doorpost.

Brenda rolled her eyes. "Can I help you?"

"Yes, you can," he said. "Chase is hogging my bed. I don't have anywhere to sleep."

"Why is Chase asleep so early? We haven't eaten dinner yet."

"I don't know, but I need my bed back." David looked extremely upset. "He's so big. I think he's gonna break it."

Brenda laughed as she got up and walked down the hall toward David's room. Her younger brother was following close behind, hoping his sister would regulate the situation and make Chase find another resting place. Brenda walked into the room and couldn't help but to laugh at the sight before her. Chase was nearly

twice the size of David's small twin-sized bed. His time
in the Navy had buffed him up and made him more
massive than his inherited form. His long legs dangled
over the bottom of the bed and he looked as if he would
fall right onto the floor if he moved even an inch.

"Brenda, make him get up," David commanded as he
pushed his sister forward.

Brenda looked down at David. "Davie, he's tired."

"So?" He crossed his arms over his chest and glared
at her.

She sighed. "Chase," she called as she walked over to
the bed. She shook her older brother's arm and called
his name over and over. Chase didn't budge. Brenda
looked at David and shrugged.

David smacked his lips and said, "I am *not* sleeping
on the floor tonight." He ran and pounced on Chase's
back and began to bounce up and down.

"Ouch!" Chase hollered as he instinctively grabbed
David by his collar. Effortlessly, swinging his little
brother around with one arm, he demanded, "What are
you doing?"

David seemed to be unfazed by his brother's tight
grip on his shirt. "I want my bed back," he said as he
gasped for oxygen.

Chase let go of his brother's shirt and David fell to
the floor. "Why didn't you just say so?" he asked as he
sat up in the bed. "Boy, I've been trained to react to
attacks. Don't jump on me like that again unless you
wanna see what I've really learned in the Navy."

David rubbed his neck and fixed his shirt. "If you
break my bed, you're gonna see what I learned in ka-
rate class last summer." He stood to his feet and illus-
trated his threat by demonstrating a simple high kick
combined with a loud, "Hiya!"

Brenda and Chase laughed, but David didn't see anything funny. From his facial expression, his older siblings could tell that he was serious, but that only made the situation more hilarious.

"Is dinner ready?" Chase asked Brenda.

Brenda was still chuckling, but she managed a shrug. "Mama is still in the kitchen so I guess not."

"Man, I fell asleep nearly an hour ago waiting for dinner and it's still not ready?" Chase complained. "I'm about to eat some leftover spaghetti."

"I'll go see if Mama's finished," David volunteered as he ran out of the room.

Brenda followed her brother out of the room, but went in the opposite direction, back into her bedroom, and logged on to her computer.

"So, are you gonna talk to me about what's going on around here?" Chase spoke from the doorway.

Brenda released a deep sigh. She had known her brother would follow her with the same question on his lips. He'd been hounding her about the situation looming over their household since he arrived last night. Brenda had successfully avoided his questions since she already knew he was in their mother's corner, but now she knew it was time to sit down and talk to him about it.

Chase came into the room and sat on her bed, waiting quietly for her to respond. Brenda took a few minutes to log in to her e-mail, so that she could check her messages. Browsing through her inbox, she found nothing of great importance, so she swiveled around in her chair so that she would be facing her brother.

"Chase, I cannot leave Taylor here by herself," she began as if he were demanding that she not take their sister with her when she left. "I'm not trying to hurt Mama. I'm trying to keep Taylor from hurting herself.

Mama blatantly stated that she was not gonna let any
of us keep her from having fun. She's made her choice
and choices always have consequences, good or bad."
She paused for only a second before adamantly stating, "Now, when I leave, it will only be a matter of time
before I come back for Taylor. That's all there is to it."

Chase dropped his gaze to the floor and let it rest
there for a while. Brenda could tell that it was hard
for him to digest, but she couldn't understand why. It
wasn't like he would be around to see Eileen drown in
her sorrows because she'd chosen her life over her children's wellbeing. Chase was acting as if Brenda were
taking *his* children away.

"Bre, I know you don't understand why *I'm* being so
defensive about this and honestly I don't either." Chase
allowed his gaze to meet his sister's. "All I know is that
Mom is gonna be miserable here all by herself. You
know she's not gonna fight to keep David and Maya.
She's not gonna fight to keep Taylor. But that doesn't
mean that they should just leave."

"Chase, if Maya and David's father wants them, and
Mama's not gonna put up a fight for them, then they
should go. And if Taylor stays here, she's gonna go off
the deep end. Why stay somewhere where you're miserable all the time?"

"To make someone else happy," Chase simply stated.

Brenda shook her head. "That's a bunch of crap,
Chase, and you know it. I'm sitting here telling you that
these kids are wallowing in misery and all you can think
of is making Mama happy. So you're saying that they
should stay here just so Mama can continue to ignore
them and do her thing out in the streets. Next thing
you know, Taylor will be out on the streets begging for
money to support her drug addiction. There's no telling
what will happen to Maya and David if they're already
feeling neglected now."

Chase stood. "Look, I'm not trying to make things worse by putting in my two cents. Why don't we all just sit down and talk about this with Mom?" he proposed.

"Mama hasn't talked to me since she found out about this," Brenda said.

"Well, I'm sure she has plenty to say about it, so let's hear her out."

Chase walked out of the room, but Brenda didn't bother to follow him. He was starting to get on her nerves. She couldn't understand why he was on Eileen's side anyway. Apparently, their mother didn't care too much about all of her children leaving because she had yet to say or do anything that would show she was going to change in order to keep her children with her. At this point, there was nothing that could change Brenda's mind about the situation unless Eileen came forward with a valid reason for the children to stay.

Dinner was spent in silence. The only sounds that could be heard were the metal utensils tapping and scraping against the plates that sat in front of each person. Brenda kept stealing looks at Chase, waiting for him to blurt out his opinion about all of the tension in the household. She knew that before the night ended, he would make them have a family talk. Chase had always been like the father Brenda and the rest of their siblings never stably had. So Brenda knew that Chase would take his stand as the dominant male in the family, and try to sort everything out.

"Mom," Chase finally spoke, gaining everyone's attention.

Brenda glared at her brother and shook her head. She wished that he would let this go. It was hard enough without him making everything worse by trying to cater to Eileen's feelings.

"Yes, Chase," Eileen responded after a few seconds.

Chase glanced briefly at Brenda and saw the cold stare she was giving him. Quickly, he turned away and returned his attention to his mother. "I've been doing some thinking. Maybe I should move back home."

What? Brenda screamed on the inside.

Eileen looked up at her oldest son. "Why would you want to do that? No one else wants to be here with me." She glanced at Brenda.

Brenda was fuming; they were acting like all of this was her idea when, in all actuality, her younger siblings had been the ones to suggest leaving once she did. She hadn't planted that idea into their heads. *Eileen shouldn't be blaming anyone but herself.* It was because of her actions that even her seven-year-old son wanted nothing more than to move away from her.

"Well, my enlistment is almost up and I only went into the Navy so that they would pay for my college education, so I figure that once my four-year term has ended, I'll move back here and go to college." Chase searched his mother's face for a response. "Maybe if I stay, the kids will too." He looked at each of his siblings, only avoiding eye contact with Brenda.

The ominous silence was killing Brenda. She couldn't tell if her siblings were happy about this, but as far as she was concerned, Chase could move back home if he wanted to. It didn't bother her at all. But she couldn't understand why he would want to move back into this house with their mother running around like she was. Brenda had been waiting forever to graduate so that she could move away from all of the drama her mother had put their family through. She didn't want to stick around to see who Eileen's fifth husband would be, and part of her preferred that her siblings not be around to see him either, but if they decided to stay home now that Chase would be moving back, it would certainly be their decision.

Taylor was the first to break the tense stillness. "I don't care if Chase moves back home," she said, keeping her gaze on her plate of steak, mashed potatoes, and sweet peas. "I still want to move with Bre. I like being around her because she makes me happy. I don't get that being here."

Taylor shifted her glance slightly to the left and caught Brenda's eye. Brenda offered her sister a reassuring smile, letting her know that she would be welcome in her home any time—well, once she found a home.

Brenda watched her mother and noticed that she didn't seem as emotional about this as she had been before. She didn't know if that meant that Eileen no longer cared about her children abandoning her, or if her mother was just holding back the emotions she was feeling so her children would just think she no longer cared.

Chase looked at his youngest siblings and asked, "Davie, Maya, would you guys stay if I came home?"

David shrugged, not wanting to say anything for fear of hurting his mother.

Maya kept her eyes lowered. "I don't know. Daddy promised me a new dollhouse. And Ms. Denise said she was gonna take me shopping this summer. And her and Daddy are gonna take me and David to Six Flags *and* Wild Adventures."

Eileen sighed and pushed away from the table. "It's okay. You guys can go stay with your daddy. Taylor, you can go with Brenda. Chase, you can go to college anywhere you want. I'll be fine. The time alone will help me understand why you guys have chosen to do this. Maybe I'll find that the reason really is me, but right now, I just don't see that."

The children watched as their mother stood up and walked out of the kitchen. Brenda watched a single tear slowly travel down Maya's cheek. David raised his head and revealed the tears in his eyes. Even Taylor was struggling with containing her emotions. Brenda and Chase locked eyes. She could see his disappointment, but something in her heart was telling her that, though they were hurting their mother, this was the right thing to do.

Chapter 37

Lauren

The Monday afternoon sun beamed down on Lauren as she walked out of her front door. Today was a beautiful day and she refused to spend the time inside of her house. With her parents at work, she was free to go wherever or do whatever she pleased. So today she decided to take a walk.

Confronting Sterling on Friday had been so liberating. It felt as if a heavy weight had been lifted off of Lauren's shoulders. She knew she still cared for him a lot, but she also realized that it would only be a matter of time before she got over what they'd shared. Part of her still regretted giving herself to Sterling, especially since there had been no emotional attachment on his part. But she was thankful for the experience because it had taught her so much about herself and the kinds of guys she had been attracted to.

Lately, Lauren had found herself thinking a lot about Jarred. She had been feeling horrible about the way she'd treated him, especially since he had been nothing less than nice and caring and he'd been the only person, besides Lauren's girlfriends, who'd truly seen her for who she was on the inside. But because of his less-than-popular status and his more-than-irritating forwardness, Lauren had used her words and actions to beat him to the ground. Now, she regretted every mean and hateful thing she'd said and done to him.

Lauren pulled at the straps of her white spaghetti-strap shirt as she continued walking down the street. When beads of sweat began to pop up on her forehead, she realized that it was hotter than she'd thought when she first came outdoors. She was glad that she'd decided to trade in her Capri pants for a pair of blue jean shorts. It had to be about eighty-five degrees. It had gotten hot early this year, just as winter had been premature in its timing the previous year. Lauren didn't complain though, because she didn't like the rain and absolutely hated the cold, so she was just glad that the rain had finally let up so that she could have a decent spring break.

A black Cadillac sitting on spinning rims caught her attention as it turned onto her street with its music blasting and bass bumping. There were three guys in the car bobbing their heads to the demeaning rap song. When they spotted Lauren, the driver immediately slowed his car to a snail's pace as he tried to match Lauren's leisurely walk. The guy on the passenger side leaned out of his window and looked at Lauren as if she were a slab of meat that he couldn't wait to dig his teeth into.

"Wassup, ma?" he hollered.

Lauren quickly looked away from him. She hated guys who did things like this. First of all, if a guy wanted to approach her, he needed to have the decency to get out of the car and introduce himself. Second, he could not be riding in an old, beat-up car with rims the cost more than the entire vehicle. She took that to mean that he had no idea how to spend his money. And lastly, she absolutely abhorred guys with dreadlocks and those who wore grills in their mouths. Neither was at all attractive to her. She liked a smile that showed off white teeth, not a mouth full of platinum and gold enhanced by diamonds and ignorant words.

"Girl, I know you hear me talkin' to you," the guy persisted. "Stop tryin' to front and come over here and talk to me."

Lauren continued walking and in the distance she could see a group of guys standing on the corner. As she neared them, she could hear them laughing and realized that they were watching her completely ignore the men who were still riding alongside her.

"Hey, girl," the guy continued to call her. "Why don't you come take a ride with me and my boys?"

Apparently annoyed from being ignored, the boy had the driver stop the car. Lauren's heartbeat quickened when she saw the man jump out of the car and move toward her. She sped up her walk and continued to disregard his constant calls for her to wait.

As she neared the boys on the corner, she noticed that they were Jarred and his familiar group of friends. She wondered why she'd never noticed how much time he spent on her block before. She didn't have time to ponder over his presence, though. The only thing on her mind was getting away from her assailant.

"Hey, Juice, man, come get back in the car," Lauren heard the driver yell to his friend. "That girl don't want you."

"Man, I got this," she heard Juice yell back.

Just as she was about to reach the corner where the group of guys stood, she felt Juice run up behind her and grab her arm. He spun Lauren around so that she would be facing him.

"Hey, girl, why you act like you ain't hear nobody callin' you?" he asked harshly. "Is you deaf or somethin'?"

Lauren looked down at his hand gripping her arm and gave him a look that said he'd better let go of her before she went off. Suddenly, she felt a strong arm around her waist. She'd never had fast reflexes, but suddenly she wished she did because she would surely give the unknown person a quick elbow in his ribs.

"Is there a problem here?" the person asked.

Lauren turned slightly to find Jarred standing next to her. She gave him a harsh look that asked why he had his hands on her.

"Naw, ain't no problem," Juice spat. "I'm just tryin' to talk to the girl. You can leave."

Jarred sucked his teeth and shook his head. "Naw, I don't think I'ma be able to do that. How would I look, walking away so you can holla at *my* girl?"

Lauren looked back at Jarred and gave him an even harsher look. He threw her a glance that told her to play along, but she was so confused that all she could do was stand there, looking dumbfounded.

"Man, this ain't your girl," Juice challenged.

Jarred shrugged. "You ain't got to believe me. Ask her." He tossed Lauren *the look* again.

Lauren watched as both guys turned to her for a response. She figured that playing along with Jarred's little game was the only way she'd be able to get this Lil Wayne wannabe out of her face. So she slyly removed Jarred's arm from around her waist and locked her hand with his.

With a plastered smile, she replied, "Yeah, I'm his girl." Her voice was tight and she was sure by her forced facial expression, Juice could tell she was lying.

She watched as the boy looked between her and Jarred, and then down at their interlocked hands. He looked back at Lauren and asked, "So you gon' make me walk back ova' to my boys empty-handed?"

Lauren narrowed her eyes and, apparently getting the hint, Juice shrugged and walked away. She watched as his friends began laughing ignorantly as he climbed back into the beat-up car and rode off down the street.

As soon as the car was out of her sight, Lauren released Jarred's hand. "Thank you," she murmured. "But I could've handled it on my own."

Jarred shoved his hands into his pockets and shrugged. "I don't think you could've."

Lauren glared at Jarred and asked, "Why do you say that?"

"You don't even know who that guy was, do you?" Jarred asked. Lauren shook her head. "Juice is a hustler who rarely ever takes no for an answer."

"He wouldn't have had a choice with me," she declared.

Jarred allowed a soft chuckle to escape his lips. "If you say so." He turned and began to walk back toward his friends.

"Hey, Jarred," Lauren called out.

When he turned around, Lauren literally had to catch her breath when the sun's rays bounced off of Jarred's pupils, causing small specks of light brown to sparkle within his dark brown eyes. For a moment, she could not find her voice.

"Lauren?" Jarred called to her. He walked back to her and searched her face worriedly. "Why are you looking at me like that?"

"Your eyes," she involuntarily whispered.

Jarred's pupils darted away from her in confusion. "What about them?" he asked.

Suddenly, she seemed to come out of her transfixed state. "Oh . . . umm, they have these little specks of brown in them."

"Oh, sometimes those show in the sun," he informed her casually. He paused and then a slight smirk spread across his face as he asked, "Is that what you called me over here for?"

If Lauren was a gambler she'd say that he seemed amused, but instead of responding to the smirk she'd noticed on Jarred's face, she simply shook her head. "No. I wanted to apologize again for how I acted at school last Monday. I accused you without any just cause. I was out of line and I apologize."

Jarred gave her a slight nod. "Don't worry about it. You straight."

"And . . . I'm sorry for the way I've been treating you the last few months," she continued. "You didn't deserve that either."

"You know, Lauren, you have the potential to be someone really special, but you come off as being snobbish. It turns a lot of people off."

"I know, but I'm really not like that."

"I know you're *really* not like that," Jarred agreed. "I don't think you'd have friends like Danielle, Jayda, and Brenda if you were. I'm just telling you that you come off as being someone you're truly not."

Lauren looked away from him and locked her gaze on his friends, who were still standing on the corner. The boys were looking in their direction as if they were trying to figure out what was taking their friend so long to return to them.

"I think your boys are waiting for you," Lauren told him, trying to change the subject.

Jarred followed her gaze and held up his index finger, signaling that he'd join them in a moment. He then returned his attention to Lauren. "We have to go to a house party in a few hours and we were supposed to hit the mall." He gazed into her eyes. "Maybe you should come . . . to the party, I mean."

"Who's throwing this party?" Lauren asked.

Jarred seemed to hesitate before offering a response. "My boy, Irvin. You know him, right?"

Lauren nodded, though she barely could remember Irvin's last name. He wasn't someone she usually spoke to in school.

"It's at his house tonight at seven," he continued. "He lives over in Sherwood Estates. You and your girls should come."

"Maybe," she responded as he walked away.

Lauren watched as he moved toward the corner where his friends had been waiting for the last ten minutes. She never noticed how confident his walk was and how commanding his presence seemed to be. Even his broad shoulders and chiseled features had been disregarded. Lauren shook her head, ashamed at her own ignorance of Jarred's beauty—inside and out.

Chapter 38

Lauren

Lauren pulled her car up to the curb nearly four houses down and across the street from Irvin's home. The street was lined with cars, and in the distance Lauren could see several people standing outside the house as if it was too crowded to go inside. She wondered why she hadn't heard about this party. With it being spring break, there were probably going to be parties every night this week. But as jam-packed as this party was, Lauren felt slightly offended by not being invited before this afternoon.

She had called her girls and asked them about attending the party with her. Jayda had declined, saying that she was going out with Evan this evening. Brenda had plans with Chase and the rest of her siblings tonight. And Danielle was supposed to be going out with her father and half brother so that they could spend some time together. So Lauren was left to attend the party alone, which would provide a more unavoidable arena for her classmates to give her the cold shoulder. But regardless of the shade her peers had been throwing her way, Lauren refused to remain in hiding. She was determined to have fun tonight.

She walked in her three-inch heels toward the ranch-style home. As she neared the house, she realized that none of the people standing outside seemed familiar to her. She looked down at her clothes when she passed a girl, positioned at the door, in a dark blue T-shirt and a pair of jeans. Maybe she was overdressed in her short, clingy party dress.

As she entered the house, the thumping music, which she could hear from outside, grew louder. The pulsating bass prevented Lauren from discerning the words of the rap song, but judging by the people dancing throughout the house, the song was apparently a crowd favorite. As she maneuvered her way through the crowd, Lauren spotted Jayda dancing with Evan in the middle of the living room floor. Pushing her way through groups of people, she moved toward her best friend.

"Hey, girl. What you doing here?" Jayda yelled over the music when she noticed Lauren standing next to her.

"This is the party I was talking 'bout coming to," Lauren told her. "I thought you said you had plans."

Jayda looked up at Evan and smiled. "I guess this was it. He never told me where we were going."

Lauren nodded and noticed that her friend was dressed in a plain brown tank top, jean shorts, and a pair of brown and gold sandals. "What kind of party is this?" she asked once she noticed she was practically the only female in dressy attire.

Jayda laughed as she glanced down at her friend's dress. "Jarred didn't tell you?"

"Tell me what?" Lauren questioned.

Jayda leaned in and said, "This is his church's youth group's party."

Lauren pulled back and looked at her friend as if she hadn't heard what Jayda had said. "You're serious?"

Jayda nodded.

Lauren looked around and noticed that several people were wearing the same dark blue T-shirt that the girl at the door sported. The shirts displayed the name of the youth group and the church they belonged to. She couldn't believe that Jarred hadn't told her what kind of party this was before he invited her. She looked ridiculously stupid in her barely covering dress and open-toe heels while everyone else was dressed more conservatively.

"I'm out of here," Lauren said to Jayda.

"Lauren, wait," Jayda called as her friend walked off.

As Lauren made her way toward the door, she could hear Jayda calling after her, but she ignored her, wanting to get as far away from the party as possible. She had been concerned about coming to this party because of how her classmates had been treating her lately, but it had never crossed her mind that she would embarrass herself in front of a completely different group of people. As soon as she stepped off the porch, Lauren heard Jarred's voice.

"Hey, I didn't know you were here," he said as he left the porch and took over Jayda's pursuit of Lauren.

"Well, just pretend like I wasn't," Lauren said. "I'm going home."

He matched her quick strides. "Why?" he questioned. "The party is just getting started."

Lauren spun around to face him, bringing his steps to a sudden halt. "Why didn't you tell me this was a church party?"

Jarred laughed. "Because it's not."

"Jarred, don't lie to me," she spat. "Jayda just told me that this is a party for your church youth group."

"Exactly. It's a youth party. Not a church party."

Her eyes revealed her irritation.

"Look, everybody's just tryin'a have fun. I know it's different from what you're used to, but I figured you could use some different surroundings." His eyes pleaded with her. "Please, don't leave."

Lauren wondered why she'd never noticed his smooth skin or his wavy hair before tonight. Even his nose and lips looked striking to her. "I'm not dressed for this kind of party." She sighed, trying not to focus on his appearance.

Jarred looked down at her party dress and shrugged. "You're right, but you look fine. Just come back in and have something to eat or drink."

Lauren glanced back at the house full of teens having fun in Jesus' name. She'd never heard of Christians partying like this before. Though there was no vulgar music, risqué dancing, or intoxicating liquor, everyone seemed to be having a good time. Maybe she should give it a try.

Danielle

Danielle sat next to Jackson in the restaurant booth. Neil and Junior sat across from them. Danielle watched as her father held Kennedi in his lap and allowed a smile to creep across her face at the sight. Though she had spoken to him over the phone several times, Kennedi hadn't interacted with her grandfather since she was a baby. Danielle wasn't surprised that her daughter had become immediately attached to Neil. Lately, Kennedi seemed to be clinging to the few men in her life to compensate for the one man who had not been there for her since she was born. Danielle wasn't too worried about the void in her daughter's life, though, God willing, Kennedi would meet her father soon enough.

Danielle allowed her gaze to move toward her half-brother. When Jackson had said that Junior favored their father a little, he had been mistaken. Junior looked exactly like Neil, even more than Jackson. Danielle didn't understand how Jackson could have never had suspicions concerning Junior's relation to the family. Danielle surely would have begun asking questions the day she had met the young boy.

Junior looked up at Danielle and slightly smiled. She struggled to return the gesture, but was sure her attempt resulted in what looked like a painful grimace. In response, Junior lowered his eyes. Danielle knew she'd given the boy the impression that she didn't care much for him, and maybe she didn't, but she was trying for the sake of her family. She knew God would want her to accept Junior as her brother, but it would take some time.

"Are you guys enjoying your meals?" Neil asked his children.

Jackson nodded. "This chicken is good."

"Mine is good too." Danielle cut a piece of her fish and stuck it into her mouth.

Junior kept his eyes lowered as he placed a chicken strip into his mouth. "I like it."

Danielle glanced at Junior and knew his mind was elsewhere. He had barely touched his food and she was sure he'd just stuck a piece of chicken into his mouth to satisfy their father. With everyone aware of the truth, she knew he felt like an outsider. He seemed to not know what to do now that he was officially a part of their family. Danielle wanted to make him feel welcome, but she honestly didn't know how.

"So what do you guys have planned for the break?" their father asked.

Jackson tossed Danielle a quick glance before answering, "I'm going to a couple of parties this week with this girl I met a few weeks ago."

Neil stared at his son. "Just don't get too out of hand with the partying."

"I'm sure we're not even going to those types of parties," Jackson responded. "This girl is different."

Danielle smiled as she noticed the optimistic look on his face. Neil noticed it as well, but he frowned and shook his head in response.

"So is this girl gonna keep you from coming back home with me?" Neil questioned.

Jackson looked away and shrugged. "I don't know. I've been looking at Clark Atlanta and they have a really good accounting program that I wanted to check out."

Neil made an incomprehensible mumble, but kept a neutral look on his face. He turned his attention toward Danielle, who had been hoping that her father would not question her about her spring break plans. She was not ready to tell him that she was in the process of reuniting Kennedi with her father. She was unsure of what her father's reaction would be, so she decided that she would leave that out of her answer.

"What about you, princess?" Neil questioned.

Danielle continued to look down at her plate. "I was just planning on hanging out with the girls—Lauren, Bre, and Jayda. We have a few places we wanted to go during the break."

"You're not going to work? I'm sure you could use the extra money," he said.

She nodded her head. "Well, yeah, I'll be working the morning shift for this week, so I'll have the afternoons and evenings to spend with my friends."

"What about Kennedi? Where's she going to be while you're with your friends?"

"She'll be with me," Danielle replied.

"So if you go to a party, you're gonna take her with you?" her father questioned.

"No, I'm not tryin'a party like that, but if I go somewhere I can't take her, I'll find someone to keep her. I know plenty of people who wouldn't mind taking her off my hands for a few hours, including Mom."

"Danni, you can't just dump your child off on someone else," Neil chuckled.

Danielle looked up at her father and raised her right eyebrow. "You did."

The sound of Jackson's fork dropping to his plate followed Danielle's curt statement. Danielle watched as her father's face dropped in surprise. Junior raised his eyes and gazed at Danielle sorrowfully. Even Kennedi was looking at her as if she had done something wrong.

Feeling a sudden surge of guilt, Danielle resumed staring at the half-empty plate in front of her. "I'm sorry," she mumbled. "I have to go to the bathroom." She moved from her seat and walked to the restroom.

She stood in front of the mirror positioned over the double-sink countertop and stared at her reflection. She didn't know what had just come over her. She had forgiven her father. She had told him that she didn't want any explanations or excuses for his wrongdoing. She didn't want to hold his mistakes over his head. She wanted to move forward with her own life and not dwell on the past. But here she was, making offhand comments toward her father, whom she had supposedly forgiven. *What's wrong with me?* she asked herself.

Danielle turned on the faucet and splashed cold water on her face. As she wiped her face with a paper towel, she hoped that whatever was bothering her about this situation would soon pass. She didn't want to be angry with her father. She wanted things to be okay between them.

When she walked out of the restroom, she was
shocked to find Junior leaning against the wall between the men's and women's restrooms. She paused
as he stood up straight and looked at her. As she studied him, she noticed that he even shared some of her
features—the full lips and broad nose she'd inherited
from her father. *This is my brother,* she told herself as
if she was trying to get used to the arrangement.

"I know you don't like me," Junior suddenly said
softly. "But I really like this family. I don't want you
guys to think I'm tryin'a take Daddy away from you,
but I need him, too." He reached up and wiped under-
neath both of his eyes as if tears were threatening to
emerge from them. "I don't have nobody else."

Danielle's eyes filled with empathetic tears. She realized that she was still apprehensive toward her father
because of Junior. He had been the reason behind her
parents' divorce and her strained relationship with
Neil. But she was beginning to understand that she
couldn't blame him for everything that had happened.
He was just a child, a little boy in need of his father . . .
his family. And she was his family.

She sighed and wiped her tears. "I do like you, Junior," she whispered. "This is just gonna take some
getting used to."

He nodded. "I know." He stood in place for a moment before moving back toward their table.

Danielle followed him and prayed that God would
make this a smooth transition for all of them.

Chapter 39

Lauren

By eleven-thirty most of the partiers had headed home. Lauren wasn't used to a party that ended before one o'clock in the morning, but she was surprisingly worn out. She had to admit that she'd had a lot of fun once she'd come back into the party. Though there was a good variety of music, most of the songs played over the sound system didn't call for group dances, and many people danced alone because they were caught up in their own praise. However, in spite of that fact, Jarred had become her primary dance partner for the night.

Lauren didn't quite understand why some of the people were so into certain songs. But Jarred had explained to her that if she just listened to the words, and not only the music, she would see what caused them to worship like they did. So when Kirk Franklin's "I Am" had begun to thrust through the speakers, Lauren had taken Jarred's advice. She listened as the lyrics spoke of overcoming the insecurities and disappointments that held people back throughout their lives, but in the end they were whatever God said they were. The song spoke to her heart and tears had begun to threaten her eyes. She refused to allow them to fall, but permitted her body to sway to the music as she nodded her head in accordance with the beat.

The song still played in her mind as she stood on the porch looking up at the full moon. She wondered if the God that she often heard Jayda and Danielle speak about was actually looking down on her right now. If He was, she wondered if He could see the pain she still held in her heart over her mistakes. She wondered if He could truly help her get past the hurt and allow her to love again. She was extremely vulnerable now when it came to her heart. She knew that she couldn't just give it to anybody because it was possible that it would be returned to her in shattered pieces. She wouldn't allow herself ever again to endure the pain she'd gone through with Sterling. But it would be nice to be able to trust someone to truly care for the person she was on the inside. Could God do that for her? She was unsure.

"Hey, girl," Lauren heard Jayda call as she and Evan stepped out onto the porch.

Lauren smiled at her friend. "Hey. You guys heading out?"

Evan nodded. "I gotta go to work at noon tomorrow and I need my rest. Did you have a good time?" he asked Lauren.

She nodded with a small smile. "It was fun. Different, but fun."

Jayda placed her palm against Lauren's shoulder. "I'm getting used to it too," she told her friend. "I'll call you tomorrow, okay?"

"Okay. Good night."

She watched as the couple descended the porch stairs and walked down the sidewalk toward Evan's car. Lauren noticed the way Evan held Jayda's waist lightly as she leaned against his side. They made such a beautiful couple, she thought. Part of her heart still wished she could've shared the same intimacy with Sterling. She still loved him, despite the issue that had separated them. But she knew she had to get over him or she would never be able to move on with her life.

A light gust of wind blew and Lauren shivered as she placed her hands over her bare arms.

"Cold?" Jarred's voice asked from behind.

Lauren turned around to face him and smiled. "A little, but I'm okay."

"Sorry I don't have a jacket. I'd give it to you," he said with his hands in his pockets.

Her smile widened as she returned her attention to the full moon. The dark sky was clear, making the brightness of the moon seem illuminating.

"It's amazing, isn't it?" Jarred whispered.

"What?" Lauren questioned, looking back at him.

Jarred kept his eyes on the moon before him. "To actually know that God created something so beautiful."

Lauren turned away from him. She had no idea how to answer his question. Anything dealing with God was foreign to her. She knew the basics: He'd created the earth and all the people in it; He had a Son named Jesus who was sent to die on the cross for everyone's sins; and when people die they either go to heaven to be with God or they are sentenced to eternal damnation, depending on how they lived their earthly lives. But even with all of that, she was still unsure of His existence. The things she was not ignorant of still often baffled her. She'd only heard of them through other people she'd encountered throughout her life. No one had actually sat down and explained things to her. So for all she knew, science could be correct in assuming that she, and every other human being on earth, had evolved from apes. Although that theory still seemed a little sketchy because then she wondered who created the apes.

Regardless of what she believed or did not believe in, getting into religious discussions never appealed to Lauren. She just wanted to live her life without worrying about where her soul would spend eternity after she died.

"So, how'd you like the party?" Jarred asked, unknowingly bringing her relief by switching the subject.

"It was fun. Everyone seemed to be into it," Lauren stated.

"I know it was really different from what you're used to, but I figured that it would be nice for you to see that you can have fun without being ratchet." He moved so that he would be standing next to her. "I hope you're not mad at me for being deceitful."

She glanced at him. "It's cool. It was nice to be around guys who don't grab on me every time their favorite song starts playing." She laughed subtly. She turned toward him, so that now they stood face to face. "I was planning on apologizing to you for not inviting you to my party, but I think you would've been uncomfortable there anyway. It was way different from this. But there were a few people, like Evan, who kept it tasteful."

"If I would've been invited to your party," Jarred began in a sincere tone, "I would've been coming for you, not to have some girl shaking her behind all in my face. It was your night; therefore, my attention would have been on you." He paused. "But, then again, I'm sure my attention would not have been well received. You probably had enough attention to keep you busy anyway."

Lauren lowered her eyes when she noticed that his gaze had become intense.

He moved his head so that he could catch her eyes again. "Don't feel bad, Lauren."

"Can I ask you something?" she inquired in a soft voice. "Did you know about me and Sterling being to-

gether before I practically announced it to the entire
school?"

Jarred turned his eyes toward the open front door
and watched as Irvin and several other people cleaned
the house.

Lauren sensed his hesitation and that provided her
with his answer. "You did," she stated quietly. "How?"

"I came to your party," he said somberly. "I came
when everyone was leaving in hopes that you would at
least accept the gift I'd bought you. I watched for a minute while you said your good-byes. You seemed to be in
a hurry because you even rushed off your friends as if
you had something better to do than to stand around
and talk to them. Then you disappeared into the hotel.
A few minutes later, I saw Mr. Sterling standing by his
car a few spaces down from where mine was parked.
I didn't know what was going on until I saw him pull
something out of his pocket. It didn't take me long to
figure out that it was a hotel key. When he hesitated a
moment before going back into the hotel, I figured my
assumption was correct. After that, I put two and two
together and then left."

He sighed heavily. "I didn't know if what I assumed
was true, but I couldn't think of any other explanation. It just seemed to be too much of a coincidence. At
school, you guys always flirted. He was the first person
you gave an invitation to your party to. Not to mention,
when he came to the basketball games, he only stayed
for the halftime show. It wasn't hard to see. It was just
difficult for me to realize that I didn't stand a chance
next to him."

Silence hung in the air between them for several long
minutes. Lauren felt even more ashamed now that she
knew someone had actually seen her foolish decisions
in action. She realized that her relationship with Ster-

ling was what caused Jarred to withdraw from pursuing her. She hated that she'd hurt the only guy who truly cared for her just so she could be with a guy who only cared about his personal satisfaction.

"Now, let me ask you something," Jarred suddenly requested.

Lauren looked up at him with a question in her eyes.

"What made you choose him?" he asked sincerely.

Immediately, Lauren looked away and shrugged.

"C'mon," Jarred urged. "There had to be something . . . besides the obvious physical attraction."

"Well, when Jayda asked me why I was going after Sterling, instead of giving *you* a chance, I told her it was because I liked a hard catch. You were within my reach because you liked me and had nothing hindering you from being with me. Sterling, on the other hand, had a lot at stake and I guess I took advantage of that. Not to mention that I felt that I loved him. I still love him," she said quietly. "He gave me a challenge and I took it."

Jarred nodded as if he understood. "So . . . have you told your parents?"

Lauren shook her head as she lowered her eyes. "I don't want them to be disappointed in me."

"You should tell them," he stated softly. "They'll love you regardless."

Silence became a third person once again as Lauren watched as Jarred stood before her with his hands still stuffed in his pockets. She wanted to ask him why he wanted her to reveal the truth to her parents, but she knew she didn't have to because the answer was already in her heart. She knew it was the right thing to do and her parents were never the type to make her feel she had to hide anything from them, not matter what it was.

"Baby girl, whenever you get yourself into trouble, you can always tell us," her father was known to say.

And her mother would follow up with, "We won't judge you. We just want to know that you're okay because we love you."

Suddenly, the loud ring of Lauren's phone disrupted the stillness and intruded on her thoughts. She reached into her purse to retrieve her cell phone and sighed when she noticed the word Home flashing across the screen.

"Hello?" she answered, and then paused. "Okay. Bye." Then she hung up. She looked at Jarred with a slight smile. "That was Daddy," she said sarcastically as she rolled her eyes. "I have to go. Thank you for inviting me here tonight. I really did have fun."

Jarred nodded. "I'll walk you to your car."

They stepped off the porch and took their time walking down the sidewalk until they stood in front of Lauren's Jetta. He held her door open as she climbed into the car. Once she was safely inside, he shut the door.

Lauren rolled down her window after turning on the engine. She smiled as she said, "Maybe I'll see you in the neighborhood."

Jarred returned her smile. "Maybe."

He stood back as Lauren drove away. She listened to the jazz station on her way home, but the music went unheard as she thought about the night's events. She'd had more fun than she'd admitted and there was something about being around Jarred that sent peace into her heart. She wondered if it was him or something inside of him. Either way, she wished she had noticed whatever it was before she'd gotten herself hurt while fooling around with Sterling. Maybe she would've had her chance at happiness with someone who would've treated her like she deserved to be treated. *Maybe there's still a chance,* she thought as she continued down the road to her home.

Chapter 40

Danielle

"Jackson, *please* behave," Danielle pleaded as she sat nervously in the passenger seat of the car.

Jackson kept his eyes set on the road before him. His jaw was tight as if he were mentally preparing himself for the encounter that was about to be made. His strong hands gripped the steering wheel so tight that Danielle could see the veins that ran up to his fingers. He already looked as if he was planning to act out.

"Jackson," Danielle called his name again as she sat up slightly to look into his face.

"Danielle, *you* need to chill," Jackson replied, annoyed. "I'ma be cool as long as he's cool."

Danielle settled back into her seat and let out a deep breath. Olivia had called her last night after she'd returned home from dinner with her family and told her that she had talked to Keenan, who had agreed to meet with Danielle. By the tone of Olivia's voice, Danielle could tell that everything was going well with their plan, but Danielle couldn't hide the fact that she was extremely anxious about this meeting.

She hadn't seen Keenan in over five years. The last time she'd laid eyes on him, she had been four months pregnant. Then, he had been five feet and eight inches tall with a deep caramel complexion, a short, messy Afro, brown eyes, and full lips enhanced by a barely there mustache. She remembered his sometimes-un-kempt appearance being overpowered by his boister-ous personality. He was loud and obnoxious and felt as if he were God's gift to women. Back then, Danielle had been attracted to him because of his social status within her class, but now she couldn't find one good reason for having been so lovesick.

She wasn't very optimistic about this meeting and didn't know what to expect from him. Keenan could agree to see her today, but tomorrow he could want nothing to do with Danielle or Kennedi. For all Dani-elle knew, if he felt taking care of his daughter would be too much to handle right now, he could be back in North Carolina tomorrow. She refused to go into this with high hopes that everything would just work out and everyone would be happy. She would not allow her daughter to be hurt if she could help it.

Once they pulled up to Olivia's house, Danielle's nerves shot to an all-time high. She wasn't sure if she was being overdramatic, but she was almost positive she could hear her heart pounding faster by the sec-ond. She turned to look at Jackson and noticed that he was standing outside of the car, waiting for her to exit the vehicle. Danielle inhaled deeply and figured that her brother had the right idea. They needed to get this confrontation done and over with. Before she had real-ized it, Danielle found herself standing in the foyer of Olivia's home.

"Please, come and have a seat," Olivia offered with one sweeping movement of her right hand.

Apparently not moving fast enough for his taste, Jackson firmly ushered Danielle toward the living room and onto the soft-cushioned couch. He glanced at his sister, and since it seemed as if she was too nervous to make introductions, he stood and offered his hand to the older woman.

"Hi. I'm Jackson, Danielle's brother."

Olivia's smile was faint as she shook hands with the young man who towered over her by nearly a foot. "Olivia Benson, Keenan's mother. He's down the hall in his room. He should be out any minute." She sat down in the wingback chair on the other side of the room. "Would you all like anything to eat or drink? I just made some homemade chocolate chip cookies and I have some milk to go with it."

Danielle could hear the anxiousness in Olivia's voice and that only made her nervousness escalate. Was this the right thing to do? Was Keenan really willing to see her and talk things through? Or was this gathering just a way for him to officially bail out of his responsibilities? Danielle had many questions, but no answers.

"No, thank you," Jackson answered after the lingering silence.

Minutes had passed and Keenan had not been seen. Danielle was growing more and more nervous, almost to the point of being afraid. She knew that she was not prepared to go through with this, no matter how much her daughter needed her father in her life.

"Ms. Benson, I think we'd better go," Danielle suddenly said. "It's apparent that Keenan's not ready for this and, truthfully, neither am I." She stood and motioned for Jackson to follow suit.

Olivia remained in her seat with a look of sorrow in her eyes as she nodded in understanding while watching the siblings move toward the door.

"I hope you're not leaving," a deep baritone voice spoke in a soft manner.

Danielle froze at the door. Every ounce of apprehension was evident in the male's voice and the quivering in his tone made Danielle's eyes water. She took a deep breath as she turned around and looked into the eyes of her first and last boyfriend. Literally having to tell herself to continue breathing, Danielle took in his appearance. He stood at least four inches taller than she remembered and his deep caramel skin glistened from his position in the brightly lit hallway. A faded cut replaced his once unkempt Afro, and his barely there mustache had grown into a neatly trimmed goatee that surrounded his still-full lips.

As he moved from the entrance of the hallway, Danielle looked up at her brother, whose anger for her ex-boyfriend hadn't changed. She could see Jackson's temper flaring and she could only pray that he wouldn't handle this situation as irrationally as he had the situation with their father.

"Please stay so we can talk," Keenan pleaded.

Danielle, moving on her own this time, slowly walked toward the couch to reclaim her seat. Jackson followed hesitantly. After they were situated, Keenan rested on the loveseat across from them.

Danielle watched as Keenan took in her appearance, just as she had his a few moments earlier. She could see the admiration in his eyes and surprisingly she inwardly smiled. She, too, had grown and matured since the last time he'd seen her. Of course, she was slightly heavier, but her inherited curves withstood the burdens of childbearing. And she was sure that in her eyes he could see the strength that life had afforded her.

"We have a lot to talk about," Keenan said, breaking the silence and keeping his eyes on Danielle.

Danielle remained quiet, but allowed her head to nod slightly.

"I know you have questions." He spoke with an inquiry in his tone. "And I have a lot of explaining to do."

"You most certainly do," Jackson interceded, breaking the calmness in the room.

Danielle instinctively grabbed on to her brother's arm and squeezed gently, silently asking him not to make this any harder than it had to be.

"Jackson." Keenan smiled as if it was his first time laying eyes on him since he'd greeted Danielle. "It's good to see you, man."

"Uh huh," Jackson grumbled in response. "I thought I'd come along for a little moral support." He placed his arm around Danielle's shoulders.

Keenan broke eye contact with Jackson and looked at Olivia. "Mom, why don't you take Jackson to the new garden you're growing in the backyard? I'm sure he'd love to see it."

Olivia opened her mouth to respond, but couldn't seem to say anything as she looked into Jackson's angry eyes.

"Jackie, it's okay," Danielle whispered softly. "I'll be fine."

Jackson released a heavy breath and stood to his feet. His cold, hard stare turned into a weary smile as he moved his gaze from Keenan to Olivia. "I would love to see what you have growing," he conceded.

Olivia nodded as she stood and the two exited the house, leaving Danielle and Keenan alone.

Keenan moved to the edge of his seat and stared intently at Danielle. He wasted no time in getting down to business. "First, I would like to apologize for my immaturity. It was wrong for me to leave you here to care for someone I had part in creating. *I* was wrong. I have been wrong for the last five years. But I'm not that same person anymore, Danni." His voice was shaky. "I would like another chance. I would love to show you that I am a much better man now. I know how to handle responsibilities . . . *my* responsibilities. I want to help you take care of our daughter like I should have been doing from the very beginning."

Danielle's eyes watered at his words. This was what she had come here for. This was what her daughter had been pleading for. Kennedi's dream was sitting right in front of Danielle and she didn't have to wait another minute. She could make all of her baby girl's dreams come true in one request. She could simply ask Kennan if he would like to take the forty-five-minute ride to Danielle's home just so Kennedi could get the fatherly hug she had been waiting nearly five years to receive. But there was something placing a damper on all of Danielle and Kennedi's hopes and dreams. There was something that was not sitting right in Danielle's spirit. Keenan had changed so much. That was apparent through his appearance and through his words, but why had it taken so long for him to come forth? And why had Danielle had to initiate this meeting if Keenan had wanted to be a part of Kennedi's life so badly? She voiced her questions aloud and waited silently for an answer.

Keenan sat back in his seat and rubbed his hands together nervously. "I don't know how you're gonna take this," he started. "But I know it's only fair for you to know the truth."

Danielle saw something in his eyes that frightened her and she prayed that his revelation wouldn't ruin any chances of him being reunited with their daughter.

"I have . . . had another . . . child. A girl."

Danielle inhaled heavily as she placed her hand over her mouth in astonishment.

Keenan continued without responding to her reaction. "I got this girl I was talking to pregnant about a year and a half after I moved in with my dad. I felt like I was having déjà vu or something. I wanted to run, like I had with you, but this time, I had nowhere to go. So I manned up and prepared myself to handle this situation like an adult. My dad made me get a job. I had to go with my girl to the doctor. I had to go to these birthing classes that lasted forever. And all the while, I was thinking about you having to go through all of that *alone*. The guilt that I hadn't felt at first from leaving you began to settle in.

"It got even worse right after the baby was born. Her mother was a habitual smoker and our baby's health must have not been as important to her as her pack of Blacks. So the baby was born with severe damage to her lungs and a few other vital organs. She couldn't breathe properly, so immediately after she was born she was placed in ICU. She didn't live past her first week." Keenan discreetly wiped tears from his eyes. "My girl was upset, but I think I was angrier than she was. Not at her, but at myself. I wanted to be there for that little girl because I felt like it would make up for me leaving you here with our baby. I thought it was a way for me to make up for my mistakes without actually having to come to you and sincerely apologize for what I had done. But I knew that it wouldn't have made anything better."

"So, what? You sat around for two years wondering how you could make this up to me?" Danielle asked angrily. "I don't get it, Keenan. Why didn't you come after that happened? It seems like that event would have made you realize that where you needed to be was here with your daughter."

"I was too scared to come here," Keenan replied tearfully. "I knew you hated me and I couldn't stand that. I felt like if I came back here after losing a child, you would think that I was just tryin'a make up for the loss instead of coming back 'cause I was wrong. Plus, I didn't wanna look into my mother's eyes and see the disappointment she felt from me having gotten into this situation in the first place." He shook his head. "There was too much pain here for me. I needed to know that I was wanted here. I couldn't come back until I knew that I was needed here.

"When my mom called and told me to come down for spring break, I could hear the neediness in her voice. She wouldn't tell me why she wanted me to come down or why she couldn't wait until the summer to see me. All she kept saying was that she wanted me to come. So I came 'cause I felt like I was supposed to be here. And when Mama finally told me why I was needed here, I knew that my second chance had come around and I didn't want to blow it." He stood and walked toward Danielle, keeping his eyes glued to hers as he sat down on the opposite end of the sofa she had been sitting on for the last thirty minutes.

"I would love it if you would introduce me to my daughter. We can do it today or tomorrow or whenever you want. But the sooner I meet her, the sooner I can prove to you that I am *not* that same thirteen-year-old boy you remember running away from his responsibilities. All you have to do is say the word."

Danielle allowed her brown eyes to search his and she saw nothing but truth and sincerity. Slowly, a smile crept across her face as the image crossed her mind of her daughter's surprised expression in response to meeting her father.

Chapter 41

Lauren

Tuesday evening the girls found themselves at Underground Atlanta, browsing through the stores, looking for nothing in particular. Danielle held Kennedi's hand as they admired the Black art on display.

"This is really beautiful," Jayda said as she gazed upon a portrait of a man standing on the beach during sunset. "Reminds me of Evan. Strong. Assertive. Confident." She smiled. "You guys, I think I love him."

"Girl, you said that the night he asked you to be his girlfriend," Brenda said, reminding Jayda of the declaration she'd made the night of Lauren's party as she had been driving Brenda home.

"Yeah, but I was just exaggerating then," Jayda admitted. "This is serious. I really do love him. He's so . . . perfect."

"Be careful," Lauren said. "The most perfect man can have the most skeletons in his closet."

"Lauren, don't rain on her parade." Danielle laughed when she noticed Jayda's face had dropped at Lauren's comment. "Let her be happy with her man."

"Speaking of men," Jayda said with a slight smirk on her face. "I'm surprised your parents let you out of the house today."

"Girl, who are you telling," Lauren replied as she remembered the conversation she'd had with her parents last night after coming home from the party.

All Lauren thought about was the secret she'd been withholding from her parents for the last few weeks. Jarred was right. She should tell them, and though the mere thought of confronting them terrified her, Lauren knew she had to do it. She walked into the house and by the surrounding darkness she knew her parents had settled in for the night. So, she walked toward their closed bedroom door and knocked softly. After being permitted to enter, she took a deep breath and opened the door.

"Hey, Mama and Daddy." Lauren prayed they couldn't hear the shakiness in her voice.

"Hey, baby girl," Rueben greeted her in return as Cathy flicked on the bedside lamp. "You know you were pushing the time tonight."

"I know. I'm sorry," Lauren said as a tear involuntarily escaped from her eye. "I kinda lost track of time."

Cathy sat up in bed and stared concernedly at her daughter. "Lauren, baby, what's wrong?"

Lauren watched as her father sat up also and it seemed that the look in his eyes told her he already knew her secret. She broke into uncontrollable tears and covered her eyes as her shoulders heaved with each sob.

"Lauren," Reuben called in an authoritative tone.

"I'm sorry, Daddy," Lauren said, trying to stop her tears, but her attempts were in vain. She looked up at her parents with tears clouding her vision. "I had sex with Mr. Sterling." She waited for a response, but her parents just sat staring at her as if they hadn't heard a word she'd just said. "Did you guys hear me?" she asked quietly as if she were unsure if she'd even blurted out her secret like she thought she had.

"Yes, Lauren, we heard you," Cathy said softly.

Reuben climbed out of bed as he added, "We also heard your principal when he called me at work last week to tell me what was going on. I knew you weren't just sick when you called and asked me to come pick you up from school that day."

"Lauren, why didn't you tell us sooner?" Cathy asked tearfully.

Lauren's eyes darted between her mother, who was still sitting, and her father, who stood with his arms folded across his chest, as her tears continued to flow. She would've never guessed that they knew a thing. Their attitude toward her had been completely normal the entire time. If they had been upset or disappointed, they'd kept their emotions hidden behind their bedroom door.

"I can't tell you how disappointed we are in you," Reuben said. "You're an adult now, Lauren, so start acting like one! How do you expect us to feel comfortable with you going off to college in just a few months if you're acting like this already?" he demanded to know.

"I'm sorry," Lauren cried. "I loved him. I thought he loved me. I thought it would be okay."

"Lauren, you knew it wouldn't be okay. That's why you hid it from us," Reuben retorted.

"I'm sorry," was all Lauren could muster as she continued to cry.

Cathy got up and walked toward her daughter. Lauren allowed her mother to embrace her, but felt unworthy of the love.

Lauren sighed as her mind returned to the present. She thought about how her parents had continuously expressed their disappointment in her. When she'd asked them why they had allowed her to lie to them for so long if they knew the truth, her mother explained that they were waiting for her to come to them. Surprisingly, they decided that they weren't going to punish her nor were they going to pursue any actions against Sterling. For one, Sterling hadn't committed any crime and anything he'd done by violating the school's code of conduct had been rectified with him being fired. They also felt that she'd punished herself enough by keeping the truth bottled up inside. Though she felt somewhat relieved, Lauren had been fully ready to receive the grounding that was sure to last until she went off to college.

"Honestly," Lauren said, "I don't think I would've told them the truth had Jarred not suggested it. I mean, Sterling told me I should tell them and I just brushed it off, but Jarred made me feel convicted."

"What *is* going on with you and Jarred?" Jayda questioned Lauren.

Lauren rolled her eyes and sped up her walk. "I am not having this conversation again," she said as she left her friends behind.

Her friends laughed as they called after her. Lauren continued walking until she reached the exit of the art shop and stood in the crisp, cool air. *Jarred*. His name alone made her smile. After spending time with him at the party on Monday night, she'd departed from him in hopes of seeing him the next day. Her hopes hadn't been in vain. As she had been sitting on her porch, earlier in the afternoon, she'd spotted him walking along the sidewalk. Surprisingly he hadn't been accompanied by his friends. After greeting him, she invited him to sit with her. He accepted and they sat in silence for several moments before he spoke.

"I'd like to get to know the real Lauren," Jarred had said. "The one your girls know. The one you say you are."

Lauren had stared at him, unable to take her eyes away from his. His gaze had captivated her and she couldn't, nor would she dare try to, break the connection. "I can make that happen for you," she'd replied.

His smile melted her heart and she wondered what these new feelings she was beginning to experience were. Jarred had never had this type of effect on her before . . . so why now?

As they shared conversation, Lauren realized that he had something she didn't. Jarred possessed the same spirit that Jayda and Danielle had received only a few weeks earlier. She could clearly see the difference between her spirit and the Spirit living inside of Jarred and her friends, and suddenly she felt herself longing for what they had.

When she had voiced her thoughts to Jarred, he'd smiled brightly as he'd said, "I can make that happen for you," causing Lauren to chuckle softly.

"Uh huh. Daydreaming about your man," Brenda broke into Lauren's thoughts.

All Lauren could do was smile because she knew her friends could just about read her mind when it came to matters of her heart.

Danielle

"Lauren, your smile is so big," Kennedi pointed out as she gazed up at her mother's friend.

"Yeah, well, your smile is bigger than mine," Lauren teased as she squatted in front of the four-year-old. "Why are you so happy?"

Kennedi glanced up at her mother with sheer excitement pouring from her very soul. "Mommy's gonna show me my daddy tomorrow," she announced excitedly. "I talked to him on the phone and he said he can't wait to see me."

Lauren smiled at Danielle knowingly. For the last several hours, all Danielle could talk about was her meeting with Keenan. Before leaving Olivia's house, Danielle had agreed to arrange a time for Keenan to meet Kennedi. She wanted to do it as soon as possible so that Keenan could spend as much time as he could with Kennedi before returning home. So tomorrow would be the big day. Danielle had been so excited that she couldn't keep the secret to herself. As soon as she'd gotten home, she ran to her daughter and spilled the surprise.

"I'm gonna see my daddy?" Kennedi had screamed with joy.

Danielle had nodded her head vigorously. "Tomorrow," she'd added.

Kennedi had jumped into her mother's arms, almost in tears from excitement. She went into every occupied room of the house to tell everyone the good news. She even walked in on Beverly taking a shower. After Kennedi had somewhat settled, Danielle gathered everyone to tell them what was going on. Her parents had been bewildered to hear that their daughter had set up everything without consulting them, but, at the same time, they were happy that she had made such a responsible decision on her own.

"I can't wait, Mommy," Kennedi had said after the family meeting. "I wanna talk to him now. *Please?*"

Danielle was shocked to hear her daughter make such a request. She knew she couldn't deny Kennedi's appeal, though, so she dialed Olivia's home number and asked to speak to Keenan. She turned on the speakerphone so that she could hear what was being said.

"Hello?" Keenan's mellow voice had greeted her, and Kennedi nearly jumped out of her skin.

"Daddy!" Kennedi had yelped without even knowing if the man on the other end of the phone line was actually her father. "Daddy!"

There was silence just before Danielle heard a deep intake of breath. "Kennedi," Keenan had replied softly.

"I can't wait to see you, Daddy," she'd said.

"I can't wait to see you either, Kennedi," he'd replied, his voice still soft.

"Tomorrow, Daddy. Don't forget."

Keenan laughed subtly. "I won't."

"Here's Mommy." Kennedi handed Danielle the phone.

"Hello," Danielle had greeted him.

"Thank you," Keenan had said softly.

"You're welcome," she'd replied. "I'll see you tomorrow."

Brenda

The girls laughed as Kennedi couldn't seem to be still as they piled into Lauren's car. Lauren turned up her Estelle CD that was playing and slightly let down all four windows so the cool air would comfort them.

"So, Bre, how are things at your house?" Danielle asked.

Brenda looked at Danielle with a disheartened expression clouding her face. "Things could be better. Mom's still in her funk, but no one has changed their minds about leaving. Chase thinks Taylor, Maya, and David should give it another year. Taylor absolutely refuses to stay. And Maya and David have been bribed with gifts and trips to move in with their dad."

"So that's it. No matter what your mom feels, you guys are splittin' for sure?" Danielle questioned.

Brenda shrugged. "It's the kids' choice. Eileen's made her bed, now she's gotta lie in it."

Brenda hated leaving her mother out in the cold, but it seemed as if Eileen had left her children no other choice. She had made her decision, and, apparently, her life didn't include taking care of her children. As soon as she graduated, Brenda would get a full-time summer job so she would be able to afford a cheap off-campus apartment. She'd probably have to find another roommate to help split the bills once she started school and would only be able to work part-time, but whatever she had to do, she'd do it. She couldn't let Taylor down. Brenda was determined not to turn out like her mother. If showing her younger sister that she could be depended upon was her first test, Brenda would pass with flying colors.

Jayda

"So, who, besides Danni, is up for church this Sunday?" Jayda asked over the music.

The car grew silent as Lauren turned the music all the way down. She came to a stop at a red light and looked at her best friend sitting in the passenger-side seat. Jayda returned Lauren's stare. She was determined to get Brenda and Lauren into a church if it killed her. She wanted her friends to have what she had shared with Danielle. She wanted them to all have something that would connect them on a totally different level. Only God could do that for them.

Lauren gave Jayda a small grin. "I hope you're not upset with me, but I was gonna ask Jarred if I could go with him."

Jayda rolled her eyes. "Girl, please. I don't care where you go, who you go with, or how you get there, just as long as you're going somewhere that's gonna help you grow spiritually."

"And don't be going just so you can see Jarred in a suit." Danielle laughed from the back. "God needs to be the only Man on your mind when you walk through those church doors."

"Amen," Jayda agreed, joining her friends in laughter. She turned slightly in her seat. "So what about you, Bre?"

Jayda gazed at Brenda as the light changed to green and Lauren proceeded to drive. "I know you realize you need to be introduced to a different environment. I don't think that you're truly happy and if God can keep a smile on my and Danni's faces, then who's to say that He can't do the same for you?" She shrugged. "It's worth the shot."

"No pressure?" Brenda asked, looking between Jayda and Danielle.

They both shook their heads.

"We've all been searching for something," Jayda said. "For me it was peace. For Danni it was reconciliation. Lauren is looking for love. And you seem to be looking for freedom from the hold your mother's life has had on you and your family."

"Jayda and I have found what we're looking for," Danielle continued as Kennedi rested against her arm. "And if Lauren keeps heading down the right path, she'll find the spiritual love she needs. Think about what God can do for you, if you just allow Him to take over and do His *thang*." She smiled.

Jayda inwardly prayed that Brenda would consent. She knew that her friend had many questions and was confused as to where to find the answers. "Any- and everything you need, Brenda, is in Him," Jayda added in order to ease Brenda's mind.

Brenda inhaled deeply and released a lung full of air before saying, "Count me in."

Danielle clapped gleefully as Jayda smiled in satisfaction. They were doing just what God wanted them to do. They had pulled their friends into the right direction; now He would handle the rest.

Reader Discussion Questions

1. If you had to describe yourself as being like Lauren, Jayda, Danielle, or Brenda, which girl would it be and why? Who are you least likely to identify yourself with and why?

2. If you could have advised any of these young women on ways to handle their individual situations, what would you have told them?

3. It is evident early on that Lauren is used to getting her way, no matter the consequences. Do you believe she was selfish in her pursuit of Sterling, going after him even after he stated the risks of them getting involved with one another?

4. There seemed to be chemistry between Danielle and A.J. from the very first day of their meeting, but the two never moved past friendship. Why do you believe their relationship flourished in the manner that it did? Do you believe A.J. would have had the same impact on Danielle's life if they had moved their relationship beyond just friendship?

5. Jayda dealt with her family's issues internally, only having one initial outburst, because she felt the need to be strong for everyone involved. In today's society, many teens have to play the same

part within their families. How do you feel this hinders their emotional and mental development into adulthood?

6. One of Brenda's greatest fears came to fruition when her focus on her schoolwork was deterred after she started seeing Ken and Zane. The second occurred when she became caught up with both guys and ended up hurting them and herself. What could have Brenda done to prevent either of these things from happening? Do you think there were signs that things weren't going as planned before the incident at Lauren's party?

7. Kennedi's strong desire to have her father in her life prompted her to seek out a father figure in A.J. Do you feel her desire was premature or is it becoming more common for young children to seek the attention of a father figure even before understanding why their father is not in their life?

8. Sterling told Lauren that if the situation/environment were different, he would love to have her as his significant other. Would you have approved of a relationship between Lauren and Sterling under any circumstances?

9. Jarred did all he could to show Lauren he truly cared for her, but was continuously dismissed by the object of his affection. Why do you feel he was attracted to Lauren and continued to pursue her despite being turned down and even disrespected?

10. Brenda's siblings were determined not to remain at home with their mother once Brenda left for

college. Do you feel that Eileen was deserving of such treatment? Do you believe that, if given the opportunity, she would've been willing to change in order to keep her children at home?

11. What do you make of the way Lauren's parents handled the situation with their daughter's relationship with her teacher? Would you have handled the situation in the same manner?

12. Danielle's relationship with her mother was impaired by Beverly's criticism of her daughter's parenting. Why do you believe Beverly was so overbearing and do you believe that reason may be justified? Do you think that the relationship between young women and their parents begins to change after they become teen mothers? If so, why do you believe this change occurs?

13. As the girls dealt with their personal issues, they never once considered confiding in one another before Jayda brought them all together. Though an individual may have the tendency to not confide in anyone, even a close friend, how important do you think it is for someone to open up when dealing with troublesome situations? Would you have agreed with any of the girls if they had refused to open up about their personal situations due to fear of being embarrassed or judged?

14. Evan, Jarred, and A.J. played pivotal roles in introducing Christ to these young women. In today's times, it is hard to find a young Black male who is proudly living for Christ without worrying about what everyone will think of him. How do these

three young men break that trend? How impera-
tive is it that the male in any relationship is spiritually grounded?

15. In life, young people are searching for things they
believe will make them happy or make them complete as an individual. However, many times, they
find that they are repeatedly looking in the wrong
places. What do you believe could help alter this
trend and aid in looking toward spiritual guidance
in order to achieve true happiness?

UC HIS GLORY BOOK CLUB!

www.uchisglorybookclub.net

UC His Glory Book Club is the spirit-inspired brain-child of Joylynn Jossel, Author and Acquisitions Editor of Urban Christian, and Kendra Norman-Bellamy, Author for Urban Christian. This is an online book club that hosts authors of Urban Christian. We welcome as members all men and women who have a passion for reading Christian-based fiction.

UC His Glory Book Club pledges our commitment to provide support, positive feedback, encouragement, and a forum whereby members can openly discuss and review the literary works of Urban Christian authors.

There is no membership fee associated with UC His Glory Book Club; however, we do ask that you support the authors through purchasing, encouraging, providing book reviews, and of course, your prayers. We also ask that you respect our beliefs and follow the guidelines of the book club. We hope to receive your valuable input, opinions, and reviews that build up, rather than tear down our authors.

What We Believe:

—We believe that Jesus is the Christ, Son of the Living God.

—We believe the Bible is the true, living Word of God.

—We believe all Urban Christian authors should use their God-given writing abilities to honor God and share the message of the written word God has given to each of them uniquely.

—We believe in supporting Urban Christian authors in their literary endeavors by reading, purchasing and sharing their titles with our online community.

—We believe that in everything we do in our literary arena should be done in a manner that will lead to God being glorified and honored.

—We look forward to the online fellowship with you.

Please visit us often at:
www.uchisglorybookclub.net.

Many Blessing to You!
Shelia E. Lipsey,
President, UC His Glory Book Club

Notes

ORDER FORM
URBAN BOOKS, LLC
97 N18th Street
Wyandanch, NY 11798

Name: (please print):_____

Address: _____

City/State: _____

Zip: _____

QTY	TITLES	PRICE

Shipping and handling-add $3.50 for 1st book, then $1.75 for each additional book.

Please send a check payable to:
Urban Books, LLC
Please allow 4-6 weeks for delivery

ORDER FORM
URBAN BOOKS, LLC
97 N18th Street
Wyandanch, NY 11798

Name: (please print): _____

Address: _____

City/State: _____

Zip: _____

QTY	TITLES	PRICE
	3:57 A.M Timing Is Everything	$14.95
	A Man's Worth	$14.95
	A Woman's Worth	$14.95
	Abundant Rain	$14.95
	After The Feeling	$14.95
	Amaryllis	$14.95
	An Inconvenient Friend	$14.95
	Battle of Jericho	$14.95
	Be Careful What You Pray For	$14.95
	Beautiful Ugly	$14.95
	Been There Prayed That:	$14.95
	Before Redemption	$14.95

Shipping and handling-add $3.50 for 1st book, then $1.75 for each additional book.
Please send a check payable to:
Urban Books, LLC
Please allow 4-6 weeks for delivery

ORDER FORM
URBAN BOOKS, LLC
97 N18th Street
Wyandanch, NY 11798

Name: (please print): _____

Address: _____

City/State: _____

Zip: _____

QTY	TITLES	PRICE
	By the Grace of God	$14.95
	Confessions Of A Preachers Wife	$14.95
	Dance Into Destiny	$14.95
	Deliver Me From My Enemies	$14.95
	Desperate Decisions	$14.95
	Divorcing the Devil	$14.95
	Faith	$14.95
	First Comes Love	$14.95
	Flaws and All	$14.95
	Forgiven	$14.95
	Former Rain	$14.95
	Forsaken	$14.95

Shipping and handling-add $3.50 for 1st book, then $1.75 for each additional book.

Please send a check payable to:

Urban Books, LLC

Please allow 4-6 weeks for delivery

ORDER FORM
URBAN BOOKS, LLC
97 N18th Street
Wyandanch, NY 11798

Name: (please print): _____

Address: _____

City/State: _____

Zip: _____

QTY	TITLES	PRICE
	From Sinner To Saint	$14.95
	From The Extreme	$14.95
	God Is In Love With You	$14.95
	God Speaks To Me	$14.95
	Grace And Mercy	$14.95
	Guilty Of Love	$14.95
	Happily Ever Now	$14.95
	Heaven Bound	$14.95
	His Grace His Mercy	$14.95
	His Woman His Wife His Widow	$14.95
	Illusions	$14.95
	In Green Pastures	$14.95

Shipping and handling-add $3.50 for 1st book, then $1.75 for each additional book.

Please send a check payable to:

Urban Books, LLC

Please allow 4-6 weeks for delivery

ORDER FORM
URBAN BOOKS, LLC
97 N18th Street
Wyandanch, NY 11798

Name: (please print): _____

Address: _____

City/State: _____

Zip: _____

QTY	TITLES	PRICE
	Into Each Life	$14.95
	Keep Your enemies Closer	$14.95
	Keeping Misery Company	$14.95
	Latter Rain	$14.95
	Living Consequences	$14.95
	Living Right On Wrong Street	$14.95
	Losing It	$14.95
	Love Honor Stray	$14.95
	Marriage Mayhem	$14.95
	Me, Myself and Him	$14.95
	Murder Through The Grapevine	$14.95
	My Father's House	$14.95

Shipping and handling-add $3.50 for 1st book, then $1.75 for each additional book.
Please send a check payable to:
Urban Books, LLC
Please allow 4-6 weeks for delivery

ORDER FORM
URBAN BOOKS, LLC
97 N18th Street
Wyandanch, NY 11798

Name: (please print): _____

Address: _____

City/State: _____

Zip: _____

QTY	TITLES	PRICE
	My Mother's Child	$14.95
	My Son's Ex Wife	$14.95
	My Son's Wife	$14.95
	My Soul Cries Out	$14.95
	Not Guilty Of Love	$14.95
	Prodigal	$14.95
	Rain Storm	$14.95
	Redemption Lake	$14.95
	Right Package, Wrong Baggage	$14.95
	Sacrifice The One	$14.95
	Secret Sisterhood	$14.95
	Secrets And Lies	$14.95

Shipping and handling-add $3.50 for 1st book, then $1.75 for each additional book.

Please send a check payable to:

Urban Books, LLC

Please allow 4-6 weeks for delivery

ORDER FORM
URBAN BOOKS, LLC
97 N18th Street
Wyandanch, NY 11798

Name:(please print):_____

Address: _____

City/State: _____

Zip: _____

QTY	TITLES	PRICE
	Selling My soul	$14.95
	She Who Finds A Husband	$14.95
	Sheena's Dream	$14.95
	Sinsatiable	$14.95
	Someone To Love Me	$14.95
	Something On The Inside	$14.95
	Song Of Solomon	$14.95
	Soon After	$14.95
	Soon And Very Soon	$14.95
	Soul Confession	$14.95
	Still Guilty	$14.95

Shipping and handling-add $3.50 for 1st book, then $1.75 for each additional book.
Please send a check payable to:
Urban Books, LLC
Please allow 4-6 weeks for delivery